"He—he's

Noah no

Fresh panic raced through me. "And he's here? Right now?"

"In the flesh."

I had the sudden urge to turn and run, to escape this bar as fast as my feet could carry me. But my legs felt like lead.

Matthias was alive. It couldn't be possible. It *shouldn't* be possible.

I turned as if in slow motion to see the vampire king in question step out of the shadows to my left, his pale gray gaze trained on me. My mouth fell open in shock. I couldn't help but be stunned to see him again—alive and well and standing right in front of me.

After all, I'd been the one who'd killed him . . .

PRAISE FOR THE PARANORMAL ROMANCES OF MICHELLE ROWEN

"I've been bitten and smitten by Michelle Rowen."
—Sherrilyn Kenyon, *New York Times* bestselling author

"Michelle Rowen never disappoints! I love her work!"
—Gena Showalter, *New York Times* bestselling author

"Michelle Rowen's books never fail to thrill."
—*Bitten by Books*

"Sassy and exhilarating . . . Epic and thrilling."
—*Fresh Fiction*

"Should leave readers breathless."
—*Kirkus Reviews*

Bloodlust

MICHELLE ROWEN

BERKLEY SENSATION, NEW YORK

THE BERKLEY PUBLISHING GROUP
Published by the Penguin Group
Penguin Group (USA) Inc.
375 Hudson Street, New York, New York 10014, USA
Penguin Group (Canada), 90 Eglinton Avenue East, Suite 700, Toronto, Ontario M4P 2Y3, Canada
(a division of Pearson Penguin Canada Inc.)
Penguin Books Ltd., 80 Strand, London WC2R 0RL, England
Penguin Group Ireland, 25 St. Stephen's Green, Dublin 2, Ireland (a division of Penguin Books Ltd.)
Penguin Group (Australia), 250 Camberwell Road, Camberwell, Victoria 3124, Australia
(a division of Pearson Australia Group Pty. Ltd.)
Penguin Books India Pvt. Ltd., 11 Community Centre, Panchsheel Park, New Delhi—110 017, India
Penguin Group (NZ), 67 Apollo Drive, Rosedale, Auckland 0632, New Zealand
(a division of Pearson New Zealand Ltd.)
Penguin Books (South Africa) (Pty.) Ltd., 24 Sturdee Avenue, Rosebank, Johannesburg 2196,
South Africa

Penguin Books Ltd., Registered Offices: 80 Strand, London WC2R 0RL, England

This is a work of fiction. Names, characters, places, and incidents either are the product of the author's imagination or are used fictitiously, and any resemblance to actual persons, living or dead, business establishments, events, or locales is entirely coincidental. The publisher does not have any control over and does not assume any responsibility for author or third-party websites or their content.

BLOODLUST

A Berkley Sensation Book / published by arrangement with the author

PRINTING HISTORY
Berkley Sensation mass-market edition / July 2011

Copyright © 2011 by Michelle Rouillard.
Excerpt from *That Old Black Magic* by Michelle Rowen copyright © by Michelle Rouillard.
Cover art by Don Sipley.
Cover design by Lesley Worrell.
Interior text design by Kristin del Rosario.

ISBN: 978-0-425-24213-1

BERKLEY® SENSATION
Berkley Sensation Books are published by The Berkley Publishing Group,
a division of Penguin Group (USA) Inc.,
375 Hudson Street, New York, New York 10014.
BERKLEY® SENSATION and the "B" design are trademarks of Penguin Group (USA) Inc.

PRINTED IN THE UNITED STATES OF AMERICA

10 9 8 7 6 5 4 3 2 1

—— ACKNOWLEDGMENTS

Thank you to Eve Silver for beta-reading and loving Declan as much as I do. To my editor, Cindy Hwang, and my agent, Jim McCarthy, for continuing to make it possible for me to share my imagination with others. To my readers for being ridiculously awesome and embracing my new, darker world of vampires. To caffeine for being my drug of choice. And to my characters for letting me be very mean to them—not that they have much choice in the matter.

1

RAVENOUS WAS THE PERFECT NAME FOR A PLACE LIKE this.

I'd arrived at the seedy North Hollywood bar a half hour ago. A friend had sent an email earlier today asking me to meet him here tonight at ten o'clock because he "had to talk to me about something very important." So here I was—ready, willing, and able to talk.

But by ten thirty he still hadn't shown. And I was getting worried.

Maybe he's dead, a little voice in my head whispered.

My chest tightened at the thought. No, he was too smart. Too wily. Too young and cocky. I refused to allow myself to believe he'd let himself get killed. Tonight he could possibly have the information that would help get my life back to normal.

Where are you, Noah?

My attention shifted to a blond guy in a leather duster approaching the far left of the small dance floor. A heavy metal tune had begun to blare through the speakers, making it difficult to concentrate. Even in the dim light of the club, his skin was so pale it seemed to faintly glow, easily making him stand out from the rest of the crowd. He scanned the few dancers, coming to rest on a petite redhead wearing a micro-short leather skirt.

When he smiled I saw the subtle glint of fangs beneath his upper lip.

She noticed him looking and smiled back at him, thrusting her ample chest forward—the universal easy-girl's signal for "Come and get me, bad boy."

The girl had no idea this bad boy was a vampire.

"For fuck's sake," I said under my breath. "Don't be so stupid."

Two weeks ago I thought vampires didn't exist. But they do. There were those who preferred to keep their distance from humans, but others like this one, well . . . they were just really hungry.

The redhead was going to die.

I wasn't psychic. I had no special supernatural powers, no superstrength, no otherworldly abilities—but I knew her fate. I saw it in the vampire's pale gaze as he flicked a smug look at his friend, also standing at the edge of the dance floor.

A large part of me didn't want to get involved. I had my own vast and varied problems to deal with. Plus, not to judge a book by its cover, but girls like this one, seemingly alone and vulnerable at this kind of dive, would likely find trouble sooner or later. If she couldn't protect herself, if she had no one around to keep an eye on her, then I didn't think her future was a bright one.

But it didn't mean I was just going to let this monster make her his nightcap.

After another quick scan for the missing-in-action Noah, I slid off the tall stool and began weaving my way through the rough-looking crowd toward the exit. The vampire and the girl were now dancing together, if you could call it that. His hand closed on her ass under her short skirt, pulling them groin to groin as he pressed his lips to her throat. It looked sexy—kind of romantic, even—but I knew it wasn't. Or it wouldn't be for long.

I froze in place as a horrible thought occurred to me. He was going to bite her right in front of everyone.

I wanted to walk away, pretend I hadn't seen the vampire, leave this club, and contact Noah another night, but I couldn't do that. I'd never be accused of being a sweet and softhearted woman who wanted to help the helpless, but if there was a problem that was standing right in front of me and I might, possibly, be able to do something about it, then I had to. My conscience wouldn't allow otherwise.

"I really don't want to do this," I whispered to myself. But I did it anyway.

I forced myself to walk close enough to brush against the vampire. He immediately caught my scent and released the girl.

I kept walking. I didn't have to look over my shoulder to know he was now following me. He was the mouse and I was the cheese. It didn't really matter what I looked like, how I filled out the thin white tank top I wore, or how long my legs were under my skirt. I was irresistible.

Believe me, I wasn't saying it to be vain. I wished like hell I didn't have this particular affect on the bloodsuckers.

I exited the club. Even though it was hot air that brushed against my bare arms and legs, I still shivered. I picked up my pace, ignored my racing heart, and walked toward the parking lot out back of the bar.

"Hey beautiful," the vampire said from close behind me. "What's your name?"

I forced myself to look coyly over my shoulder. "Sorry, I don't talk to strangers."

"Oh, c'mon, don't be like that." He was right next to me now, and he stroked a long strand of black hair off my forehead, pausing to roll it between his fingertips. He held it up so he could inhale its scent and his eyes darkened with lust and hunger. "Damn, you smell good. Where are you going, honey?"

I shuddered. "Back to my motel room."

"We can keep you company." He glanced at his friend—dark hair, sallow skin, and a slow smile stretching his gaunt cheeks. He bared his sharp fangs as if he didn't care who saw that beneath his human facade he was a monster.

I'd just wanted to lure the vampire away from the girl. I didn't want this, but it did come with the territory. I tried my best to stay calm. "I don't want company. Really, just leave me alone."

"And what if we don't want to leave you alone?"

"Then you're in serious trouble."

He grinned at that, then inhaled deeply and thin, dark veins branched along his jawline and down his neck. Each vampire showed their hunger slightly differently—it was like a fingerprint, and along with their fangs it revealed them to be much different from humans. The black of his pupils spread out to cover the pale gray of his irises.

His hand shot out and he grabbed me by my throat. I clawed at his arm as he dragged me around the corner into an alleyway, and then he threw me roughly at his friend.

"Hold the bitch still," he snapped.

I tried to struggle against him. I'd hoped very hard it wouldn't come to this, but I'd overestimated how much control a hungry vampire had. Fear laced through me as the blond's lips peeled back from his fangs.

"No, wait—my blood—" But I wasn't able to finish my sentence. He wrenched my head to the side so violently he easily could have snapped my neck. I gasped in pain as his fangs sliced into the soft flesh of my throat.

The vampire's friend had grabbed my left breast and was squeezing it so hard that tears sprung to my eyes.

"She tastes incredible," the blond growled as he slurped at my blood.

A moment later, he gasped and pulled back from me, his black eyes registering surprise now that he realized that my incredible blood came with a bit of an aftertaste.

"What's wrong?" his friend asked.

"I don't know." The vampire's mouth gaped open and

he touched his lips, looking down at the unnaturally dark crimson color of my blood on his fingertips. His brows drew together in confusion before he staggered back a few steps from me.

When he screamed, fire poured out of his mouth. In mere seconds, the only thing that remained of Thirsty Vampire #1 was a fall of fiery ash, turning the hot July night into a Christmas card from hell.

The paralyzing effect of the bite disappeared and I clamped my hand to my neck to stop the flow of blood. I felt weak and my legs threatened to crumple beneath me. I had to struggle to remain standing. The vampire's friend moved his shocked gaze to me. His hunger showed along his hollow cheekbones, the sallow skin etched with a spiderweb of dark blue veins, his eyes soulless and black as pitch.

"You're the one I've heard about, aren't you? Your blood is poison to us." His voice was a whisper, but his hands were clenched, his jaw tight. Anger and grief flashed through his eyes as he came at me, not waiting for my answer.

He wasn't going to bite me. He was going to kill me just as I'd killed his friend.

Before his hand did more than brush against my throat, someone grabbed him, spun him around, and a scarred fist slammed into his jaw, knocking him backward.

"Don't fucking touch her," the man attached to the fist growled. His gaze flicked to me, resting on my injured throat for a split second, before returning to the vampire.

I pressed back against the cold wall as the vampire recovered quickly and launched himself at his attacker. Silver flashed, too fast to fully register. The blade sank into the vampire's chest right up to the hilt. He attempted to pull it out, but didn't have enough time. His hands burst into fire along with the rest of his body and he exploded outward into another ashy cloud.

The knife clanged to the pavement and the man crouched to snatch it up and slide it into the sheath he wore at his hip.

Then he glared at me through his right eye. The left was covered by a black patch. He'd lost the eye a long time ago in another fight with a vampire in which he hadn't fared quite as well as this.

I hadn't realized I'd been holding my breath. I finally released it and inhaled shakily.

He was well over six feet tall, heavily muscled, and covered in ragged scars, including those on his face, branching out from where his eye patch sat, down his cheek and jaw and along the left side of his neck. His dark hair was cut very short, almost shaved. He wasn't the type of man you wanted to meet in a dark alley like this. Not if you valued your life. Declan Reyes was scary as hell.

My hero.

I finally allowed myself to relax just a little bit and I wiped my tears away.

He came toward me and roughly brushed the hair back off my neck. "Let me see."

I reluctantly pulled my hand away from the bite wound.

"Damn it, Jill." His lips thinned. "What the hell did you think you were doing just now? Trying to get yourself killed?"

"They were going to kill a girl in there. Right in front of everyone."

"So you offered yourself up as a willing sacrifice instead?"

"I thought I could distract them without getting bit. I guess I was fooling myself."

"Where's Noah?" He pulled a clean rag from his pocket and held it against my throat.

"He hasn't shown yet."

"Then you shouldn't have stuck around." He glanced over his shoulder in the direction of the bar. "You need to stop trying to protect others all the time. You have to focus on protecting yourself."

Declan had a tendency to see me as way more altruistic than I actually was. "So I should have just stood by and watched them tear her throat out?"

"Next time come find me first before you decide to play the pied piper to vampires." He touched my face gently. "Are you okay?"

"I'll be fine." I searched for some emotion on his battle-scarred face—anger, fear, maybe even annoyance—but came up empty.

"We need to go," he said.

"But Noah—"

"Isn't here. Something must have gone wrong. We'll wait for him to contact us again."

"Don't you think we should wait just a little while longer?"

"No. Best to cut our losses and try again later."

I felt the thud of disappointment push away the small amount of hope I'd allowed myself to feel earlier. Declan had chosen to remain outside when we'd arrived just before ten o'clock. While it wasn't the classiest bar in Los Angeles, the way he looked—like death incarnate, which as a vampire hunter he came by honestly—might have gained us a bit too much attention.

Declan was a dhampyr—human mother, vampire father. While this gave him a great deal of extra strength, it wasn't nearly the same as being fully vampire. He healed much faster than a human, but every single time he received a flesh wound it left a scar behind as a reminder of the horror he'd been through.

It was Declan who'd kidnapped me, kicking and screaming, from my normal life two weeks ago. It may as well have been two years by how different I felt and looked. It was the Nightshade formula I'd been injected with that had changed my hair and eyes to black. It was the Nightshade that meant any vampire who drank my blood would die a horrible, fiery death.

Declan stopped a dozen feet away and glanced over his shoulder at me. "Are you coming?"

When I moved closer to him he turned his face away so the scarred side would stay in shadows, away from the light shining down on us from the street lamp. The undamaged side of his face showed the man he could have been in a different life—a handsome, if a bit rough around the edges twenty-eight-year-old. Same age as me. Very different lives.

I wanted to touch him, but I restrained myself. "Don't hide from me."

"I'm not hiding."

"You asked me how I was feeling, so now I'll do the same. How are you feeling right now?"

His jaw tensed. "I'm fine."

"The new serum is—"

"Holding strong. Much better than before."

Better. It wasn't exactly the word I'd use to describe the experimental drug he'd been pumped full of a week ago.

His now-deceased adoptive father, Carson Reyes, had been very concerned about Declan's dhampyr nature. So much so that he'd developed a special serum that had to be injected every three hours since Declan was a child. This serum was meant to curb any vampiric tendencies he might have—violence, bloodlust, erratic behavior of any kind. The serum also restrained his emotions so much that he appeared to have none. This made him the perfect weapon who could follow orders to the letter and not give his father or anyone else any problems. He'd been an effective killing machine who felt nothing apart from getting the job done.

Shortly after he'd met me he'd been forced to stop taking his serum regularly when it was stolen. I'd been worried that the violence and need for blood might overwhelm him, but it hadn't. Instead I'd met a different Declan, one who felt emotions strongly and wanted more from life than merely being a blunt instrument sent out to kill monsters.

Carson was still convinced he was right, that dhampyrs like Declan were dangerous and unpredictable. He'd been developing another serum—one that was meant to be permanent. He'd forcibly injected Declan with it, hoping it would save his son from giving in to any bloodlust. Ever. But that also meant that his emotions—including love, compassion, and sexual desire—would be permanently dampened.

I needed answers. "I'm going to check the bar one last time."

Declan shook his head. "Not a good idea."

I felt the resolve flow through me. It helped me to ignore the stinging pain from the vampire's bite. "Five minutes, I swear. Wait for me here."

"Jill, no—"

Before he could stop me, I turned and quickly reentered the dark and musty interior of Ravenous. Keeping a close eye on my surroundings, wary of anyone who looked suspicious—and, admittedly, a lot of people did—I made a beeline to the bar where I'd been sitting earlier. The newspaper I'd been flipping through still lay closed on the scarred wooden bar top. On the top of page twenty-two I'd seen a small black-and-white picture of me and a heartfelt plea from Cathy, my older sister, asking anyone who knew my whereabouts to please contact the police immediately.

I forced myself to look away from the newspaper toward the bartender.

"Have you seen a guy in here tonight?" My words came out in a rush. "Early twenties, about five-ten, sort of thin. Light brown hair. Looks a bit like a frat boy?"

He eyed me as he ran a wet rag along the countertop. "Not a lot of frat boys come in here."

"No shit." I hissed out a sigh of frustration.

"But, yeah, I think I've seen the guy you're looking for."

My breath caught in my chest. "Really? Where?"

His gaze moved over my shoulder. "Right behind you."

I spun around to see Noah standing ten feet away after coming out of the restroom on the right side of the club.

A wide smile spread across his boyish features and he closed the distance between us in a few steps. "Jill, I wasn't sure if you were here or not."

I hadn't realized until this very moment how incredibly worried I'd been that he was hurt . . . or worse. The last time I'd seen him he'd been recovering from a bullet wound.

"Where the hell were you? You said you'd be here over a half hour ago."

His smile widened. "Good to see you, too."

I hugged him tightly. "I thought you were dead."

"I'm not. But, ouch. Be careful. I'm still recuperating."

"Sorry." I released him, and he placed a hand over his chest wound hidden under his dark blue shirt.

"Don't worry about it. But if this was a normal world I'd likely still be in a hospital bed slurping up Jell-O cubes." His amiable expression faded and he touched my face. "Christ, you look like hell."

I'd take it as an insult if he didn't look so concerned. "I feel better than I look, believe it or not."

"You're paler than last time I saw you. Maybe it's just the new hair color. I mean, don't get me wrong. You're still hot. You're a hot chick who looks like she hasn't slept in about a decade."

"I'll go heavier on the under eye concealer the next time I enter polite society."

"Are you in any pain?"

Having poison in my veins came with a whole set of issues, a couple of which were excruciating pain and nausea. I'd been given another drug, a fusing potion, meant to bind the Nightshade with my blood on a cellular level. Since then, things had been better.

"Other than feeling headachy and weary, kind of like a constant low-level hangover, I haven't experienced any severe pain since taking the fuser."

"Not yet, you mean."

I cringed. "Thanks for the reminder."

"I got more fuser for you so you can take it regularly. I know it doesn't exactly go down easily, does it?"

"It sure doesn't."

The fuser ramped up the pain I felt about a hundred-fold before it started to work. As the saying went, it was always darkest just before the dawn.

"A spoonful of sugar helps the medicine go down," he said.

"Thank you, Mary Poppins. If I didn't have to inject it, I'd be happy to swallow a bucket of sugar with it." I reached for his sleeve to draw him closer when some other rough-looking bar patrons moved past us. "Is that what you wanted to see me about tonight? The fusing potion? I thought you might have some other answers."

His expression tensed. "Not yet, I'm afraid."

I felt a stab of disappointment at his answer. "Oh."

"Where's Declan?"

"Waiting vigilantly outside. Armed to the teeth."

"That's surprisingly reassuring to know." He glanced at my neck as I twisted a lock of hair around my finger. "Making new friends?"

I touched the fresh fang marks. Luckily for a newly designated pincushion like myself, a vampire's bite healed in a matter of a few days, leaving no scars behind. It was small comfort since they stung like a bitch. "You kept me waiting too long. I met a couple guys who liked the way I smelled."

He grimaced. "Sorry. I take it they're gone now?"

"Permanently." I glanced around. "Now that you're here, I do want to talk to you about Declan's new serum."

Noah looked nervously over his shoulder. "Yeah, sure. But . . . listen, Jill, there actually *is* another reason why I needed to see you tonight. And it's not because I enjoy the dulcet tones of Black Sabbath and the smell of sweaty leather."

"What is it?"

Noah shot another look over his shoulder. "Jesus, Jill, when he contacted me yesterday it scared the shit out of me. It was the last damn thing I expected. He wants to see you, but he didn't want me to mention that until you got here."

My heart sped up. "Who?"

Noah met my gaze and held it. "Matthias."

There was a long moment of stunned silence before I

gathered my thoughts together enough to answer him. "He—he's alive?"

Noah nodded.

Fresh panic raced through me. "And he's here? Right now?"

"In the flesh."

I had the sudden urge to turn and run, to escape this bar as fast as my feet could carry me. But my legs felt like lead.

Matthias was alive. It couldn't be possible. It *shouldn't* be possible.

I turned as if in slow motion to see the vampire king in question step out of the shadows to my left, his pale gray gaze trained on me. My mouth fell open in shock. I couldn't help but be stunned to see him again—alive and well and standing right in front of me.

After all, I'd been the one who'd killed him.

2

THE REST OF THE BAR BLURRED IN MY PERIPHERAL VI-sion and the throb of the music dulled in my ears. When Matthias got within six feet of me he slowed and dark veins faintly surfaced on his pale cheekbones.

"I'd almost forgotten how powerful it is," he said so quietly I barely heard him. "I hadn't properly braced my-self for your scent."

"I can't believe this." The shock made my words sound hollow. "You died right in front of me. Fire, ash, you were gone."

"A parlor trick I'd planned well ahead of time for just such an occasion. That, along with a sliver of mental in-fluence helped me to cloud minds and escape. It was all smoke and mirrors, Jillian."

I'd known Matthias had a love of magic. He'd even been friends with Houdini himself once upon a time. It was a possibility to me that it had all been a trick, but with each day that had passed since it seemed less and less likely.

He'd drank my blood—the same blood that killed every other vampire who'd tasted it.

I moistened my dry lips with the tip of my tongue and flicked a nervous glance at Noah, who stood with his arms crossed and a worried expression on his face. My attention returned to the former vampire king. "So my blood doesn't kill all vampires."

"No."

"You proved once and for all that the ritual—your brother's ritual—worked."

"In part."

While vampires had the potential for immortality, they were still vulnerable and could be killed by a wooden stake or silver blade through their hearts, by decapitation, by fire.

In their search for true and inarguable immortality, a secret group had formed called the Amarantos Society. They believed that the blood of an infant female dhampyr imbued a vampire with that immortality.

Thirty years ago, Matthias's brother, Kristoff, murdered his own daughter and forced Matthias to drink her blood alongside him.

Just thinking about it made me feel physically ill.

"You wanted to talk to me." I tried very hard not to let my voice tremble. I failed, but at least I tried.

He nodded, his gaze traveling over my face and down my tank top and short black skirt. I felt chilled even though it was warm in the bar with all the human bodies milling around generating an unpleasant sticky heat. When his gaze returned to mine, I fought the urge to look away. Matthias appeared to be no more than thirty, a handsome man with dark blond hair that fell nearly to his shoulders, but I knew he was at least four hundred years old.

Vampires, especially those as old and powerful as Matthias, could easily manipulate a human's mind. I knew this firsthand because he'd once manipulated mine.

"Where is my daughter?" he asked after a moment.

Just before Matthias faked his death, he'd asked me to take care of his baby daughter, who'd been born in the research compound where Declan and his father lived.

"She's safe."

"Where is she?" he asked again, sharper. "Tell me."

"Jill doesn't know." Declan's voice made me jump. He'd entered the club despite his earlier protests. I could see he'd already attracted the wary glances of others around us in the bar. His gaze narrowed on Matthias. "And this is not a discussion to have in public."

Matthias eyed Declan, as if sizing up the dhampyr. "I disagree."

"Your daughter is in good hands. You have nothing to be concerned about."

"But you won't tell me where she is, will you?"

"No, I won't. Not now."

Matthias's attention shifted to me and I could see his frustration. "Jillian would tell me."

"Don't be so sure. She doesn't know you very well and I'm sure she doesn't trust you."

"You're sure about that, are you?" Matthias's strained expression now showed a trace of amusement. "I'll assume she hasn't told you much about the time we spent together alone in my chambers."

Declan's jaw tightened. "The subject hasn't come up."

"I can still feel her body against mine, see her bare skin flush with desire. She has a tattoo on her left hip—a small Japanese symbol for strength, isn't it?" He glanced at me. "Do you remember that, Jillian?"

"Go to hell." My face was hot with anger and embarrassment.

"Hell, heaven . . . sometimes it's hard to tell the difference." A smile played at his lips.

"Enough." Declan's voice was harsh, although Matthias's words hadn't seemed to put much of a dent into his cool composure.

It had put a big dent into mine. What happened between me and Matthias had been a huge mistake, one brought on by that strong mental influence of his. What I'd felt for him for a few brief moments hadn't been remotely real. It had been more of that smoke and mirrors he'd spoken about earlier.

Declan didn't trust Matthias to start with, and it looked as if the feeling was mutual. The dhampyr had been raised to hate vampires all of his life and he didn't disappoint. It was one of the reasons he'd taken his original serum so religiously—because of his hatred of his vampire father who'd allegedly raped his mother.

All of his life he'd been led to believe that monster was Matthias himself. But that had been a lie.

Declan moved his seemingly unaffected gaze from the vampire king to Noah, ignoring the previous bait Matthias had thrown out. "Do you have any information tonight that can help Jill?"

Noah cleared his throat. He'd been watching our uncomfortable exchange like a spectator at a tennis game. "Still working on it, Dec. It's not easy now that I'm away from the compound since all the research material's there, but I'm doing my best. I'm gathering info on your new serum, too. That's not quite as top secret, so I expect to have some solid news soon."

"If you have nothing useful to tell us, then being here tonight is a waste of our time. Jill was attacked earlier."

"I know, but—"

"When and if you learn anything that can actually help us, please contact us again." He wrapped his fingers around my wrist. "We're leaving."

I expected Matthias to try to stop us, but he didn't. He stood in place, his hands fisted at his sides, and silently watched us leave the nightclub.

DECLAN AND I RETURNED TO OUR MOTEL NEAR VENICE Beach, the latest in a succession of motels we'd stayed at for the past week. It wasn't The Ritz or even the Holiday Inn, but it had a bed and a TV and a bathroom that actually worked. It was a one-story U-shaped motel with a vacancy sign flashing out front of the small parking lot where our ten-year-old Buick—admittedly acquired through less than legal means—was parked along with a couple other cars.

My entire life now easily fit into a tote bag and had been purchased entirely at Walmart. Including the tote bag. It definitely made it easy to leave a location quickly without worrying about forgetting anything important. But it wasn't exactly what you'd call a life of luxury.

Back home in San Diego, working as a temp, I hadn't had tons of money and clothes. At twenty-eight, I'd still had a roommate to afford rent downtown as I figured out what I wanted to do with the rest of my life. I'd lived paycheck to paycheck. But this was much different than even that modest lifestyle. All I could do was hope that one day very soon things would return to normal and I could stop running and hiding like a criminal who'd escaped from prison.

Declan hadn't said anything to me on our half hour drive back here. I'd stayed quiet, trying very hard not to let what had happened since arriving at the bar only an hour and a half ago haunt me. My neck stung and I immediately went into the tiny bathroom to clean the vampire bite with a damp facecloth.

"He won't just let the subject of his daughter drop, you know," I said, glancing over my shoulder.

Declan stood by the door, his arms crossed over his hard muscled chest. He didn't reply.

"Declan, are you listening to me?"

He finally looked at me, his gray gaze flat. "He shouldn't be alive."

"But he is."

"You said he drank your blood. That he killed himself right in front of you."

"It was a trick so he could escape."

"Did you know it was a trick?"

"I . . . had a feeling it might be." Just before he'd bitten me, an act of rebellion against a woman who meant to use Matthias as a stud to breed dhampyrs, he'd whispered that he'd find me.

He did. It was just a bit quicker than I ever would have imagined.

"I see." Declan watched me dab at my injured throat with the cloth.

"About his daughter . . ."

"I told you that she's somewhere safe. Somewhere she can be looked after. We don't have the means to properly take care of a baby. It would have been too dangerous to keep her with us."

"I know that." Frustration welled inside of me. "But why can't you tell me where she is? Don't you trust me?"

"I trust you. I don't trust Matthias."

"She's his daughter."

"And she's a dhampyr. She's very valuable. Her blood is worth more than diamonds to those interested in the immortality ritual."

I was surprised by how cold he sounded. "He wouldn't just hand her over to the Amarantos Society."

Declan regarded me a moment longer. "Then you have much more faith in him than I do. But I suppose I now have a good idea why that is."

I felt myself pale. "If you're talking about what he said earlier . . ."

"It doesn't matter."

I hissed out a breath. "It does matter. If it's bothering you . . ."

"It's not bothering me."

"Fine." I nodded stiffly. "Then let's just forget about it."

Declan moved to the small window at the side of the door and opened the gingham curtain so he could look outside. The nearly full moon hung heavy above the parking lot, the only light apart from a couple lamps around the motel's cement lot. There was one sorry-looking palm tree out front next to the sign, but that was about it for greenery in the general vicinity.

"You said his name in your sleep last night," he said after a moment.

The facecloth froze at my neck. "What?"

"I heard you. You were dreaming and you said his

name. I thought maybe you were having a nightmare about what happened, but now I'm thinking it wasn't a nightmare at all."

I'd all but forgotten about it until this very moment. It hadn't been a nightmare. It had been a dream in which I'd been seducing Declan, feeling his warm hands sliding over my body, when suddenly it had turned into Matthias's cool touch. It wasn't the first time I'd had the dream this week and I worried it wouldn't be the last.

My face burned. "There's no reason for you to feel jealous."

"I'm not jealous."

"I didn't sleep with him."

Declan brushed his fingertips lightly against his eye patch, then scrubbed his hand back and forth over his scalp. "So he lied? He made it sound like you were in his bed, naked, while he explored your body enough to know you have a tattoo on your hip."

"He influenced me."

"To have sex with him."

I shook my head, wishing I could rewind this conversation and try again. "He was trying to test himself, see if he could be close to me without giving in to the need to taste my blood. It was a power thing for him, that's all."

He studied my face. "I know vampires are very powerful. That bastard could have made you do anything. I just wish you'd told me. Is there anything else you're keeping from me?"

I shook my head. "It happened. It's over. It feels like a million years ago. And it's not going to happen again."

At the time I'd believed Declan was dead, a horrible lie told by Matthias himself as a means to manipulate me. But as a human, one look in the vampire's eyes was all it took to make me forget all of that, for me to strip off my clothes and climb into his bed at his command. And I'd come very, very close to letting him have sex with me as he tested his limits by using me as a guinea pig.

I looked at Declan, surprised by his lack of reaction to this news. "You really don't care, do you? You're only asking this out of curiosity, not jealousy."

"Do you want me to be jealous?"

"That another man nearly manipulated me into letting him fuck me? Yeah, a little jealousy might make everything start to make some kind of sense again."

"The serum won't allow me to feel jealousy."

"Must be great to be emotion free. Keeps things nice and simple." The words tasted sour on my tongue.

His jaw tensed. "You know it isn't like that for me. And now that I know what happened, it all makes much more sense."

I raked my hand through my hair until it caught on a tangle, then went to toss the facecloth back into the bathroom sink. "None of this matters. And it's just distracting us from the real problems we need to deal with."

"You're right. That is, unless you'd rather be with him right now."

I almost laughed. "You manage to make that sound more like a bland question than an accusation."

"I swore to protect you, Jill. To do everything in my power to get you through this and back to your regular life."

I swallowed hard, my anger quickly being replaced with anxiety. "And now?"

"Nothing's changed."

He came closer and touched my chin, raising it so I'd look directly at him. I wasn't sure what to expect after our little conversation about Matthias. I didn't feel particularly better about having it all out on the table even though it had been weighing on my conscience for days. Even though it hadn't been full intercourse, I still felt as if I'd cheated on Declan.

I wanted him so much, but I couldn't have him. I was coming to terms with this very slowly. It was likely the reason behind my disturbing dreams about both Declan and Matthias. One was shut off from me sexually and emotionally, and the other—wasn't. But only one was the man I truly wanted to be with.

"I'm sorry for everything you've had to go through since we met," he said softly. "It's all my fault."

Strange. I hadn't expected an apology from him at the moment. My heart, which felt rather battered and tender tonight, grew a few degrees warmer. "If my life hadn't been completely turned inside out, I never would have met you."

He snorted humorlessly. "Some prize."

I placed my hand on his broad chest to feel his heart beating under my touch, then slid up to his throat, letting my fingertips trail over his scars. "It has its moments."

It might have only been my imagination, but I thought I saw something in his gaze then—a softening, a yearning.

He shook his head. "I can't be who you want me to be, Jill. Not anymore."

"Then I guess I'll have to take what I can get." I went up on my tiptoes so I could brush my lips against his. His body felt like a statue, so hard and unyielding. He let me kiss him without attempting to pull away. His mouth felt hot against mine and after a moment his lips parted so I could deepen the kiss. I even imagined that he was kissing me back.

His thumb moved across my throat, over the vampire bite from earlier.

"Jill . . ." he whispered against my lips.

"You want me to stop?"

"No. Don't stop."

I pulled back a little to look up at him, surprised by the sound of his voice. It was deeper and raspier than before. It held desire, the same desire I swear I now saw in his gaze. "Your serum . . ."

"It's like a cloud lifted just now. At this very moment, I can barely feel it at all."

I was confused. "And how before you didn't seem to care about what happened with Matthias . . ."

His eye narrowed. "Right now I want to fucking kill him for touching you. For manipulating you like he did."

I frowned. "Wait. But you—"

He didn't let me finish. He kissed me this time, crushing his mouth against mine, his fingers digging into my sides so hard it nearly hurt. He groaned as his hands slid down over the curve of my buttocks and he brought me up firmly against him, enough that I could feel him hard against my stomach.

I wasn't sure what was happening. The serum made him completely impotent, the perfect soldier unaffected by emotion or desire—one who could focus all of his attention on hunting and killing vampires. One who didn't have to worry about the lustful nature of his vampire side that might lead to the same violent crimes his father had been accused of. Bottom line: Being on the serum meant no sex.

When he'd been off the serum I'd been the first to . . . well, I'd been Declan's *first*. And there had only been the one time between us before his father injected him with the new and improved permanent drug.

This didn't feel all that permanent to me.

I slid my hand down between us and over the front of his jeans to make sure his erection wasn't simply a figment of my overworked imagination. It wasn't.

He groaned again. "Jill . . ."

"I don't know what's happening right now."

"It might not last very long."

Hope rushed through me making me dizzy. "Then"—I kissed him again—"there's no time to waste. I want you. I need you. Right now."

"I thought you said there were more important things to deal with."

"They can wait."

"Agreed."

He gathered me into his arms and carried me to the bed, laying me down on top of it. His kiss was so hard it felt like it was bruising me. His tongue slid over my jaw, down my throat to my chest. He pulled up my tank top to bare my breasts and his mouth closed over my right nipple, sucking it in hard, his tongue swirling over the very tip. I gasped from a mix of pleasure and pain. He raised his gaze to mine and I saw a desperate need mixed with a heavy dose of caution.

I shook my head. "It's okay. Don't stop."

"I want you so much." His voice caught on the last word.

"I want you, too."

His hands moved to my skirt, unzipping it and pulling it off me as I removed my top all the way. He tore off my panties with one quick pull, then returned to cup my sex, sliding his fingers back and forth between my legs.

"Declan . . . please . . ." It was little more than a moan.

Maybe this was another dream. If so, I wasn't going to waste a second of it. I forced myself to sit up and quickly undid his pants, sliding them down over his hips. His erection jutted out long and thick and all I wanted was for him to be inside of me.

"Take off your shirt," I told him, knowing I sounded demanding.

He hesitated before he pulled the black T-shirt off over his head. I got up on my knees on the bed in front of where he stood and ran my hands over his chest, over the scars that showed where he'd been wounded so many times in the past. I kissed his lips and then ran my mouth over those scars as I wrapped my hand around his length and slowly began to stroke him.

"Jill—" There was more than a hint of desperation in the way he said my name.

I smiled and kissed him again. "This is a sign."

"A sign?"

"That it's all going to be okay. That we can be together."

"I don't know how long this will last."

Hooking my hands behind his neck, I pulled him down with me on the bed.

"Make love to me," I whispered, then moaned and held on to him tighter as he began to push himself into me. His hands trembled as they gripped my thighs.

"Like this?" he asked gruffly.

All I could do was nod.

He had next to no experience with sex, but damn, he was a natural. It was so good to feel him sliding inside of me. I'd tried very hard not to think about this, knowing it wasn't a possibility. Most of the time he was simply my emotionless traveling companion, my platonic protector, and hoping for more could only lead to disappointment.

"Fuck, Jill. You feel so good. You smell so good. *Too* fucking good. I think you're driving me crazy."

That made two of us.

I couldn't think, only feel. The worries of the Nightshade, of my blood, of the vampire who'd attacked me earlier, even of seeing Matthias again, faded away to nothing. There was only this incredible moment with Declan and I wanted it to last forever.

"Declan—"

I arched my back and cried out with pleasure as he began to move inside of me with long, deep thrusts.

After a moment, his tone changed. "Jill . . . fuck, there's something wrong. Your scent . . . it's—it's too much . . ."

I leaned back and grasped his face in my hands and looked up at him. I gasped as I saw that his eye had changed from gray to black, his upper lip peeled back from his teeth in a fierce grimace.

"What is it?"

His thrusts became quicker and harder, and he clutched my shoulders painfully hard before his hands moved to my throat. Fear ripped through me.

"No," he growled, his teeth clenched together. "I want to . . . fuck—I want to taste your blood, sink my teeth into you—"

He growled again, only this time it sounded like a wild animal. He let go of his crushing grip on me and a split second later I heard a loud rip. Shocked, I looked to see what was happening. He'd grabbed the mattress to either side of me and shredded it to ribbons.

His face loomed over mine, red and furious. A vein stood out on his forehead and the blackness of his eye scared the hell out of me. It was the same as a vampire's eyes when they were hungry and ready to attack.

I was suddenly and completely afraid of him. Afraid he was going to lean over and tear my throat out while he still moved inside of me.

"Declan, no—" I braced my hands against his chest, my previous desire for him turning to cold fear. "You need to control yourself."

"Fuck," he snarled and finally pulled out of me. He pushed back from the bed, staggering back a few steps, then tucked himself back into his jeans and zipped them up.

"What the hell is wrong with you?"

"It's—" His jaw was clenched so tightly it looked painful. He grabbed hold of either side of his head. "Fuck!"

Then he raised his still-black gaze to mine again. Mixed with the rage there I could have sworn I saw hate. His hands became fists and he moved toward the bed again.

Panic clutched at me. He looked ready to kill.

I scrambled back, falling right off the bed, and landed hard on my ass, then crawled backward from him as he drew nearer. I held a hand up. "Declan, try to think. Something bad's happening and this isn't you."

"This *is* me."

"What's going on? Please tell me. I can help you!"

"You can't help me. This is *because* of you. My need for you turned into *this*. You don't know what's going through my head right now. You wouldn't like it very much."

I didn't need to know for sure. I could see it. He wanted to tear me apart.

He swore and came at me fast, his bare arms flexed, showing taut, sinewy muscle.

"No, Declan, don't—" A scream caught in my throat. I

was certain he was going to hit me, but instead he plowed his fists right through the wall, above where I was pressed up against it, reducing the drywall to a splintered crumble.

His breathing was erratic, his face only inches from my own.

I shook with fear, afraid to touch him, afraid to move. "What is this?"

"I can't touch you, Jill. Not again. Not like this. Not even when it's all I fucking want in the world."

Before I could say anything, and I wasn't even sure what I could say, he grabbed his shirt and left the motel room, leaving me there alone, naked and shivering on the floor.

My blood might not kill a dhampyr. But it made him want to kill me.

3

AN HOUR LATER, DECLAN HADN'T RETURNED. IT GAVE me way too much time to worry about what had happened.

It was like a stranger had been looking out at me through his eyes. While he and I didn't exactly have a long history together or, for that matter, anything in common apart from our current on-the-run predicament, we had an understanding, both spoken and unspoken.

He'd chosen to leave the government-funded research compound to accompany me. To protect me. To . . . be with me.

A lot of money had been spent developing Nightshade. The person who'd created it hadn't left any written notes behind; the formula was entirely in his head.

I shivered and pulled my thin sweater closer to me as I sat on the edge of the bed staring at the door of the motel room, waiting for it to open.

It was my blood that had set him off. Declan was affected by it—his vampire side was. My blood wouldn't kill a dhampyr, but it would weaken him—we learned that lesson when a scientist we'd gone to for help had used it against Declan to try to kill him. The scent, however, now triggered his bloodlust.

It might be true that he was an assassin who'd killed countless vampires in his life, but he would never deliberately hurt me. Once I'd gotten used to him and his fearsome appearance, I knew this for a fact. I felt safe with him.

However, I hadn't felt very safe an hour ago. I'd felt scared to death—for him and for myself.

I paced back and forth in the small motel room between the bathroom and the window, so many times that I practically wore a line in the carpet. I went to the window and peered outside at the dark and nearly deserted parking lot, a million questions racing through my mind. Where had he gone? Was he okay? Was this—whatever it was—going to wear off? Get worse? Hurt him?

I tried to think about something else because this was eating me up inside. My mind wandered back to being at the bar and reading the newspaper. My picture, my sister's plea for help. She had no idea what had happened to me that day—a day that was still crystal clear in my memory.

I remembered the chemist—the *para*chemist, since he dealt in formulas meant for preternatural uses—who'd grabbed me and put me between him and Declan. Declan wanted the prototype formula he'd had. It was only in its initial stages. One sample. And it had been injected into me.

My sister knew nothing about this. She might have seen some security camera footage of the hostage situation, the standoff between Anderson and Declan, but she'd have no idea how it had turned out. Just a fleeting image of me running away and being pursued by a large, scary-looking man with a gun who'd just shot someone in the head and left his dead body bleeding on the lobby floor.

With a shaking hand, I picked up the motel phone and held it to my ear. I pecked out the numbers and waited as the phone rang once, twice, three times. Voice mail picked up and the familiar sound of Cathy's voice brought the sting of tears to my eyes.

She lived here in Los Angeles. From where this motel was, her house was only about ten miles away. Despite speaking to her weekly on the phone and sending tons of emails, I hadn't seen her or my nieces since Easter when I'd stayed at her house for the weekend. I missed her so much.

I opened my mouth to say something after the beep, but pressed my lips together. The silence stretched like bitter taffy until I lost my nerve and hung up. This wasn't the time. And it wasn't fair to just leave her a message that explained nothing.

The moment this was all over—if I found my way out of this mess—when I finally saw my sister, I swore I'd never leave again.

I leaned back on the bed, trying to ignore the huge rips in the mattress from Declan's violent burst of rage. A bare spring poked into my back.

The next moment I sat bolt upright when someone knocked on the door. Declan wouldn't knock. And no one else knew we were here.

Heart racing, I slipped off the bed as quietly as I could and went to the window to glance outside. I gasped. Matthias stood outside the door with his hand pressed against it, a half smile on his face.

"Jillian—" The eerie singsong way he said my name carried easily through the thin door. "I know you're in there. Your blood . . . it calls to me even from a distance."

Cold sweat slid down my spine.

He could smell me. It was a chilling thought. I guess I couldn't exactly pretend that no one was home. However, I wasn't about to swing the door wide open and roll out the welcome mat. The memory of what he'd done to me the last time we were alone spiraled in my head.

I hated this guy.

The erotic dreams I'd had about him since he'd disappeared in a fiery burst of ash were meaningless. I couldn't control what my unconscious came up with.

"What the hell do you want?" I didn't bother to raise my voice since I knew he'd hear me anyway.

"Let me in."

"No, thanks."

He sighed. "Open the door, Jillian."

My hand curled into a tight fist at my side. "Why are you here?"

"To see you."

"You saw me earlier."

"Only for a moment."

My shoulders tensed. "Declan will be back any minute."

His pale eyes moved to where I peeked through the window and locked with mine. "Then we best hurry this up. I get the distinct impression he doesn't like me very much."

He was so insightful.

I shook my head. "Not a good idea."

"I'm not planning on ravishing you, if that's what you're thinking." He looked way too amused by my protests. "I've brought you something."

My guard was up. "What?"

He pulled a small leather case out of the pocket of his black pants. "Noah tells me you'll need this soon. It's a vial of fusing potion."

My attention narrowed skeptically on the case. "Why didn't he bring it himself?"

"He doesn't know where you are."

"But you do."

He shrugged. "I followed you."

"From the bar." My fingernails dug sharply into my palms.

"Yes."

"So that means you've been lurking around here for more than an hour."

"*Lurking* makes it sound rather vile, Jillian. I was waiting for the right time to visit you."

My stomach churned. The curtains hadn't been drawn earlier. If he'd been spying on me and Declan when—

Well, he would have gotten an eyeful. My face grew warm with embarrassment, which led directly into a fresh burst of anger. I went to the door and opened it a crack so I could glare out at him and his smug expression. "You're supposed to be dead."

"I thought we already discussed this." He put his hand on the door and pushed it open farther while I tried to stop him. He was strong. I wasn't. He won.

His gaze swept the small room in an instant, resting on the shamble of a wall and torn-up mattress. His attention returned to me and he raised an eyebrow. "Having some fun to pass the time?"

I tried to keep a lid on my anger and eyed the case he held. "How do I know that's the real thing?"

"You don't trust me?"

"Sorry, no."

"It's real. I mean you no harm, Jillian, whether or not you believe me."

I studied him for a moment, but couldn't read his intentions. Finally I held out my hand. "Okay. Thank you for bringing it to me."

He hesitated a moment before handing over the case. I was surprised he did so without further argument. I noticed there were dark circles under his eyes as if he hadn't slept in days.

"Feeling okay?" I asked.

"Who me?"

"No, the dethroned vampire king standing behind you."

His lips stretched over white teeth until I could see the sharp tips of his fangs. In the movies sometimes they were able to retract like a switchblade, but in real life they were always there, sharp and ready to pierce their next victim's flesh.

"I'm feeling fine. Although, I must admit, being this close to you still fills me with a difficult to resist need even knowing about your very powerful blood. It's interesting to me."

Unease continued to flicker inside me. "I guess I should be extra careful around you now. You could come back for second helpings now that you know my blood won't kill you."

Something unpleasant slid behind his eyes then, but I wasn't sure what it was. "Maybe you shouldn't have opened your door to me."

"If I hadn't, you could have broken it down. Vampires don't need an invite inside people's motel rooms. Do you?"

"No, we don't."

He didn't look so well. I hadn't noticed it at the bar earlier, I'd been too shocked at seeing him walking and talking that I hadn't paid close attention. But he looked very pale, thinner than before, and those dark circles seemed strange to me, although I wasn't sure why. If he was human, I'd say he looked sick.

"What do you want, Matthias?"

"You know what I want."

"I'm not inviting you in here with me."

His gaze flicked to the destroyed mattress. "I'm not asking you to."

"Then—"

"I saw your picture in the newspaper today. Your sister is worried about you. I'm surprised you haven't contacted her yet."

I swallowed. "It's not the right time."

"Your little nieces will wonder where their aunt has disappeared to." He grinned at my look of shock. "Not hard to find out information when you have a name and a city."

"Leave them alone."

"I wouldn't dream of bothering them. I simply wanted to learn more about you."

My face felt tight. I didn't like him knowing about my sister and nieces. It felt too personal. "There's really not much to know."

"Where's my daughter, Jillian?" Again the amusement on his face disappeared and he was all business.

A breath caught in my chest. "I don't know. Don't you believe me?"

"Look at me."

I was tired and unprepared to deal with him tonight. The moment I looked into his eyes he captured me there immediately. It was like being instantly hypnotized. All of my fear and apprehension and anger disappeared completely. A warm and pleasant sensation flowed over my skin and I found I couldn't look away.

He leaned against the doorframe. "That's much better."

"Damn you, Matthias." It sounded much more conversational than angry now.

"I know you don't like it when I do this."

"You're right, I don't."

"It can't be helped."

"It's cheating."

"There are other methods I've used to get someone to talk. Believe me, this is much less painful for you."

He drew closer, and I didn't attempt to step back. I couldn't move and at the moment I was perfectly fine with that. He'd influenced me to be calm and I was calm, even face-to-face with the vampire who'd told me he'd personally ripped the hearts of traitors out of their chests. Side by side, he didn't look as dangerous as Declan. But he was.

"Where is she?" he asked evenly.

"I don't know."

"Declan took her somewhere and didn't tell you where."

"That's right." I now understood all too well why Declan hadn't told me anything about this. It was because my mind was too easily influenced. I would have blurted out her location to Matthias already if I'd known the truth. "But Sara's safe. I know she is."

His pale brows drew together. "Sara?"

"Yes."

"You named my daughter?"

I nodded slowly, studying his face, which looked so tired it made me think he hadn't slept much in the past week. "Sara means princess. I thought it was a suitable name for a vampire princess."

"Half-vampire."

His eyes were the same pale gray as every vampire's. A dhampyr's were a couple shades darker, but still colorless. I wondered what color Matthias's eyes had been when he was human.

"Jillian," he said sharply, drawing me a little out of my trance.

"You—you can name her something else, of course. I just wanted to call her something other than *baby*."

"Sara's a fine name." He studied me closely for a moment, then stroked a line down the side of my face, over my throat where the fang marks were. I leaned against his cool touch, enjoying it more than I wanted to. "Did you miss me when I was gone, Jillian?"

It felt as if I was floating in warm water. "Yes."

He smiled at that answer.

I hadn't meant to say that. I'd felt badly that I'd been to blame for his death—or my blood had been, anyway. But as far as him being gone after all the trouble he'd caused . . .

I *hadn't* missed him. I didn't even like him.

"Are you working with Declan to destroy me now that you know I'm still alive?" He took my chin firmly between his cool fingers so he could hold my gaze.

"No."

"And your blood—Noah doesn't know where all this will lead. Do you think you're going to die from the poison in your veins?"

"Yes, I'm dying." I couldn't lie even if I wanted to.

His expression was as unreadable as Declan's usually was. "How long do you think you have left?"

"When the fusing potion wears off I don't think I'll

survive it. I might mentally be able to handle the pain, but I don't think my body can. It's going to give out. I figure I have a couple of weeks. If that." My throat felt thick as I spoke about my own death sentence. I tried not to think about it much, but it was the truth.

"How does the dhampyr feel about that?"

"He doesn't like to talk about it."

"He hurt you." His gaze moved to my throat that showed fresh bruises from Declan's crushing grip on me earlier. "Do you want to leave him?"

"No."

"He's dangerous. And he'll only become more dangerous."

I shook my head. "The scent of my blood triggered something bad in him earlier, but it wasn't his fault."

His lips pressed together. "What happened has little to do with your blood."

"You're wrong. My blood sparked the violence in Declan. He would never hurt me."

He smiled humorlessly. "Don't be so sure about that. He's a dhampyr, and because of that he's automatically a threat to anyone who gets too close to him." He hissed out a breath. "There's no time to worry about these peripheral issues right now. My questions have been answered. Good night, Jillian."

He stepped back, and his mental influence over me vanished and the calm I'd felt disappeared like an icy wash of water had been thrown at me. Anger at having him mess with my mind shot forth.

"Wait." I grabbed his arm before he walked away. "Declan isn't a threat. It's my blood and his serum that's messing him up, it's not him."

He eyed me. "You've seen other dhampyrs, haven't you? The other kind?"

Just the mention of them sent a shiver through me. Declan was a very rare kind of dhampyr. The more common ones were hunched-over monsters that weren't capable of human reasoning or thought. They were more savage than a pure vampire and once they got the taste of blood, they were completely deadly. It was the reason that most human women who became pregnant by a vampire got an abortion. If they didn't and they bore a monster dhamp, they never survived the birth. The dhampyr clawed its way out of its mother's womb, ready to feed on her before it moved on.

"Declan's nothing like that," I said under my breath.

"For now." Matthias turned and began walking away, throwing a glance at me over his shoulder. "Just be careful with him or your two-week estimate for living may be drastically reduced."

I followed him out into the deserted parking lot, drawing my sweater closer to me, chilled despite the hot night. "What are you talking about?"

His gaze swept me. "The dhampyr is dangerous. I sensed something earlier at the bar from him. It was one of the reasons I followed you immediately. He is . . . close to the edge of his control. And I was right."

"You were spying on us earlier, weren't you?"

He didn't flinch at the accusation. "You once accused me of being violent toward women. I hope by now you see that's not true."

"I saw you kill a woman."

"A traitor who meant to kill me and was conspiring behind my back."

I couldn't argue with that. "Declan is a good man."

"But he scares you, doesn't he?"

I looked up at him. "You scare me more."

His lips curled. "Your loyalty to him is admirable. But that"—he nodded toward the motel room—"is just the beginning of the troubles you'll have with him. All dhampyrs descend into violence or insanity at his age. I know the original drugs he took curbed this, but that's the past and what happened earlier is what the future holds."

I didn't want to believe what he was telling me. It was my blood. It was the new serum that was messing him up. This wasn't anything other than that.

But what if Matthias was right?

"So what am I supposed to do?" I whispered.

"Leave him."

I shook my head. "There has to be another way."

His jaw clenched. "This wasn't my purpose in coming here tonight. What happens with that vampire hunter is not my concern."

Something in the way he said it made my breath catch. "There is a way to help him, isn't there? And you know what it is."

"Yes, there is a way. The only way. But you won't like it very much."

"What is it?"

He studied me for a moment. "Why would I tell you?"

"Because I—I'm asking you nicely."

He laughed out loud at that. "Jillian, I don't think you're capable of asking for anything nicely." I could have sworn I saw some irritation and impatience in his gaze before his expression softened a fraction. "Find out where my daughter is being kept and I will tell you how to save your dhampyr lover. I'll be in touch soon."

"Matthias, wait!" I chased after him as he began walking away again. Suddenly, he turned and grabbed me hard, dragging me backward. I shrieked out loud.

"Someone's here." He pulled me around the corner of the motel before releasing me. "Go back to your room. Don't come out or they'll be able to smell you."

Before I could ask another question he stalked back around to the empty parking lot. He was twenty feet away from me when I saw the dark shadows of three men stretch across the pavement.

I pressed back against the wall, but I didn't leave. Not yet. I needed to know who they were and what they wanted. Maybe they were after Declan and me. He'd said they could smell me, so that meant they were vampires.

It was the small man wearing glasses and a three-piece suit, flanked by two larger ones, who spoke first. "Your majesty."

"Meyers." Matthias's back was to me. He stood as if blocking my location. "How did you find me?"

He didn't sound totally surprised to see these people. His voice was curt and lacked friendliness. This wasn't a welcome visit.

Meyers ignored the question. "We've come for the key, your majesty. It's time."

The line of Matthias's back stiffened. "You were a loyal blood servant to me. I trusted you above all the others."

"The key, your majesty."

"Twenty years. I was about to finally sire you, give you eternal life. And this is what you do? Betray me along with all the others?"

There was some strain visible in Meyers's face. He removed his glasses and cleaned them on the corner of his shirt before putting them back on. "I have no choice."

"Kristoff cannot be released. I locked him away with very good reason. You know this."

"Kristoff will be awakened and returned to the throne that you stole from him. Your majesty, it's always been a matter of time before this day would come. You must have seen that." Meyers scanned the area. "The woman is here, isn't she? The one rumored to have poisonous blood."

"She's not here."

"No one understands why you'd continue to protect someone like her. It only alienates you more from your former subjects. They demand that Kristoff permanently take your place. You will never be king again."

"Don't be so sure about that."

Meyers smiled. "Your optimism is admirable, if unwise. There's no other way this will go. It's too late to make amends. And your dealings with the woman is only another sign of your growing weakness."

"Meyers," Matthias said evenly. "You said yourself this woman is likely a rumor. Very few claim to have seen her. It's merely a myth created to unsettle us by a group of human hunters—a ruse to shake confidence in my ability to rule. She doesn't exist."

Meyers flicked his chin at his two hulking companions. "Hold him in place."

They moved so quickly I could barely follow it, each grabbing one of Matthias's arms. My fingers dug into the brick. I expected him to slough them off easily, to pound them into the ground. I knew he was strong and dangerous and I'd seen him kill several people without a moment's hesitation.

But he didn't.

Meyers produced a knife and brought it up to Matthias's throat. "I only know where you keep the key because you told me yourself."

"Consider my confidence in you now at an end."

"I don't enjoy this, your majesty. Don't think I do."

I didn't understand why he wasn't making mincemeat of these people. What the hell was he waiting for? This wasn't right.

"Why do you need the key?" Matthias said. "You're one of the few who knows where he's being kept. You can just break in and let him out."

Meyers smiled. "Breaking the lock will cause the room Kristoff is being kept in to be destroyed, including those who attempt to release him. There are no secrets, Matthias. I know all, and I'll use my knowledge to free the rightful king. His gratitude to me will be endless."

"You have no idea what monster you'll be unleashing upon the world," Matthias growled.

"Quiet him," Meyers instructed.

One of the thugs plowed his fist into Matthias's gut, then drove an uppercut into his jaw. Matthias spat blood and snarled at him like a cornered wild animal.

Meyers walked a slow circle around the vampire king. "There was a rumor you'd been weakened from drinking some of the Nightshade-tainted blood when you had the woman in your bedroom before you disappeared. Your weakness tonight proves it's true."

Matthias clenched his teeth. "I'm just having an off night."

The rumor that he'd drunk my blood was true. The rumor that it had been in his bedroom was not. I looked around frantically for someone to help, someone other than me to witness this, but there was no one around.

"You should have sired me years ago," Meyers said. "Maybe then my loyalties wouldn't have shifted."

Matthias jerked his chin at the vampires who held him in place. "Why don't you get one of your new friends to sire you?"

"I wanted the blood of a king so I'd be stronger than the others. And I'll get it. But first, I need that key." Meyers sliced the knife down the front of Matthias's shirt, splitting it open, then pushed the thin material down over the vampire king's shoulders so his pale chest and abdomen were bared.

"How did you find me, Meyers? You didn't answer my question earlier."

"There's a tracking device I had placed under your skin by one of your more amorous consorts six months ago. Perhaps you thought she only scored your back with her sharp fingernails in a moment of passion. For a random whore she was very adept at her job, don't you think?"

"Brilliant, actually." The blood from Matthias's mouth trickled down over his chin.

"I thought so." Meyers pursed his thin lips. "I do apologize for betraying you in this fashion. But once you were deposed, my loyalties to you were no longer part of my job requirement. I'll be loyal to Kristoff. Hopefully he'll acknowledge this by not making me wait twenty more years before he sires me."

"Or he'll just tear off your head and drink his fill to regain his strength. I wouldn't stand too close when you awaken him."

Meyers's mouth twitched. "It's a risk I'm willing to take."

"My brother is a sociopath. His passion is pain and making others—human and vampire alike—suffer. It's

Pandora's box you're playing with—you don't know what horrors will emerge when you open it."

Meyers smiled. "What's life without a little risk?"

Without another word exchanged, he sliced the knife deeply into Matthias's stomach, cutting upward, and then plunged his hand inside the gaping wound.

4

I CLAMPED MY HAND OVER MY MOUTH TO KEEP MYself from screaming.

Matthias didn't scream either, but dark, pained snarls came from deep in his throat as Meyers searched inside his gut.

"It's here somewhere. I know it."

"I'm going to kill you, you fucking maggot." Matthias's words were barely understandable.

"Shh. It will only hurt more if you keep struggling."

Vomit rose in my throat but I choked it back as hot tears slid down my cheeks. I couldn't move. I felt powerless to do anything to help him. All I could do was stand by and watch this horrific attack.

"Here," Meyers said after a torturous wait. "I think I have it."

He pulled out his hand, dark and wet nearly to the elbow, dripping with Matthias's blood. Matthias buckled over, gasping.

"Nearly thirty years," Meyers mused. He pulled a

handkerchief out from his pocket and wiped off the small metal object he held in his bloody hand. Then he held it up to the light enough for me to see that it was a key.

I found it hard to believe that Matthias had kept the key to Kristoff's secret prison hidden inside his body, but he had. And Meyers had just ripped it out.

Meyers thrust his chin toward the thugs. "Let him go."

"You will regret this," Matthias said, pained words, as he collapsed to his knees on the pavement.

"I'd kill you myself, but I get the strange feeling that your brother will likely want to do it himself."

With the steel-toed tip of his boot, one of the thugs kicked Matthias in his shoulder, knocking him backward. Then, without another word, they left. Moments later there was the squeal of tires as a black car in the shadows drove out of the parking lot.

Shaking, I finally left my hiding spot, my breath coming in gasps. I quickly made it over to where Matthias lay on the ground unmoving.

I didn't want to look at his wound but I forced myself to. It was horrible, a big gaping hole pouring blood. But there was more than torn skin and blood; I could see the glisten of his intestines as well. I gagged, clamping my hand over my mouth.

"That bad?" His voice was so weak I could barely hear it.

"Worse." It was difficult to breathe. "My God, why didn't you fight them?"

"I *was* fighting them. I'm not quite as fit as I was a—a week ago."

"Why not? What's wrong with you?"

He finally opened his eyes. They seemed even paler gray in the moonlight than they normally did. "Your blood is what's wrong with me."

I shook my head. "It didn't kill you."

"No, it didn't. I was immortal. The ritual . . . my brother's ritual . . . it was all that allowed me to survive the

Nightshade. But the . . . poison stripped that away. I'm not immortal anymore. I've been weakened for the past week—it's what kept me from finding you sooner. My strength . . . it's nearly gone completely."

I felt cold. "What are you saying?"

He looked at me. "I'm dying. I can feel it deep inside of me. I have days left, if that."

"You're dying? How is that possible?"

"Your blood stripped away my immortality. I'm now no more able to cheat death than any other of my kind."

I felt stunned—was what he was saying true? He'd lived for four centuries. And now he was dying. Because of my blood.

It was a Nightshade success story. And it made me feel like hell that I was responsible for the pain he was going through right now.

He watched me through half-closed eyes. "Does the thought of my death upset you?"

I sucked in a shaky breath, trying to compose myself. "Not nearly as much as the sight of your internal organs spilling out on the pavement." Anyone else—anyone *human*—would already be dead from an injury this bad. "Shouldn't you have started healing by now?"

His expression was tense. "This injury . . . it's too severe for me to heal as I normally would."

"What does that mean? Can you bleed to death?"

"Yes, I believe so."

I'd normally look at Matthias as a threat, not a potential victim. But here he lay, his life spilling out of him, his immortality a thing of the past. I didn't want to feel empathy for him, but I did anyway. "You need to tell me how to save Declan."

He laughed at that, before the sound was cut off with a groan. "As my life spills out on the ground with only you to witness the end of me, your thoughts are with your soon to be uncontrollable dhampyr lover."

I squeezed my eyes shut for a moment. I didn't believe

what was happening to Declan was because of him simply being a dhampyr. His serum was to blame for his violent outburst earlier. But . . . I could be wrong. All I knew was Matthias couldn't die. He knew too much. And that information was very valuable to me.

I touched Matthias's shoulder, glancing again at his horrible wound. "You said you know how to help him."

"I do. And if I die right now, you'll never find out how." It sounded like a threat.

I crossed my arms, trying to stop my hands from shaking. "Do you want me to call an ambulance?"

His grin looked more like a grimace. "Human hospitals can't help me."

I craned my neck, but no one was around. It felt as if the entire world was asleep or that it had abandoned us. "Then what can I do?"

"Come closer . . ."

I frowned before leaning over toward him. He raked his hand into my long black hair and drew me even closer so he could whisper in my ear. "Blood."

I jerked back from him. "What?"

"I need blood. It will help me heal. You need to help me, Jillian."

I scrambled up to my feet, noting that the spiderweb-like indication of his hunger had quickly appeared on his face and his gray irises had turned black. Matthias needed a victim—that's what he was asking for. Since he couldn't sink his fangs into me to get healthy again, he was willing to see other people.

At the moment he was too mortally injured and bleeding out onto the pavement of the motel's parking lot to help himself. The dark puddle he lay in was growing with each minute that passed. He couldn't find the blood he needed without my assistance.

"I don't have much time left." His voice had grown weaker. "Help me, Jillian. And I will help you."

A steady flow of tears stung my eyes but I squeezed

them back as I tried to figure this out. There weren't very many answers to this particular problem. In fact, there was only one.

My entire body felt tense. "Promise me that you won't kill anyone."

"I'll try."

"Not good enough."

He sighed and it was shaky. "You don't understand what it's like, Jillian. How the hunger takes us over. I'm normally very well fed in all aspects of my life, but right now, I'm not sure. Once I taste blood I might not be able to stop."

Fresh anger flowed through me at his words. "Couldn't you just lie to me? Couldn't you just say you won't kill anyone? I thought you said you wanted my help."

Where the hell was Declan? He'd know what to do right now.

But he wasn't here. I was on my own with a dying vampire on my hands and on my conscience.

If I truly believed the world would be better off without him in it, I'd let him die right here. I wasn't a total pushover. I wasn't pro-life when it came to vampires, that's for damn sure. But Matthias wasn't just any vampire. And he also knew—or claimed to know—how I could help Declan.

"They took my key," he whispered as I drew closer again.

"Keeping it in your gut was an interesting hiding place." I glanced down at his injury and winced. "You might want to invest in a safe-deposit box next time."

"There won't be a next time. My brother will be awakened very soon." There was so much pain in his voice. "You don't understand what this means. The risk of one human life tonight is nothing compared to countless lives in the future if I can't stop him."

If he killed someone tonight, could I live with myself that I'd helped him?

I'd heard enough about Kristoff to make me fear what he would do when he was released from the prison Matthias had trapped him in decades ago. He was a monster, a sociopath, someone who shouldn't be allowed to live—that is, if he wasn't already immortal. Matthias had locked him away because he'd had no other choice. And now Kristoff was going to be released so he could pick up where he'd left off.

And if Matthias was being truthful and what had happened with Declan was only the beginning of a horrible downslide into becoming more like a monster dhamp than one who could be reasoned with, one who couldn't be controlled by any serum or drug—

He was frustrating, aggravating, challenging—but there was something about Declan that I knew I couldn't lose.

I had to stop overthinking this. There was no time. There was only one answer that I could wrap my head around right now. It didn't mean it was a good one.

"Fine." The word came out like a sob. "Tell me what I need to do."

He forced himself up to a sitting position, holding his intestines in with his right hand. His abdomen was a ragged ruin of flesh and blood. His handsome face had paled more than I thought possible considering how white he was to start with, and the dark circles under his eyes had only grown darker. His blond hair was streaked with his blood. His eyes black. His cheekbones and jawline were covered in those scary-looking thin dark veins. He looked like an angel of death.

"Get me to a human with blood flowing through their veins. Anyone will do."

I didn't think. I just moved. I helped him to his feet and his weight slumped against me, almost knocking me over.

He groaned. "Please hurry. Right now, your blood is nearly impossible to resist. This time I know it would kill me in seconds."

I gritted my teeth as I half pulled, half dragged him across the lot back to the motel. "I'll keep it in mind for the future."

"There," he said after a minute.

I looked forward to see there was a motel door he was pointing at. It was on the side opposite to mine. I figured that there were only a few occupied rooms in the cheap motel and the rooms on either side of my room were currently empty. It was the only explanation for no police banging on the door after Declan had made like a rock star and trashed the place.

"There's someone in there?" I asked.

"A woman. Alone."

A chill shot down my spine. "Please don't kill her, Matthias."

"Go back to your room. You don't need to see this."

Before I could say another word, he knocked on the door, much as he'd done to mine earlier. I half hoped she wouldn't answer it. What sane single woman opened her motel room door in the dead of the night? Then again, this wasn't exactly a prime location for the sane.

After a few moments, the door creaked open.

"What the hell do you want?" the woman said. She was a bleached blonde who'd hit her prime of beauty at least twenty years ago. Her eyes bugged as she took in the terrifying sight in front of her. "Wait a minute—no—"

She went to slam the door shut, but Matthias blocked it.

"Look at me," he said.

She whimpered with fear, but then looked at him and he captured her immediately in his gaze.

"I will try to make this as easy as I can on you. Is my influence working?"

"Yes." The tremble in her voice had vanished.

"Matthias—" I began.

"I said for you to go." He shot a look at me, and then pushed the woman inside her room, slamming the door behind him.

He was going to kill her.

Do as he said and go, I thought.

But I didn't do that. I couldn't. Instead, I moved to the window. The drapes were open a crack. This time *I* was the Peeping Tom.

The woman staggered backward, not taking her eyes off Matthias. He looked more demon than angel now. In the light of her room his veins were easily visible and now appeared to cover most of his face. His eyes were as black as death. His cheekbones had sunken in, giving his face a skull-like appearance.

He reached out a bloody hand to her, while keeping the other tight against his split-open gut, and swept the brassy blond hair off her shoulders. Then he grabbed the edge of her leopard print teddy and pulled it down over her shoulder till it was low enough to expose a large, sagging breast. He did the same to the other side. The trashy garment fell to the floor, leaving her completely naked.

"Jesus," I hissed under my breath, gripping the edge of the window. I could barely breathe. I shouldn't be here, watching this. I felt sickened and afraid, but I couldn't turn away.

Matthias didn't waste any more time. He bent over and sank his fangs into her throat and red blood slid down to her shoulder as he began to feed. I half expected the woman to fight, but of course, she couldn't. His bite had paralyzed her and her arms hung slackly at her sides. However, her head was turned toward me and I could see the expression on her face. It disturbed me as much as anything else I'd witnessed tonight.

She looked orgasmic.

My hands trembled and felt cold despite the heat of the night, so I rubbed them together. I knew I had to wait there. I had to make sure he stopped before he killed her. Another glance in the window showed that he now had her limp, naked body pinned on her bed, her legs spread, his hand sliding down the length of her.

The whole scenario made the memory of what had happened to me in Matthias's chambers come back vividly. Other than the blood-drinking it wasn't that far off. I hadn't been afraid when I was in his bed. His influence worked to make everything seem okay, even desirable, even when it wasn't.

After another minute, I sank down to the ground, covered my face with my hands, and started to sob.

Weak and pathetic. Yeah, I know. It had been a difficult couple of weeks.

I jumped nearly out of my skin when the door opened a few minutes later and Matthias emerged. The veins were gone from his face and his eyes had returned to their regular color, but his mouth was smeared with blood. He wiped the back of his right sleeve over his lips as he continued to hold his stomach with his left hand.

"She's still alive," he said. "She'll be weakened for a while, but she'll recover. I promise."

I got shakily to my feet and looked in the window. The victim was in bed, the sheets pulled up to her chin. Her chest moved so I could tell she was still breathing. He didn't hurt her. He'd drank enough blood to fix himself and then he'd tucked her into bed and left.

I was surprised. Truly, completely surprised. Relief moved through me so quickly it nearly made me dizzy.

"Good." I turned away from him and walked back to my motel room. He was behind me, and without asking permission, he entered behind me and closed the door. I tensed. "Matthias, I want you to leave."

Before he said anything, his knees buckled and he sank to the floor, his eyes rolling back into his head.

Shit.

I waited for a moment for him to wake up, but he didn't. I worried that the woman's blood hadn't been enough. I crouched next to him and pulled at his hand so I could see his bloody wound.

I ran into the bathroom, and my hands were trembling violently as I wet a towel, then returned to kneel beside him so I could clean the wound a bit to check how severe it was. I braced myself for the worst. It wasn't nearly as bad as it had been before. I watched in disbelief as the skin a couple inches above his navel knit together like magic over the next couple of minutes.

I'd watched Declan heal like this before, knife and gunshot wounds that needed to be cleaned and taken care of before they had a chance to properly heal. The speed was nearly the same, but the results were very different. While Declan retained a scar to show where the injury had been, a raised reddish pink patch of hardened skin before it faded with additional time, Matthias's skin healed flawlessly. Not a single mark remained after ten minutes had gone by of the injury that had almost introduced his internal organs to the cold, hard pavement.

I rubbed the damp towel over where the wound had been only minutes before, then touched the healed flesh with my fingertips just to prove I wasn't imagining things.

"A little lower, please. And feel free to kiss it better."

I yanked my hand back. Matthias watched me with half-lidded eyes and a pained smile stretching across his face.

"I'll pass, thanks."

His amusement faded. Even though he'd been healed from this injury, it didn't change anything. He believed he was going to die soon from drinking my blood a week ago, and I had no proof that he was wrong about that.

"You look worried about me," he said.

I swallowed hard and turned away from him. "You think so?"

"Yes."

I wanted to argue, but I couldn't find the strength. I had cared if he lived or died tonight, and I couldn't simply say it was only because of the information he had about Declan.

Maybe I was more softhearted than I gave myself credit for.

"You thought I was going to kill that woman," he said.

I bit my bottom lip. "I thought it was a distinct possibility. I mean, you *are* a vampire."

"I could have killed her easily. But her death wouldn't have made any difference in strength to me. I took what blood I needed and that was all."

"So getting her naked first was just personal preference?"

He raised a pale eyebrow. "Keeping watch, were you? I never would have guessed you were a voyeur, Jillian."

I hated that he was able to make me blush. "I guess I don't understand how biting someone's neck requires them to show their tits and ass."

"No." He began to push himself slowly up to his feet. "You wouldn't understand."

I watched him warily. "So make me understand."

"Bare skin allows me to feed better. After all, I don't just feed on blood. At my age, I can feed on a human's sexual energy as well, which I could tell at a glance she had in spades. I needed all the help I could get." He smiled. "I really wouldn't worry. I think she enjoyed herself. And when she wakes, she'll remember nothing from the incident. No damage done. Is it still sick to you now that I've explained it?"

My face felt tight. "I don't know."

"Now I'd like to use your shower to clean myself up." His smile widened. "You're welcome to join me if you like. I may not be able to drink your blood, but I can still feed off your desire."

I stood up and moved back from him, feeling that I'd been a bit too friendly with the former vampire king and given him the wrong impression. "Listen, Matthias. Let's get one thing straight here. What happened between us— well, it was completely fake. It was no different from what just happened with you and your random blood donor just now. The only difference is you didn't do me the courtesy of letting me forget about it."

His amused expression held. "Of course, whatever you say. Now, your shower?"

"If I say no, will you leave?"

"You make an excellent point." Without another word he walked to the bathroom and closed the door behind him. I heard the water turn on a moment later.

To say my feelings toward the former vampire king were conflicted would be a vast understatement. My current emotions included dislike and discomfort, as well as grudging admiration that he'd managed to survive being gutted enough to be a cocky asshole about it. I didn't know what else to do other than stand there awkwardly and wait for him to be done.

Declan returned before the shower turned off. The door swung open slowly and he seemed surprised to see me standing there.

I tensed the moment I saw him. It felt as if he'd been gone a day, not just a couple of hours. "Where did you go?"

"I—I needed time to clear my head. I wasn't thinking straight before."

No shit. I exhaled shakily, hating that I felt fear at seeing him again. "And now?"

"I'm better. Whatever that was—it passed. It took a while."

I grabbed his hands so I could see them closer. His knuckles were red and it looked as if they'd recently healed from a more serious injury. I looked up at him. "Punching somebody?"

"Some*thing*. A wall. Concrete."

"Did it help?"

"A little. Although the wall might disagree." He glanced at the bed and at the damage he'd done to this wall earlier. His face showed strain. "I'm so sorry."

I shook my head. "Don't be sorry. It's okay."

His brows were drawn closely together and he studied the floor. "How can you say that? I could have hurt you."

"You didn't. And you wouldn't." I believed it. I didn't care what Matthias had told me, Declan wasn't like that. This was an isolated incident only.

"Nothing like that's ever happened to me before. But . . ."

"But what?"

"I've felt that rising violence inside me in the past, but it was something I could control. Distant. Fleeting. There was no control for me earlier."

The water in the bathroom turned off a moment later and Declan's head whipped in that direction.

"Who's here?" he asked sharply.

Damn. I'd forgotten about the showering vampire king for a blissful moment.

5

MATTHIAS EMERGED FROM THE STEAMY BATHROOM wearing nothing but a white towel wrapped low around his hips. His pale skin was scrubbed clean of any trace of the blood or injury that had been there. "Thank you, Jillian. I feel much better now."

I'd wanted him gone. I'd helped him get his blood, heal himself, but he refused to tell me how to save Declan—if he even *needed* saving—until I found out where Sara was. I'd had enough trouble to deal with tonight.

Declan's arms were flexed, his hands fisted, and veins had popped up in his neck and forehead.

"Why the fuck are you here?" The words weren't much more than a growl.

Matthias raised his eyebrow. "Declan. You're back."

"Answer me."

"Noah wanted me to deliver a vial of fusing potion to Jillian. During this delivery I was attacked and sliced open by a former blood servant and needed some time to recover."

Declan's gaze turned to me. "Is that true?"

I nodded. "Yes, but it's all right now and Matthias was just leaving after he, uh, cleaned himself up."

Matthias glanced at me. "Are you certain you feel safe alone here with the dhampyr?"

This earned him a fierce glare from Declan.

Declan had a lot of Matthias issues, starting with the lies he'd been told about the vampire that originated with Declan's birth mother. She was dead now and you wouldn't be seeing me putting any flowers on her grave.

Dr. Monica Gray had been the head of the research program that developed the Nightshade formula. and she was Carson's boss. Her entire agenda wasn't to destroy the threat of vampires as she would have had everyone believe. No, it was to destroy Matthias alone—the man who stood in the way of the release of her former lover, Kristoff.

Kristoff was Declan's real father.

Declan didn't know this because I hadn't told him yet. Maybe I figured he'd been hurt so much, physically and emotionally, that one more blow might break him.

Stupid thought. Declan wasn't that fragile.

"Your blood servant followed you here?" Declan said after the uncomfortable moment of silence passed between the three of us. He didn't address Matthias's comment about my current safety and neither did I. "How would they know where you are to begin with?"

"There's a tracking device planted under my skin I didn't know about until tonight." Matthias's jaw tensed. "It needs to be removed immediately. Will you help me?"

He wasn't looking at me.

Declan stared at the vampire for a long time before he nodded. "Of course."

The news of a tracker hidden under the vampire's skin didn't make him so much as blink.

Matthias sat on a wooden chair he pulled out from the small corner desk and sat on it backward. The towel split, showing off a long line of his pale thigh right up to the hip.

"It's below my right shoulder blade and very small. So

small that I never knew it was there. But now that I do, I was able to find it easily during my shower."

Declan pulled his silver blade from the leather sheath at his right hip. He used that blade to kill vampires when he wanted a change from the gun he kept filled with silver bullets. One to the heart did the trick as well as a knife would, provided the bullet penetrated all the way through.

He approached Matthias with the knife in hand. I was surprised Matthias trusted him enough to do this. Not only to turn his back on a known vampire hunter, but to do so willingly. However, a glance at his knuckles showed they were white as he clutched the side of the chair, which told me he wasn't as at ease with the situation as he might want us to believe.

I tried very hard not to think about what had happened between me and Declan earlier, but it was impossible. The look in his eye—that rage that seemed to be completely gone now, that had come out of nowhere—it bothered me a lot.

Matthias said it wasn't because of the serum or my blood, it was simply because he was a dhampyr. And it was only the beginning.

The thought chilled me as I touched my tender throat, the throat I'd thought for a split second he'd wanted to tear out.

"Here?" Declan touched the spot Matthias mentioned.

"Yes."

"I feel it. It makes me wonder how you didn't notice it before. It had to get in here somehow."

Matthias turned his head. "My play is sometimes a little rough. Spilled blood—mine or another's—can be part of the fun."

"Your *play*."

"Sex, dhampyr." Matthias's lips curled. "A woman's fingernails can be used to show her passion. I've found that the harder they scratch, the more they are enjoying themselves."

Declan's jaw clenched. "Or the more they're trying to fight a man taking them against their will."

"I've never taken a woman against her will. I think you have me confused with my brother." He hissed as Declan sliced into his skin. "No warning?"

"Hurts less if you're not expecting it."

Declan spread the cut flesh and felt about for the tracking device. A fresh well of blood spilled down Matthias's side to stain the stark white towel. He didn't move, but his face grew more tense.

It reminded me too much of earlier and seeing the blood servant with his hand deep in Matthias's gut, searching for the key.

"If Kristoff's really so bad, you don't think Meyers will have second thoughts about freeing him?" I asked, although I already knew the answer to that.

Matthias's pale gaze moved to me. There was sweat on his brow and pain in his eyes. Declan wasn't trying to be particularly gentle during this operation. "No. I have no doubt he'll free my brother, but I didn't think it would be so soon."

"What are you talking about?" Declan asked.

"I had a key surgically hidden inside of my body from the time I imprisoned Kristoff. The room my brother was placed in is rigged with explosives if anyone attempts to release him without the key." His expression darkened. "I told only two people the location of this prison and where the key was. I trusted both of them. One is dead. The other a traitor who carved the key from inside of me less than an hour ago."

I remembered the greed in Meyers's eyes as he pulled the bloody key from Matthias's body. "He seems very determined to have Kristoff sire him."

"I'll kill him long before that happens. But I must also find a way to kill my brother. It should have been done decades ago."

Declan yanked out something from inside Matthias's flesh and the vampire king gasped in pain. I ran to the bathroom, wet a facecloth, and returned to press it against Matthias's new wound. This one wasn't as bad as I thought it was and it didn't take very long before it started to knit and heal right in front of my eyes.

Declan held the tiny piece of metal in the palm of his hand. "What do you want me to do with it?"

"Destroy it."

Declan placed it on the carpet and slammed the hard sole of his boot on top of it, leaving a bloody stain and a destroyed tracker behind. Between that and the mattress and wall, I hoped not to be here when the maid stopped by to clean up. She was going to be pissed.

"You should have killed your brother before he became immortal." Declan wiped his hand against his thigh to remove the blood. "Evil like that shouldn't be allowed to live. Same goes for the rest of your kind."

Matthias took the cloth from me and dabbed at his side a bit harder to clean it up. "Contrary to what you believe, we're not all soulless monsters. We require blood to survive, and blood doesn't come cheaply. However, many of us have chosen not to take from those we consider innocent. When I drink blood it's usually from a willing donor."

"*Usually*," Declan repeated.

Matthias grabbed his clothes from earlier and began to get dressed right in front of us. I automatically looked away when he dropped the towel. "I know you don't like me, dhampyr, but I'm not the biggest threat you'll be faced with. If you knew my brother—" He broke off for a moment. "He's different from most others. I know better than anyone what he's capable of and what his plans were before I put him into that prison."

"What were they?"

"To infiltrate society. To slowly turn all humans into blood servants. To have vampires become the dominant species on earth."

Declan shook his head. "It's impossible. There aren't enough vampires."

"That's because I've kept our numbers small. Not everyone who wants to be sired has been granted their wish. There are currently less than a thousand of us worldwide. But Kristoff will change that. He'll begin to sire many new vampires immediately after his awakening. It'll grow faster than anything you ever imagined—like a virus."

I felt ill at the thought. "You really think he can recover that quickly from being locked away for nearly thirty years?"

"I don't know for sure what will happen." His jaw clenched. "But the moment blood touches his lips again, he'll regain a great deal of his strength. And I'll know the moment it happens."

I frowned. "How will you know?"

He walked to the window to look outside. "Because we're twins we've always had a very strong psychic bond with each other. When we were sired, this connection became stronger. There were times when we could even read each other's minds."

I stared at him, dumbfounded. "You and Kristoff are psychically connected twins."

"Yes."

"*Identical* twins?"

He nodded.

"You've got to be kidding me," I said under my breath. This was like a bad soap opera.

I already knew Kristoff and Matthias were brothers, but I had no idea that they were twins. I studied the two men standing before me. Declan's scars and eye patch, as well as the thirty-plus pounds of muscle he had on Matthias were definitely distracting. But if I ignored that, I thought I could see a slight family resemblance. The line of their jaws. The shape of their noses. The curve of their upper lips.

Matthias raked a hand through his hair. "I only hope I'll have enough time to find a way to destroy him before it's too late."

Declan crossed his arms over his chest. "What do you mean?"

Matthias rubbed at a large bloodstain at the edge of his sleeve. "I believe the Nightshade in Jillian's blood stripped away my immortality. I can feel my life fading. I don't have much time left."

We were both dying. The thought made my throat thicken. I wondered which one of us would last longer.

Declan stood there stoically, seemingly unmoved by the announcement. "So what's your plan?"

"When Kristoff is awakened, I think he'll be able to find me through our bond. I know he'll come for me—out of revenge for what I did to him. He'll want to kill me. This will be my only opportunity to kill him first."

Declan snorted. "You think you can kill an immortal when you're not even immortal anymore?"

"I need to try." Matthias's gaze narrowed. "And I need to know the location of my daughter. In my final days, knowing she's safe is all I actually care about."

"Father of the year," Declan said dryly. "But I'm not telling you where she is."

Any warmth drained from Matthias's face. "Why?"

"Jill might believe that you're on our side, but I'm not quite as trusting as she is."

Declan shot me a look and I shot it right back at him. Trusting? I didn't trust anyone except for him, and after what happened earlier I was a little iffy on the unconditional confidence I'd had in him before I'd seen his desire for me turn to hate and rage. But I sure as hell didn't trust Matthias as far as I could throw him—except when it came to Sara.

Matthias's expression was tense. "You can trust me when it comes to the safety of Sara."

"She's a dhampyr. A female infant dhampyr."

"Your point?"

"I know about the immortality ritual you participated in."

Matthias shook his head. "That was against my will, the final straw in my dealings with Kristoff. That he'd sacrifice his own child—"

"For the chance to live forever. That's right. Drinking the blood of a dhampyr like Sara could give you that immortality back couldn't it, Matthias?"

I felt cold. "You're not suggesting—"

"That Matthias would sacrifice Sara in order to save his long life?" Declan's face was stony. "Actually, that's exactly what I'm suggesting. And it's all the more reason why I won't tell him where she is."

I watched Matthias, worried about how he'd react to this. He drew closer to Declan and he didn't look happy. In fact, I could see a slight tremble to his fists he clenched at his sides.

"She's my daughter. Other than Kristoff, she's my only family."

Declan shook his head. "This doesn't give you any right to be near her in your current condition. You're the one who's admitted you're near death."

"You don't trust me."

"That's right. I don't."

Matthias looked at each of us in turn. "Then how do I gain your trust?"

Declan frowned. Perhaps he was expecting Matthias to throw a temper tantrum, but he didn't. I felt his sincerity that he meant his daughter no harm. It made my heart ache a little for him.

Still, I was conflicted.

I wasn't sure why this conversation was making me so emotional, but I felt tears sliding down my cheeks. "You're wrong about one thing, Declan, I don't trust easily. I don't trust Matthias in many matters, but when it comes to Sara, I . . ." Both men were staring at me now with strange expressions on their faces. "What's wrong?"

"Jill—" There was a catch to Declan's voice. "Your face . . ."

I reached up to wipe at my tears. When I pulled my fingers back I saw that they were covered in blood so dark red that it was almost black.

A moment later a curtain of pain descended over me,

making me collapse to my knees. I braced myself on the floor, hunched over, and saw the blood drip to the cheap beige carpet there.

After a moment, all I could feel was agony. All I could see was blood.

And then darkness claimed me.

6

THERE WAS LIGHT STREAMING IN THROUGH THE WIN-dow when I woke. I sat bolt upright in the bed, but felt a firm hand on my shoulder.

"No, Jill. Lay back."

I blinked and the world became less blurry. Declan was beside me. A quick scan of the motel room showed we were alone.

"What—?" I touched under my eyes.

"It stopped. The blood stopped right after you passed out. Are you in any pain right now?"

I felt achy, like I'd run a marathon, but there was no intense pain like I'd felt before. "No, I—did that really happen?"

"I'm afraid so." His expression was stony, cool, and collected, but his hands were warm as he stroked the hair off my forehead. I settled back down on the pillow. "I was worried about you."

"You don't look worried."

His gaze moved to my face and there was again that frustrating flatness to his gray eye thanks to the serum.

"My emotions were all fucked up last night, but I'm back to normal now. But don't think for a moment that I wasn't worried. That I'm not worried now."

"The Nightshade," I said, my voice shaky. "It's killing me, Declan."

There was a flicker of something this time in that single eye of his. He knew I spoke the truth. "There's no reason to believe it's that serious."

My throat felt thick and the fear I'd felt before came flooding back. "It felt pretty fucking serious to me. I was bleeding out of my eyes."

"It stopped."

"So what happens next?" My voice caught.

"I don't know."

I laughed a little and it sounded slightly hysterical. "Well, at least you're honest."

He brushed away a tear sliding down my cheek with his thumb. The color of it was clear, not dark red, which was a relief. "I'll never be anything but honest with you, Jill."

"Thank you." I felt guilty for holding information back from him, like who his father really was, but it still didn't feel like the right time.

He stood up from the side of the bed and walked toward the window to look outside. "Matthias isn't here anymore. Your blood was too much for him to handle. I guess when it's inside of you he can find a way to control himself. When it's not, he needs to be controlled. For his own good."

I glanced around the room again, this time registering uneasily that several things were askew and there was another deep splintered dent in the wall near the door as if a body had been slammed into it. The lamp was on the floor, broken, as was the television, its screen cracked.

"Looks like there was a fight in here."

"It was over quickly. The vampire was weakened, so I handled him easily." At my look of shock, he continued, "I didn't stake him, even though I was tempted. He seemed as worried about whether you'd live as he was thirsty for your blood."

I grimaced. "I don't suppose there's a Hallmark card for that, is there?"

"I've contacted Noah." Declan pulled his cell phone out of his pocket and glanced at the screen before putting it away again. "He needs to step up his game and find out more about the Nightshade formula and what the hell we can do to fix this."

"You really think he can get that information?"

"I hope so."

"Me, too." The achiness was fading away, so I sat up again. "I think I'm okay, at least for now. I feel much better."

"Good. I got you some breakfast in case you were hungry when you woke up." He sat down at the small table in the corner of the room and pulled a large muffin wrapped in cellophane and a small bottle of orange juice out of a brown paper bag.

"Haute cuisine." I got up from the bed, testing my legs. Declan looked ready to come to help me the moment I showed any signs of needing him, but he stayed where he was. "Thank you."

His attention didn't leave me for a moment as I made my way over to the table. I was dressed, but the sweater and jeans I'd been wearing last night had been replaced by a large black T-shirt—one of his. I looked down at myself.

"You cleaned me up?"

"I couldn't let you lay there covered in blood."

I had to smile. "So romantic."

He looked vaguely uncomfortable with the comment. "Eat something. You need your strength."

"What would I do without you, Declan?"

His lips thinned. "Likely you would have lived a long and healthy life."

"What's the fun in that?" I was trying to make a joke to help push away the anxiety I felt, but knew I was failing miserably. "Maybe I should inject the fuser potion Matthias brought me last night right away."

"I think we should wait. The fuser itself is too hard on your system to use it after one incident. We'll use it only for emergencies."

"That felt like an emergency."

"But it passed, and it was different from the original symptoms you had from the Nightshade."

Right. That was pain, nausea, and vomiting up a nasty black inky substance.

Will the fun ever end?

Sure it would. With my impending death.

A distraction would be a good thing. Luckily, there were plenty to choose from. "If Matthias couldn't even hold his own against you, what chance does he have against an indestructible immortal vampire like his brother?"

"He has no chance."

"There you go again with the brutal honesty." I unwrapped the muffin and began to pick at it. I was hungry, but my stomach felt unsettled. "We can't just sit by and let Kristoff start working on his new world order like a Hitler with fangs."

"No, we can't."

It felt too big to me to wrap my head around, especially since I'd never met Kristoff before. All I had to go by was Matthias's opinion of his brother, but that was enough to make me terrified of him.

But how could he be stopped if Matthias was in such bad shape?

Suddenly something occurred to me. "What if Kristoff bites me?"

"What?"

I touched the fang marks on my neck from the blond vampire from last night. "What if he bites me and my blood strips away his immortality like it did to Matthias? Then he could be killed."

"That's not going to happen."

"But—"

"No, Jill." Although Declan looked emotionless, there was command in his voice. "Put it out of your mind. It's a stupid idea."

I felt his words like a slap. "It's not a stupid idea. It could work."

He exhaled. "Okay, maybe not stupid. But you're being naïve. There's already a rumor about a woman with poisoned blood. He'll know it's you. If Matthias can usually control himself around you, then so can Kristoff. If the Nightshade was given to a number of humans, then maybe there'd be a better chance. But there's only one of you, and I won't let you put yourself in that kind of danger." I opened my mouth to say something but he held up his hand. "The discussion is over, Jill."

I wanted to argue with him. One of the reasons I'd had a hard time keeping a job back in my regular life was that I was allegedly "difficult to manage." I liked to do my own thing even if it didn't follow the rules to the letter. This didn't go over well with management—any management. I guess I just had a very specific way of thinking that didn't jive with most other people. When I got an idea into my head, it was nearly impossible for me to ignore it. Even if it was a shitty idea.

This wasn't a shitty idea, but I did get why Declan had a problem with it. He didn't want me to get hurt. He didn't want me to put myself in harm's way. It was what he fought against on a daily basis. He tried to protect me, even from myself. He even refused to teach me how to use a gun even though I'd asked him several times. His theory was if I stayed out of trouble, I wouldn't need one. It was one of the many things we disagreed about.

I inhaled deeply. "I'm not that naïve."

"Sometimes you can be when it comes to shit like this, Jill. And that extends to your dealings with Matthias, as well."

My jaw tightened. "Which means what?"

His knuckles grew whiter on the edge of the table he currently gripped. "He's not a noble knight on a quest to save humanity. He's a vampire who drinks blood and lived a selfish life of luxury, using the fear of his subjects to keep them in line, at least until that luxurious existence of his was taken away."

My mouth felt dry and sour so I took a swig of the sweet orange juice. "I know all of that. But I honestly don't think he'd hurt Sara. He might be a bastard when it comes to a lot of things, but I honestly think he's"—I hissed out a breath as I tried to think of the right word—"*sincere* when it comes to his daughter."

"He would have sank his fangs into you last night if I hadn't stopped him. And if he was right about his lacking immortality, your blood would have killed him. He still couldn't resist it. That worries me about his impulse control."

My grip tightened on the bottle. "And what about you?"

"What about me?"

"You said my blood . . ." I hesitated. "Last night when you—when you lost control. I'm worried that could happen again."

He stood up from the table so fast that I jumped. "Last night my mind was elsewhere. But I can control myself when my head's in the game. Your blood is distracting to me, but it's not torture being around you because thankfully I'm not a full vampire. For Matthias, I believe it is."

"Quite a compliment," I said dryly. "I'm torture to be around."

"If Anderson had lived to see Nightshade in action, I'm sure he would have been proud to see how successful it is."

I shivered at the memory of my bloody tears. "Matthias really couldn't stop himself?"

"That's right."

I thought it through. "So if we use my blood to get to Kristoff, I'll have to cut myself first. Make sure I'm bleeding. Then, just like Matthias, he'd have a harder time controlling himself."

Declan looked at me directly. "I advise you to let this subject drop, Jillian."

I bit my bottom lip. "Uh-oh. Full-name usage. Somebody's not happy with me right now." My gaze moved from him to something laying on the table next to us. It was a file folder. "What's that?"

He put his scarred hand on top of it. "Some research I've been doing."

"On what?"

"Dhampyrs."

"What about dhampyrs?"

He eyed me. "Sometimes I forget how many questions you ask."

Despite everything, I almost grinned. "If you want answers, you have to ask questions."

He flipped the folder open and inside I saw printouts, photos, handwritten notes, and other typed documentation. "I've been looking into other dhampyrs that have existed in the area, trying to understand more about what I am. Carson never wanted me to learn about this. But the events of the past couple of weeks, his association with Dr. Gray all of these years, and everything he kept from me, have made me question a lot about what he always told me and what he made me do."

"Like the original serum."

"Yeah." He paced to the other side of the room and back, his arms crossed over his chest. "When I went off it I felt fine, other than having to suddenly deal with my fucked up emotions. So I thought he was wrong about everything he'd ever told me. He made me believe that without the serum I'd eventually become just like the monster dhamps."

My chest tightened. I wasn't sure I liked where this conversation was headed. It reminded me too much of the one I'd had last night with Matthias on this very subject.

Declan's emotionless face was like stone as he looked down at the research he'd gathered. He said nothing for so long that I reached out and touched his hand.

"Declan . . . what's wrong?"

He blinked. "I don't want to be a monster, Jill."

He said it flatly, but there was pain in his expression. "You're not."

He shook his head. "I've killed a lot of vampires in my life and I've done so without any guilt because I hate them. But . . . but last night . . ."

"You didn't hurt me."

"I wanted to. For a second, I wanted to. And that's not acceptable to me."

"It's the new serum that caused that," I said firmly. "It's a shitty side effect, and with Noah's help we're going to find a way to get it out of your system completely. It's simple."

"You're right, it is simple, but not for the reasons you're thinking."

"Then what?"

He glanced at the damage he'd done to the bed last night before looking at me. "My father was right about everything."

I shook my head, panic rising inside me again. "No, he was only saying those things to keep you in line."

"He was saying those things because they were the truth. I didn't want to believe it, but it's the truth. And the research I've been doing the last week has led me to that conclusion."

"Research," I repeated, glancing at the thick file folder. "Is that where you head off to all alone?"

"Yes."

"And that's the reason we're in Los Angeles right now?"

"I had a few things I needed to check here."

So much for him not keeping secrets from me. But I didn't hold it against him. Sometimes you had to handle personal matters personally. And this was about as personal as it got. But now that it was out in the open . . .

I grabbed the file folder and looked at some of the pages. Each one seemed to be a case study with a name at the top and a date. Two dates. The birth date and the date of death for whomever was mentioned.

My hands felt cold as I flipped through the papers. "And what did all of this tell you?"

He scrubbed a hand over his scalp and came to stand next to me, looking down at the papers. "It tells me that my father was right. A dhampyr born with the human side dominant will become more violent the older they get. In fact, there are very few dhampyrs who live beyond three decades."

My gut churned. "Why? Do they get sick?"

He shook his head. "Nearly every case I've found, the dhampyr has been killed. Usually in self-defense. I only found one other than me that's still alive and in the area. The rest are dead." His face had paled and the scars on his left cheekbone looked like shiny streaks. "Look for yourself at my notes. They're murderers, rapists, child molesters. At a certain point, even if they are on medication like I was, it stops working. The proof is right there."

"You're different," I said without hesitation, although my heart was sinking. This is exactly what Matthias had told me. I hadn't wanted to believe it then, either.

"When I was on the regular serum, I *was* different, because that side of me was repressed. But the new serum can't control the monster that's waking up inside of me. There's no going back."

My eyes burned. I closed the folder and stood up. "I don't accept that."

He snorted. "You don't?"

"No."

"Just like that."

"That's right. Let me tell you something, Declan. I know you. Sure it's only been a couple of weeks and those weeks haven't exactly been a joy ride, but you're a good man. You're one of the best—if not *the* best—men I've ever known in my entire life."

He shook his head. "Jill—"

"No, you have to listen to me. This"—I pointed at the

folder—"means nothing. You're different. You're better than this."

He looked at the folder, his expression bleak. "How can I be different or better when the proof is right there in front of us?"

"You can be different because anything else is unacceptable."

His gaze snapped back to me. "So whatever you say goes, is that how you want to play this?"

"Pretty much."

"And last night . . ."

"Last night was a little glitch."

"I wouldn't use the word *glitch* to describe what happened. I could have hurt you—I could have *killed* you."

"But you didn't. And I'm still here. I'm not running away because I believe in you. Everything's going to be okay."

I meant it, too. I'd never been a major optimist in my life, but one of us had to be. I had to find out what Matthias knew, how to fix this and make it so Declan could be different from the others. But I didn't understand—if there was a way, why wasn't it common knowledge to prevent disasters like the ones in the folder?

His expression tightened. "It might be a good idea if I left. Sorted through this on my own."

The panic I felt deepened. "No. That's a seriously bad idea."

"You'll be better off without me, Jill. And if you're not going to leave, maybe I should."

"No, Declan. Please—" My voice cracked. "Say you won't leave me. Say you'll stay with me no matter what."

He was silent for a long moment, studying my face. "Why do you want me to stay?"

"Because I—" I swallowed hard. "I need you. I think I'd be lost without you."

"I get the feeling that Matthias would be happy to help you find yourself if you let him."

I glared at him. "Fuck Matthias. Seriously."

That earned a full, deep laugh from him. "I think he'd like that, actually. Just try not to bleed around him."

I was surprised how emotional I was getting over this. I prided myself on being fairly tough, considering everything that had happened. I might not have Declan's muscles, but I was a survivor. I did what I had to do. But this had thrown me. It hadn't occurred to me—even after the close call with Declan's violent side last night—that he'd suggest leaving me. "Say it, Declan. Please. Say you're not going to go anywhere."

His Adam's apple shifted as he swallowed hard and stared at me for a long moment. "Fine. I'm not going anywhere."

I inhaled. "Promise me."

"I promise." He shook his head and a humorless smile played at his lips. "I'm all yours, come what may."

I grinned shakily. "You and me till the end."

"Let's just hope it doesn't come to that." He drew closer to me, took my face between his hands, and looked deeply into my eyes. "You scared the shit out of me last night."

"Bleeding from my eyeballs isn't a very good sign, is it?"

"No, it sure the fuck isn't."

I wanted to touch him so badly, but I kept my hands at my sides. While I didn't want to believe what he'd said—that being a dhampyr went hand in hand with what happened between us—I didn't want to play with fire. I didn't think the motel could take any more damage.

I frowned. "Did you say that one of the dhampyrs you found is still alive?"

"Yeah. It's a female, too. She's in her early thirties. An impressive age, given what I've recently learned."

"Show me."

He went to the file folder and sifted through the papers for a moment before he pulled one out. "The source I was talking to said she's being kept at a vampire-run amusement park not too far from here."

"Being kept?"

"As a prisoner."

I drew in a breath. "How can you say that so calmly?"

"Which part? The dhampyr being kept against her will or the fact that there's an amusement park run by vampires?"

"The first part. Although the second is equally as disturbing." I looked at the handwritten piece of paper. Declan's penmanship left a lot to be desired. Attached to the location and name, which was Jade Connolly, was a picture. "This is her?"

"According to my source."

She was pretty, with freckles on her nose, and long flowing red hair. She didn't look like much more than a teenager in this picture, so I figured it was probably taken at least ten years ago.

I chewed my bottom lip as I stared at the picture. "Wouldn't she be in danger from the Amarantos Society? She's female."

"From what I've heard, the dhampyr must be less than two years old in order for the immortality ritual to work properly. Unlike Sara, she's in no danger from them."

I almost jumped right out of my skin when there was a sharp knock at the door. Declan pushed me behind him before he moved toward it, glancing out from the curtained window before opening the door.

"How did you know we were here?"

"Hey, Dec." It was Noah's familiar voice. "Great to see you, too. Lovely day today, isn't it? Matthias told me where you two lovebirds were holed up."

Declan opened the door wider so I could see Noah standing there wearing jeans and a tan T-shirt under a leather jacket.

"Jill!" He was smiling. "You look—well, uh, you look pretty good all things considered."

"Thanks," I said dryly. "I feel like a million bucks."

He stepped into the room and glanced around at the damage and bloodstains. "Is this one of those theme motels? Like this is the death and carnage room?"

I grimaced. "Not exactly."

"Then I'm hoping you didn't pay with a credit card because they are so going to charge the shit out of you if you did."

I tried to keep my hope at seeing him from rising too much. "Have you found out anything about the Nightshade since last night? About Declan's serum?"

His cheery expression faded. "I've been trying. Really. But I'm not having much luck. I'm sorry, Jill. It's just that the parachemist who developed it didn't keep any notes other than those in his head, which, of course, Declan put a bullet through. I downloaded the computer files and some email exchanges between him and Carson before I left the compound, but there's nothing that I'm finding very helpful."

I felt a fresh well of disappointment flow through me, but I couldn't say I was surprised. "And what about Declan's serum?"

"Same people developed it as his original dhampyr serum. Nothing nefarious there."

"Forget about the serum," Declan said. "Jill had an issue last night that's very serious."

"I know." Noah grimaced and shot me a pitying look. "Matthias already told me about it. Bleeding eyeballs are not a good sign, like, ever. Looking into removing the Nightshade is a lost cause. It's too late for that."

"So what I do I do?" I asked. "Just give up?"

"No, don't be ridiculous." He took a deep breath. "I've been thinking about this pretty much nonstop for the last week. I've decided the fusing potion is the best bet for your continuing survival. It's what Dr. Gray said before the monster dhamp ate her." He cringed and glanced at Declan, but he didn't react at all to the mention of his birth mother's violent demise. "I think if Jill takes a shot of it every two weeks like clockwork, it'll keep things steady. I brought another vial of the fuser for you to keep in reserve." He pulled it out of his pocket and placed it on the table. "Ta-da."

I eyed it. So that was my Plan A. I'd been hoping for a nice and easy Plan B, but that hadn't happened. Instead I'd met face-first with a brick wall. "I guess that's that then."

"I'm sorry I couldn't be more help."

I shook my head and reached out to touch his arm. "I hoped for a miracle, but didn't really expect it. This will have to do."

I didn't let on how I really felt. That he was wrong, that Dr. Gray was wrong, and that the fuser wouldn't make much of a difference in the long run. My days were numbered. I didn't know how I knew it for sure, but I did. This was only duct tape to bind together a rusty car that was steadily falling apart. A human couldn't survive long with poisonous blood flowing through their veins. I was already living on borrowed time.

Noah looked at Declan. "Why are you looking at me like that?"

"Like what?"

"Like you want to rip my head off."

Declan snorted humorlessly. "I'll try not to kill the messenger."

"This messenger appreciates it."

Declan's eyes narrowed. "Didn't realize how friendly you and Matthias were."

Noah laughed nervously. "We're not."

"Friendlier than I thought," Declan said pointedly, and Noah flinched.

Noah had been working as Matthias's informant long before Declan knew anything about it. The news had not gone over very well. Declan had trusted Noah since he'd come onboard Carson's research project and they'd forged a bit of a friendship. Declan didn't trust easily—about as easily as I did—and when that trust was shattered, it was difficult to piece it together again.

"He's dying, you know," Noah said.

Declan's flat expression didn't change. "Can't honestly say I'm too upset about that."

"I know you don't like the guy, but think about it, Dec.

If Matthias bites it, then who's going to stop Kristoff when he's awakened?"

"I will."

I looked at Declan. He hadn't mentioned this to me before and I didn't like the sound of it. "You're going to stop an immortal, indestructible vampire."

"Matthias did nearly thirty years ago. Even if he can't be killed by normal means, I can find a way to lock him away again, and this time I'll throw away the key."

"Why don't you just get him to bite Jill and then—" Noah began, but then stopped talking when he saw the unpleasant look on Declan's face. "Oh, I see. You've already had this discussion, haven't you?"

We'd had the discussion, all right. The one where Declan refused to let me even think about putting my neck on the line. And yet, here he was willing to do the exact same thing.

"How long do you think Matthias has?" My voice was tight. "He seemed to think it was only days. And he didn't look so good."

Noah shrugged. "No idea. Nightshade's supposed to kill vamps right away, not give them a terminal illness."

I walked over to the table, glancing at the file folder with all of Declan's research in it. "Noah, what do you know about dhampyrs other than Declan?"

"A little. Not much. They're rare. Like, really rare. And most of them are big, black-eyed monsters without the charming personality Dec has."

If he was trying to break the icy feel in the room with some humor, he was failing miserably.

Declan moved toward me and grabbed the folder off the table. "I found another dhampyr nearby. A thirty-two-year-old female."

"A female?" Noah brightened. "For real? Talk about a needle in a haystack."

Declan glanced down at his notes. "The older the dhampyr is, the more unpredictable their violent natures become."

"You're worried about that?" Noah asked.

"The new serum isn't working properly. There have been issues." He didn't look at me. "And I need to figure out a way to deal with them. And more serum isn't the solution. I thought doing some research on others who've existed might help, but I haven't found anything that I could use." There was an edge of defeat to his voice that worried me.

No, he hadn't found anything helpful. All he'd gathered was a pile of notes. Research material was great at giving an overview of a subject, but to really understand what was going on, he'd need to talk to one of the dhampyrs face-to-face.

I stood up from the table. "If Jade's really being held prisoner at that vampire amusement park we need to rescue her. She could help us understand what's happening to you."

"You want to rescue her?"

"I'm surprised you don't. If we talk to her, question her, she could help you figure out what to expect. Maybe she's different from the others, which is why she's still alive." Suddenly it sounded like the best idea I'd had in a very long time. "Besides, no one should be kept anywhere against their will. Your informant said she was a prisoner there. Why would they be keeping her?"

"An adult female dhampyr?" Noah said. "Shit. A female her age has blood that can cure a vampire's aches and pains and severe injuries. The female dhampyr has always been revered, almost like a goddess. Her blood is even painted the color of gold in some illustrations I've seen to show how valuable it is. Her blood wouldn't be able to give actual immortality, but she'd be able to heal—" He stopped talking and looked at me. "She'd be able to heal *Matthias*."

A breath caught in my chest. "How do you know all of this?"

"Consider it a bit of a side project I've been working on. I'd hoped it would benefit a friend of mine before he decided he hated my fucking guts." Noah flicked a glance at Declan. "Oh, and by the way, Molly's fine. I set her up

with a family who love cats, even one-eyed flea-bitten
bitches like yours. No offense."

His voice was distant to me now because I was trying
to sort out what he was saying. Jade, the dhampyr, wouldn't
have blood that could imbue true immortality like a
child's, but her blood would be able to heal Matthias and
give him his strength back.

Then he could go and stop Kristoff when he was awakened. And Declan could put going after the vampire king
out of his mind. I didn't want Declan to die. Dhampyrs
weren't immortal. They might be able to heal horrific injuries in record time, but they lived the same lifespan as
a human. *Less* by the sound of it.

A glance at the dhampyr in question made me realize
that he'd been following my train of thought and the expression on his ragged face wasn't one of approval.

"You'd offer up this dhampyr to Matthias and let him
drink her blood to heal him?" he asked.

"Yes," I said without hesitation. "In a New York minute. Are you in?"

"I'm not sure I feel quite as strongly about Matthias's
recovery as you do."

"Then do it for purely selfish reasons. She can help
you, too." I turned to Noah. "Tell Matthias we're going to
get her tonight."

"Awesome." Noah nodded, although he looked nervous. "I love amusement parks. Do you think they have a
Ferris wheel?"

7

THERE WAS A FERRIS WHEEL. A BIG ONE. TO THE LEFT of the expansive beachfront grounds of "FunTown," the full moon shone high above the Pacific Ocean.

I hadn't known what to expect of an amusement park owned and operated by vampires. I guess I thought it would be something horrible. Something with an aura of danger and death about it.

I did feel dread at the sight of it. But it was coming from me, not the park itself. I'd even been to this one a while back with my sister and her two daughters. It had been during the day then. We were here an hour after sunset due to the fact that Matthias was going to be joining us. Yes, it was me and Declan. Noah and Matthias were arriving in another car. All of us together at the park. Somehow my love of cotton candy and arcade games wasn't the first thing on my mind tonight.

We were going to rescue the dhampyr. And she was going to help heal Matthias and figure out what was going on with Declan. Finding her and safely getting her the hell out of here as quickly as possible was the only thing I wanted to focus on.

"Stay in the car," Declan advised as he shifted the car into park in a spot a couple dozen feet away from the entrance walkway to FunTown.

I just looked at him. "I want to help."

"It's too dangerous."

He'd gone out for the better part of the afternoon in search of more dhampyr information. Despite his emotionless ways, he seemed to be in a foul mood tonight. It was another sign that his serum was not working as well as originally advertised.

We wouldn't be returning to the motel room again. I felt a bit of guilt at what the maid would think when she opened the door on the damage and bloodstains we'd left behind. But it couldn't be helped. Declan left a stack of bills on the ruined bed that would cover most of the damage.

I put my hand on his thickly muscled arm. "It's going to be okay. Once we get her, she'll be able to help us. And there's no way I'm waiting in this car." I frowned at the strained expression on his face. "What is it?"

"You don't get why I'm trying to keep you from all of this, do you?"

"All of what?"

"Everything. Vampires, death and destruction, pain . . ."

"Because all of that stuff sucks ass?"

He shook his head. "Sometimes I feel as if I kidnapped an angel and dragged her into the belly of hell."

I stared at him before I smiled. "I never knew you were so poetic. But if you're calling me an angel, I think you're a bit delusional."

He twisted his fingers into my long black hair, looking at it for a moment, before his gaze locked with mine. "The more I try to protect you from all of this, the deeper you sink into it."

I knew Declan had me on a bit of a pedestal. I represented a normal life to him—a normal woman who'd been forcibly taken from her regular life and plunged headfirst into his. And he was right in some ways. I had one of the most average lives of anyone I knew. Didn't mean it was all that happy. I had the scar on my left wrist to prove that. The deep depression I'd sunk into after the deaths of my parents five years ago caused me to take a razor blade to my wrist one horrible night.

The pain had given me second thoughts, but the scar was there to remind me that hope was not something I wanted to lose again. That moment when I touched the blade to my wrist and pressed down to see the blood well up was, emotionally, far bleaker than anything I'd had to face since meeting Declan. That darkness had come from inside of myself, not outside. Big difference there.

While I'd been through a shitload of trouble and pain and misery in the last two weeks, that tiny spark of hope hadn't completely extinguished for me, although it had come very close a couple of times. I was still fighting. I hadn't given up. Part of me knew there was a way to crawl out of this rabbit hole I'd fallen into. It wasn't going to be easy, that was for damn sure, but I still had hope it was possible.

And when I found a way out of this dark hole and into the sunshine again, I planned to bring Declan along with me.

My fingers tightened on the small photo of Jade Connolly that Declan had in his dhampyr files that looked as if it had been taken well before she'd been kidnapped by vampires. Pretty girl. Red hair, bright gray eyes. Smiling for the camera.

It reminded me of the picture of me in the newspaper. Someone who had no idea of the danger waiting just around the next corner.

For the moment, I would gladly put aside all of my problems to deal with hers. A day ago I didn't know she existed, but now my goal was to free her from this place no matter how we had to do that. If we did and she was okay and healthy, it would prove to Declan that he didn't have to worry quite so much about his future. That he wasn't slowly turning into a monster that I needed to fear.

A car pulled up alongside us. I could feel the vampire staring at me even before I turned in my seat to confirm it was Matthias and Noah.

I was glad I'd been unconscious last night during the fight between him and Declan. I hadn't witnessed Matthias losing his shit before, and I didn't think I wanted to.

"I've been thinking about Matthias," Declan said quietly.

"What have you been thinking?"

"Maybe I was wrong about him."

I turned away from the vampire in the car next to us. "You're going to have to be a bit more specific."

"About Sara. Maybe I'm wrong to keep her location from him."

That was surprising. "You were so certain about it last night."

"I was."

"So what changed your mind?"

"You did. But there was also something in his eyes when he spoke about his daughter. All he cares about is her safety. He desperately wants to protect her." Declan's own gaze was distant. "And he'd kill anyone who tries to hurt her."

"You saw that in his eyes?"

"Yeah."

"And how do you know for sure it was for real?"

He blinked. "Because it's the same way I look at you."

I steeled myself against the lump in my throat. "Declan—"

Noah rapped on my window, jolting me out of the moment. Declan was seriously the most frustrating man I'd ever met. He was stone-cold emotionless one moment, and then said stuff that made me want to throw my arms around him and never let go the next.

Declan exited out of his side of the car and so did I. Matthias stayed back about ten feet from me, his hands clasped in front of him.

"It's all right," Declan said.

Matthias looked at him with confusion.

"You can come closer," he clarified. "I want to give you something."

"What?" The vampire's voice was guarded.

"The address of the woman looking after your daughter."

Matthias frowned. "Why would you do that for me?"

"Because you deserve to know."

"After last night with Jillian, I thought—" He broke off. "I was certain you'd never tell me."

Declan fished into his pocket and pulled out a small spiral-bound notepad and a pen that he used to scribble something down on the paper. "I've faced a lot of vampires in my life and not many showed the slightest bit of remorse for what they did. I haven't always been the best judge of character, but—" He hissed out a breath. "Don't make a fool out of me, Matthias. I swear, if you harm that child I will personally hunt you down and kill you."

He held out the piece of paper. Matthias looked at it for a moment, before moving close enough to take it and study the address.

"She's here?"

"Yeah. It's Carson's sister, actually. She took care of me when I was a kid and she's probably the only reason I'm not more fucked up than I already am. She's a good woman. I strongly suggest you leave Sara with her for now, but if you want to see her, I won't try to stop you."

Matthias nodded his head once. "I appreciate this more than you know."

I felt a huge sense of relief. Not only did Matthias know where his daughter was now, this might mean he'd tell me how to save Declan. It was very nice to know there would be options.

Matthias tucked the paper into the pocket of his black pants and regarded the entrance to the park. "I'm familiar with the clan who run this place. It would be better if we don't come face-to-face with them."

He said it lightly, but it made a shiver run down my spine. Stealing a valuable dhampyr from right under their noses wouldn't be something they'd be happy about.

"We'll be quick. Jill has a picture of the dhampyr." Declan held out his hand and I gave it to him. "Noah, you wait by the cars with Jill while Matthias and I locate the dhampyr. If there's any sign of danger, leave immediately."

I wanted to help. I hated the idea of waiting and not knowing what was happening, but I stayed silent.

"Fine with me." Noah rubbed his chest. "Really. I've had enough drama to last me a decade and I'm still nursing my last life-threatening injury."

Matthias crossed his arms. "The clan lives underground as I did, only their dwelling is on a much smaller scale. They have humans run the park. It's only a cover for them."

Declan nodded. "Then we'll have to go below and check things out."

I felt bad that I'd come all this way and wouldn't be any help in the rescue, but the logical part of me saw it was for the best. It was crowded and busy aboveground. Lots of kids and teenagers and families and people on dates. There was safety in numbers. Not so much safety in underground lairs with vampires who hated trespassers, especially since I could attract them like bees to honey.

Having me along would only be a burden. I understood. Didn't like it, but I understood.

I touched Declan's arm. "Be careful. Both of you."

Declan held my gaze for a moment longer, then nodded and walked with Matthias into the park. I watched until they were swallowed by the crowd. A chill went through me despite the warm evening.

"They'll be fine," Noah said. "Seriously. The two of them together? Death incarnate."

"That's not terribly comforting."

He leaned against Declan's stolen car, eyeing me cautiously. "How are you feeling tonight?"

"I'm all right. But last night . . . Noah, I haven't felt pain like that for over a week. Before it was in my gut, but last night it was in my head. Felt like it was going to explode."

"Luckily it didn't." There was a catch to his voice so I turned to look at him directly to see that his bottom lip was quivering.

"What's wrong?"

He shook his head. "I hate seeing people suffer."

"I'm not suffering at the moment."

"I wish I could find another solution for you."

I swallowed. "I know."

Noah wiped at his face. "I like you, Jill. You know that, right? I don't want bad shit to happen to you. You don't deserve that."

"Right back at you."

"At the very least, I think you're safe at the moment," he said.

"How do you figure?"

"Because there are so many scents here—good and bad ones—that even a vamp nose would have a hard time locating you."

"That is oddly comforting."

"I'm here to help."

He was right. Even from where we stood near the entrance, the familiar carnival sounds and smells were strong and brought me back to a simpler time. There was no admittance fee to the park, so the entrance was wide and we could see almost everything at a glance.

To our right, I watched a mother lift her little boy up so he could throw a baseball toward a carnival game. The boy missed, but the mom celebrated the throw anyway. The carny gave the kid a small plush toy for his efforts.

A flash of red hair caught my eye as a woman moved past them. She turned a little so I could see her face.

I gasped.

"Ouch. What are you doing?" Noah asked. I realized my fingernails were digging into his arm. I loosened my hold a little.

"Noah, that's her."

"Her who?"

"Jade. The woman with the red hair. I—I'm sure it's her."

He frowned. "I thought she's being kept prisoner underground."

Jade held the hand of a little blond girl eating an ice-cream cone. I watched as they waited briefly in a short line up to get on the Ferris wheel. I moved toward them as the ride began to move and Jade and the girl rose high into the air.

"I'll call Declan and tell him we found her." Noah fished into his pocket for his cell phone and pecked in the numbers, then held it to his ear. After a few moments. "Voice mail. He's not picking up. I'll text him."

I didn't want her to get away from me so I followed after the ride let off a few minutes later and they entered the crowd again.

"Jade," I called out.

She stopped walking and turned slowly to look at me with a quizzical expression on her face.

It was her. I was sure of it. That hair was unusual and vibrant. Her face was older, but still beautiful. Her gray eyes scanned me. I felt a mix of apprehension and elation churning in my gut. Matthias and Declan were looking in the wrong place. She wasn't hidden somewhere underground. She was right here, right in front of me. And if I hadn't been asked to wait by the cars, I never would have seen her.

She looked normal, totally normal and completely in control. Hope swelled inside me as I walked right up to her.

"I'm sorry." She frowned at me. "Do I know you?"

This wasn't remotely how I'd pictured our meeting, but I could work with it. In fact, this was way better than a smash and grab rescue mission.

"I'm Jill. Uh, this is Noah." I wasn't prepared, so I felt

a bit uncertain about exactly what to say to her. I still held tightly onto Noah's arm, but he wasn't complaining anymore. "We really need to talk to you."

"I'm sorry, Jill, but my daughter and I were just leaving." She turned away.

"Wait! I know what you are."

She froze and glanced over her shoulder at me. "Who are you?"

My heart pounded hard and fast. "I'm a friend."

She hesitated, then crouched down next to the little girl and put her hands on her shoulders. "I'm going to talk to this nice lady for a minute, okay? Go find your father."

"Yes, mommy." The girl licked her ice-cream cone, glanced up at me curiously, and then walked off into the crowd.

I watched her wander away. "Is that a good idea? She's so young."

"It's fine. This is our home. We live here with some people who take care of us."

I glanced at Noah. He was staying quiet, but his presence next to me was reassuring.

"Listen, Jade—"

"What is it you know about me?"

I held my breath a moment, before letting it out. "You're a dhampyr."

I braced myself for her reaction, but after a moment of silence a slight smile flickered at her lips. "Yes, I am. But I still don't know who you are or why you're here."

The confirmation made me light-headed. "I'm someone who really wants to help you."

"I don't need help." There was a barely noticeable tightness to her cheeks and her gaze moved away from me to scan the crowd.

I wasn't crazy. She *was* a prisoner. She seemed so gathered and in control wandering around the park with her daughter, but this woman was being held here against her will. I wasn't sure exactly what was going on. Maybe the vampires were threatening her daughter if she tried to escape. It made sense and would be a big enough threat to get her to behave.

"There's someone I need you to meet," I said. "He's a dhampyr, too."

Her eyes widened. "Another like me?"

I nodded.

"I've never met another one. Is he here?"

I nodded. "He's close. Will you come with me? Will you talk to him?"

Her gaze darted around. "It's not safe out here. Come with me. Right now. They could be listening to us and they wouldn't like that."

At the far left of the park was a large building with an iron door. When we reached it, Jade pulled a key she wore on a long gold chain from beneath her blouse and unlocked it.

If she had a key, if she had the means to escape, then this situation had to be because of her daughter. Those bastards were threatening to hurt her daughter if she tried to escape. The thought made cold anger rise inside of me and I swore I'd do anything I could to get her and her little girl out of here tonight.

She pushed open the heavy door. "Come with me quickly."

We followed her into the large room and the heavy door closed behind us.

I looked at Noah. "Have you reached Declan yet?"

He looked down at the screen of his phone. "He hasn't replied yet. And there doesn't seem to be any service in here for me to try again."

The moment Noah was able to contact Declan, we were out of here. I just wish the little girl hadn't wandered away. Declan said we could leave without him. Noah had the keys to the car he'd arrived in. That was probably the best bet.

"Where's your daughter?" I asked, moving farther into the large room, which was a storage area for old and broken amusement-park rides. There were a couple of rusty detached cars from a Tilt-A-Whirl over to my left. "Did you say that she went to her father? Is he in here or out there?"

Jade ran a hand through her red hair. "Oh, no. Her father died a long time ago."

I blinked. "I'm sorry? Did you say he's dead?"

"Yes."

"Then how can she—"

"Her name is Patricia."

"How can Patricia see her father if he's not alive?" Seemed like a reasonable question to me.

Jade had a serene look on her face as she pressed her hand against her chest. "Because he's in her heart. And our hearts are always with us, aren't they?"

"Oookay," Noah said, glancing at me.

That didn't sound all that rational to me. The burst of adrenaline and hope I'd had minutes ago faded a little bit. Dread was already waiting in the wings to take its place.

"Will Patricia be okay wherever she went? Shouldn't we try to find her?"

Jade smiled. "Patricia can take care of herself very nicely, don't you worry about that. It was so sweet of you to want to meet me. I can't wait to meet your dhampyr friend. I'm sure he's lovely."

"*Lovely*'s one word I probably wouldn't use to describe Dec," Noah mumbled.

I pushed away my frustration. "We're not just here to meet you, Jade. We're here because we want to help you."

"Help me." She cocked her head to the side. "How do you plan on doing that?"

I finally let go of Noah and we exchanged a glance. "I know they're keeping you here, whether it's by force or by threat. We came here because we want to rescue you."

Jade sniffed the musty air. "You smell very strangely to me. There's something unusual about you, isn't there?"

I hadn't seen it outside, but I did now. Jade wasn't quite all there. Then again, being held against your will by a group of vampires had to be taxing on one's mental health.

At the other end of the dim storage room there was a flight of stairs leading downward. She stood at the top and gazed at me as I approached her cautiously.

"I didn't want to go to the fair for too long, just long enough for Patricia to have an ice cream." She closed her eyes and inhaled. "Yes, that's what you smell like. Ice cream. Sweet, thick, delicious. It's your blood, isn't it? They'll like you, I think."

A cold line of sweat trailed down my back. "Who'll like me?"

"My family." She glanced at the stairs. "They're waiting for me in the parlor. I'm a bit tardy, but it can't be helped. Patricia had to have her ice cream. She's very insistent, you see. Sweet child, but with a mind of her own."

She was crazy. The sudden realization made tears burn in my eyes. Matthias said dhampyrs became violent or insane as they aged. She wasn't the exception like I thought she might be and she couldn't help us. She was just more proof that everything Declan had learned and everything Carson had preached was the truth.

I'd wanted her to be different.

I felt sorry for Jade. This wasn't her fault. She needed to be in a hospital with people who could help her, not the prisoner of a clan of bottom-feeding vampires.

However, despite my sympathy toward her, my back was now up. Way up.

"I don't want to meet your family," I said slowly and firmly. "We need to leave right now. I promise that you'll be okay, but we need to find Patricia and take her with us, too."

Jade turned her face toward the door. "We don't have to find her. She's already back. She likes to stay close to me."

The iron door behind me creaked open, and the little girl entered the empty room. She also wore a key on a chain around her neck. "Mommy, there you are."

"Yes, darling. I'm here. Come, let's introduce our guests to the family."

Noah cleared his throat nervously. "Uh, Jill? I'm thinking maybe we should go now. Okay?"

"Yeah, okay." Damn it. I didn't want it to end this way, but it would have to. We had to find Declan and Matthias and tell them about this. The last thing I wanted was for Jade to ignorantly announce our presence to the vampires downstairs.

"He looks like a nice man, Mommy."

I watched warily as the little girl approached Noah and looked up at him.

"Who me?" Noah pointed at himself. "I don't know. I try to be a good guy. Don't always succeed. Kids like me, though. It's a gift."

Jade nodded. "He does seem like a nice man, Patricia."

Patricia held a hand out to him. "Will you be my new daddy?"

"Uh . . ." He glanced at me as if looking for guidance. "Not so sure that's a good idea, kid. I'm really more of a dog person."

When the little girl giggled I finally saw her fangs.

"Oh shit," I said under my breath as my heart slammed against my rib cage. I instinctively moved backward toward the stairs so she wouldn't be able to smell me from where she stood. I didn't have the smells of the amusement park to help mask me in here. "Jade, what is this? I said that we're here to help you."

She nodded. "You're too kind. Really, you must stay for dinner. Meet the others."

"Noah, get away from her! She's a vam—"

Jade shoved me hard, showing her dhampyr strength for the very first time.

I fell backward down the stairs and just before my head hit the railing, I heard Noah scream.

8

WHEN I WOKE, MY BODY WAS SORE FROM HEAD TO foot. I stayed still for a moment and concentrated, trying to determine if anything was broken. I didn't think so. I was lying on my back in a cold, dark room. The air felt thick and smelled stale.

"Noah?" My voice creaked out. "Are you there?"

I shrieked as someone grabbed me by my hair, dragging me up to my feet. I stumbled along on weak legs as whoever it was didn't slow their pace to let me catch up. Finally, I was thrown forward and I landed hard on my knees on a stone floor.

The first thing I saw when I pulled my hair back out of my eyes was Noah. He sat ten feet away from me, his back against the wall in the corner of the room. His throat was torn open and bloody and he stared at me through glossy, half-shut eyes. His chest moved with rapid, shallow breath, but that was all the movement I could see. He looked like an animal had attacked him and left him behind to die.

"What have you done to him?" I choked out.

"I just nibbled on him a little," a small voice said. "I'll finish him later."

I struggled to breathe and slowly looked to my left. The blond girl stood there holding hands with a tall, dark-haired man with pale gray eyes. Another man with very short blond hair stood alongside them. They watched me carefully as I got to my feet.

They were vampires. The same vampires Matthias said we should avoid coming face-to-face with.

There was no time to let myself fall apart, but fear ate at my insides. Noah was dying, and we were trapped in the basement of an amusement park with a clan of blood-thirsty monsters.

"Who are you?" the dark-haired man asked.

"I—I'm Jill." I tore my gaze away from Noah. "Who are you?"

"I am Isaiah. This is Ethan. And I believe you've already met Patricia." He studied me for a moment. "Why did you come here, Jill?"

I licked my dry lips. "I—I'm here because I wanted to rescue Jade."

Sometimes the truth will set you free. I was fairly certain this wasn't one of those times, but lying to vampires didn't serve any purpose. They could make me tell them the truth with a look. And if they found out I was lying, it wouldn't do much to help me get out of this in one piece.

Showing my fear right now would only mark me as a victim. I took a deep breath in and let it out slowly. I had to stall for time. I had to get Noah help as soon as possible. That wound looked really, really bad.

If Declan and Matthias were nearby, they might be able to help.

A horrible thought occurred to me. Maybe they'd received Noah's message and they'd left the park to look for us, thinking that all was well and that we'd found the dhampyr with no problem and already taken off.

Shit.

"Why would you want to rescue her?" Isaiah asked.

I forced myself up to my feet and was surprised that I was able to do so without discovering a broken ankle or a more severe injury. I felt shaken and sore, but nothing more than that. Small mercies.

"I think keeping someone prisoner so you can suck their blood whenever you want isn't exactly fair to her." Bile rose in my throat as I looked at my friend bleeding to death in the corner.

I swallowed back tears. *Noah, I'm so sorry.*

"You're being honest with me," Isaiah said. "I'm surprised."

I forced myself to meet his gaze. "If I wasn't, you could just influence me to tell the truth."

"We could. So the two of you decided to come here to my park and steal my dhampyr."

"That was the original plan."

He pressed his lips together, his gaze cold and detached as if analyzing a small insect under a magnifying glass. "Kill her."

Another vampire I hadn't seen emerged from the shadows behind me and grabbed me in his crushing grip. I fought against him, but he easily wrenched my head to the side and I felt his cool breath on my throat.

"No, wait! My blood is poison!"

"Stop." Isaiah held his hand out. "What did you say?"

The vampire holding me didn't let go, but he didn't bite me, either.

"My blood is poisonous to vampires," I said shakily.

What might seem like an asset to me right now really wasn't. The moment the vampire holding me bit me and then died from it, my secret would have been revealed anyway. There were too many vampires in the room. They would have killed me before I had the chance to take another one out. Admitting it up front was my only chance for my life not to end in the next minute or two.

"She smells so good," the vampire holding me said,

and he drew his nose along my throat. "I have to taste her. It's driving me mad."

"Taste her and I'll kill you myself." Isaiah approached me slowly, cautiously, and walked a slow circle around us. I watched him warily, my attention flicking with concern toward Noah again. If I died here, he would, too. No matter what, I had to be strong for the both of us.

Isaiah looked into my eyes. "You're the one they're talking about, the mythical poisoned human meant to bring death to us all. Were you sent here to assassinate me?"

I felt his influence wrap around me. While it did nothing to lessen my fear, it did freeze my body in place so I couldn't struggle any longer. I became as limp as a rag doll. "I don't even know who you are."

He flicked his chin at the vampire behind me, who finally and begrudgingly let me go. Then Isaiah clutched my throat so tightly it cut off my breath. I couldn't move, not even to grab his wrist. He inhaled and his eyes blackened and the veins branched across his forehead and down the sides of his face. "You're a great danger to us."

He released his hold enough to let me gasp for breath, but didn't let go of me completely. He nodded in Noah's direction. "What is that man's name?"

"It's . . . Noah. He—he's hurt. Please, you have to let me get help for him. He's going to die."

"Yes, you're right. He will."

"The little girl bit him." I squeezed my tears back. She more than bit him by the looks of it. The little monster had gnawed and torn at his throat to get to his blood rather than simply pierced his flesh with her fangs.

"That little girl is much more dangerous than she looks," Isaiah said. "She's over a hundred years old, even older than I am."

I gasped. "She looks like a child."

"She is a child. Frozen forever at five years of age, mentally and physically, only with an eternal thirst for blood and difficulty following the rules we set forth for all who live here. We try not to let her attack anyone without supervision, or she tends to make a mess like this. She doesn't understand that there's a much more civilized way to feed."

"I've tried to teach her table manners." Jade's voice made me strain to look to the left but Isaiah held me in place until the dhampyr came into my peripheral vision. "But she's a naughty girl sometimes. And she doesn't use her napkin to clean up after teatime. It makes quite the mess."

I swallowed hard. "Why does Jade think Patricia's her daughter?"

Isaiah sighed. "She lost her own child years ago in an accident and never recovered from it. We choose to go along with her fantasies since they make life around here much more pleasant."

"She needs help."

"No, she doesn't. Besides, Patricia likes having a doting mother again as well as living so close to an amusement park. Children." He smiled, showing his fangs. "Such simple creatures."

I honestly didn't give a shit about Jade anymore, all I cared about was Noah. I felt bad that she was crazy and stuck living with vampires, but my priorities had quickly shifted. I didn't want to let myself lose hope, but the sand was falling through the hourglass at a furious pace.

"Your blood, it's intoxicating . . ." Isaiah's face looked monstrous and his upper lip peeled back from his teeth.

"Bite me and you won't like it very much. That warning has to be worth something to you. I could have let your friend die."

His jaw clenched. "Yes, of course. How rude of me. Your warning is appreciated." He brought a sharp silver blade up against my throat, pressing deep enough to sting and I whimpered at the sensation of warm blood sliding down my skin. He touched it and raised his fingers to look at the nearly black shade of it.

My teeth were now clenched. "You need to let me go."

"I can't let you leave here."

Panic sliced through me. "I told you who I am. I warned you about my blood. And now you need to let me help my friend. We won't come back, I swear it."

Isaiah shook his head, the knife now pressed to my jugular just above his grip on my throat. "No. What I need to do is to kill you."

"No—"

"I promise to make it fast—" He stumbled forward a foot, pushing me backward. The influence he'd had over me suddenly lifted and it was as if a cold glass of water had been thrown into my face. I leapt back from him as his hand fell slackly to his side. The knife clanged against the ground as he dropped it. He moaned, and it was a pained sound deep in his throat.

I didn't know what had changed to make him release me, but then he turned and I saw what it was. There was a knife with a familiar carved silver hilt sticking out of the back of his skull. Isaiah grappled for it and pulled it out with a sick, smacking sound. He fell to his hands and knees on the cold stone floor.

I half expected him to burst into fire and ash, but a knife to the brain, even a silver one, just wasn't enough to kill a vampire. I looked over to see Declan standing under the archway leading into the cavernous room. He looked furious enough to kill after throwing the knife at the vampire's head as if he'd been playing a game of darts—hard enough to penetrate a skull.

Declan flicked a glance at me. "I thought I asked you to wait in the fucking car."

He did have a point there.

I didn't have a chance to say anything before three vampires including Ethan swarmed toward him.

Declan dodged out of the way just in time to miss a knife aimed for his throat. He knocked it out of his attacker's hand, snatched it up, and sank it into the vampire's chest. Before he'd exploded into fiery ash, Declan had his silver stake in hand and was ready for the next.

The second vampire growled, crouching low like a wrestler, then jumped at Declan, grabbing him and throwing him to the ground hard. I didn't see the weapon make contact this time, but the vampire was gone in an instant. Declan's stake skidded on the ground, coming to rest a few feet away from me.

Ethan's fist connected with Declan's jaw and he staggered back, hitting the wall behind him. He was out of weapons. I grabbed for the stake as fast as I could.

"Declan!"

When he looked at me I threw it at him. He snatched it out of the air and sank it into his attacker's heart.

It had all happened in less than fifteen seconds.

Declan's head was bleeding from hitting the wall. He wiped at the wound by his temple absently as if it was more of an annoyance than an actual injury.

I thought the attack was over, but then Patricia raced across the room, hissing and screaming like a child possessed. Declan grabbed her by her long blond hair to hold her back from him.

"What in the hell is this?" he growled.

"A vampire."

Patricia screeched. "Let go of me! You're a bad man! I hate you!"

Declan look over at me with shock and disgust etched into his features. "What kind of monster would do this to a helpless child?"

My face felt tense. "That helpless child did *that* to Noah."

He glanced over his shoulder at Noah, his expression turning from disgust to grim concern. He let go of Patricia like she was on fire and she scrambled back from him, clawing at the air like a deadly kitten.

Jade had stood silently in the shadows of the room watching everything, not moving or speaking. The woman made me very nervous. Finally, she came forward, wringing her hands.

"This isn't good." She shook her head back and forth. "All I wanted was to introduce you to my family. This isn't good at all. They're all dead now and who will come to dinner? The Ferris wheel keeps spinning and spinning and no one shall ever ride it with us again."

Declan stared at her for a moment. "*This* is the dhampyr."

She looked up at him. "Oh my, yes. Dhampyr, dhampyr. That's what I am. You are like me, just like me. We shall be marvelous friends, won't we? All I want is for all of us to get along like a happy family. Can that be? Please? Will you stay for dinner, sir? We're planning a lovely buffet and shall make all the food forget after the meal is over."

My heart broke to see the bleak expression on Declan's face as he regarded the crazy woman. He hadn't let on that he'd had any hope about finding her alive and well, nonviolent and sane, but he must have had a lot of it. That hope was what I saw fade away from his gaze as he realized that his one clue to his future was a babbling lunatic.

"Declan, it doesn't matter," I said. "We have to help Noah."

He drew in a breath. "You're right."

He turned to Isaiah, who was recovering slowly from his head wound.

"Kill me," the vampire gasped. "And be done with it."

"Why would I want to kill an old friend?" Matthias asked, finally entering the room, glancing around at us each in turn.

"Your majesty." Isaiah raised his gaze to the former king.

"I thought it was your clan here, Isaiah, but I wasn't sure. I would have predicted that you were one of those who set up camp so close to so many warm and happy potential victims. You were always lazy that way."

"I've followed the rules, your majesty. We don't murder humans when we feed from them. And we make them forget immediately. There's no harm done."

Matthias glanced at Noah, whose breathing had become less noticeable. "Doesn't look like it from where I stand."

"That was a rare mistake. But we don't claim to be perfect." Isaiah struggled to stand, but failed. The wound in the back of his head had already begun to heal, but he still seemed worse for wear. Even a vampire couldn't bounce back immediately from having their brains scrambled like a dozen eggs.

What the hell were they waiting for? I forced myself to remain in one place and swallowed back the panic about Noah. I hated to think it was too late. If we could get him to a hospital he might still have a chance.

"I know you've sided with those who believe in awakening Kristoff," Matthias said.

Isaiah looked nervous. "It's a lie."

"You don't know what a mistake it will be when he—" Just then, Matthias clutched his hands to either side of his head and a ragged scream escaped his throat. He collapsed to his knees.

"Matthias!" I ran to his side and grabbed his shoulder. I looked at Declan whose brows were drawn tightly together.

"What's wrong with him?"

"I don't know. Matthias, what the hell's happening to you?"

Matthias turned and clutched my upper arms so tightly I thought he was going to break them off from the rest of my body. The next moment Declan was there, pushing him away from me.

"It's Kristoff." Matthias looked as if he'd seen something that scared him. "He's being awakened right now. I can clearly see it in my mind's eye. I can see his mind, everything, every thought that's going through his head. It—it can't be stopped now. He's drank the blood of a dozen human sacrifices. He's covered in it. It fills his mouth, his hands, his senses—the smell, the taste, the feel—he's awake. And he can see me, too, right now . . . and he wants to kill me."

Goose bumps had broken out all over my skin. I didn't like seeing him like this, filled with pain and fear. I much preferred the cocky, powerful vampire king to be totally in control of himself, but this—this was despair. Defeat. All because of something he saw in his head. He had a psychic connection to his twin brother. That sounded scary as hell to me.

He blinked hard. "It's already gone from my mind. It shuttered off as if he didn't want me to see any more of his plans. The—the bond is stronger than it ever was before."

"He's free," I said. It wasn't a question.

"What I've been trying to prevent all of these years, it was in vain. Kristoff is king again and every vampire currently in existence must follow his rule if they don't want to be hunted down and brought in front of him to face his wrath. This is only the beginning." He slowly got to his feet and, looking drawn and terrifying, he loomed over Isaiah. "You would really side with him over me?"

Isaiah shook his head. "I side with whomever is king. I have no choice."

"No, I suppose you don't. And neither do I." He glanced over at Jade. "I need your dhampyr's blood to heal my recent injuries."

Isaiah's jaw tensed. "If I give her to you will you let me live?"

"Yes, you may live."

"Then take her. Take anything you want. Kill her if you have to."

Matthias didn't hesitate. He went toward Jade, grabbing her arm tightly. Jade let out a frightened shriek that didn't sound human.

"You can't kill my mommy!" Patricia screamed and she moved like a pale streak through the room.

I watched in shock. "No, Matthias! She has a knife!"

But it was too late.

The girl launched herself at him and plunged the knife deep into Matthias's back. He growled in pain, let Jade go, and swatted at the child vampire. She fell to the ground in a tiny heap.

Matthias swore loudly and reached backward to grab

the knife and pull it out, a mirror of what Isaiah had done only minutes ago.

Jade cowered away from him, reaching out for Patricia. "Come here," she cried.

"He's a bad man." Patricia was back on her feet, grabbing for the discarded knife. Despite her small size she looked like a monster ready, willing, and able to kill.

Declan snatched her right out of the air by the back of her blouse as she jumped toward Matthias again, this time aiming for his chest. She hissed at him and instead tried to stab him with her weapon, but he grabbed it out of her hand and threw it to the side before placing the child firmly on the ground.

"Behave yourself," he growled.

Isaiah crawled over to her. "I'm sorry, your majesty. Patricia shames us all, both with what she did to your friend, and what she's tried to do to you."

Matthias glared at him. "There are more important things than this to deal with right now. I'll heal."

"No, she must be punished immediately."

I saw him snatch the knife off the ground. The next moment I heard a sharp, bloodcurdling scream and then saw a small burst of fiery ash.

There was absolute silence in the room for several moments as I registered with horror what he'd done.

A keening wail filled my ears. Jade scrambled forward, gathering Patricia's ashes in her hands. Tears streamed down her cheeks. "You bastard! You murdered my baby!"

Isaiah looked at her with pity. "She wasn't your baby. She was and always has been an abomination that never should have been allowed to—"

And then he was gone as well. As the ashes cleared, I saw Declan standing there, stake in hand, a look of red-hot fury replacing his normally cool, stoic gaze.

"Declan—" His name caught in my throat.

"That fucking monster killed that child."

"She wasn't a child. She was old—a vampire, just like the others."

Declan dropped the knife and squeezed his eye shut. "This is what comes from me helping a vampire in the first place." He opened his eye and pointed at Jade. "You cannot drink her blood, Matthias."

Matthias straightened his shoulders even though it looked as if it caused him pain. His new wound would take a little longer to heal. "Don't you understand? My brother is awake now. You know what this means."

"I only know what you've told us."

"It's the truth."

"You really believe that all that stands between you and the power to stop Kristoff is forcing this dhampyr to give her your blood?"

Matthias's expression turned icy. "That's exactly what I believe. And if you stand in my way there will be repercussions."

"I'll stop Kristoff myself," Declan snapped.

"You can't."

He frowned. "How can you sound so fucking sure about that?"

"Because he'll have power over you, dhampyr. And he won't hesitate to use it."

"Power over me? Why?"

"Because he's your father."

I felt as frozen as when Isaiah mentally influenced me. How did Matthias know that? I hadn't told him. He was already gone when Dr. Gray shared that information with me.

Declan reacted to this as if he'd been punched in the stomach. He even took a step backward. "What the fuck did you just say?"

"Kristoff was Monica's lover twenty-nine years ago shortly before I imprisoned him. Her *only* lover. He kept her on a tight leash and his jealousy was not something anyone would have wanted to face. I'm certain that you're his son."

Declan's gaze shot to me and he looked confused by the bleak look he must have seen on my face. He didn't speak for a moment. "Did you know this?"

My stomach sank. I'd wanted to tell him, but it never seemed like the right time. I should have told him anyway. "I didn't want you to find out like this."

"You knew?" His voice was barely audible.

I felt ill. "Noah needs help. Now. Please, Declan. Anything else can wait."

I ran to Noah's side and sank down beside him. His pulse was weak. His forehead felt cold and clammy. His throat was open and ragged and bleeding profusely. I wasn't sure if he was unconscious or if he simply didn't have the strength to keep his eyes open.

Declan crouched beside me and checked Noah's vitals before shaking his head. "There's nothing we can do for him."

"No." I felt like hyperventilating. "He can't die."

"He's already lost too much blood."

"We have to do something. What are we supposed to do without him?"

Declan looked at me and there was a strange set to his gaze. "Noah lies here bleeding to death after you drag him into this mess, and all you care about is that when he dies he won't be able to help us anymore, is that it?"

I struggled to breathe. "I didn't mean it like that."

I didn't. I wasn't being a mercenary. It wasn't all about my needs, my problems. I cared about Noah deeply, but he *was* an integral part of this puzzle. I hadn't given up yet— on myself, on Declan, on anything. And I wouldn't give up on Noah, either.

But Declan didn't seem to understand that. He stood up, leaving me on the floor.

"I'm sorry about your friend," Matthias said. "But it changes nothing. Kristoff needs to be stopped and I need the blood of this dhampyr. Will you stand in my way?"

Declan hissed out a long breath. "If you kill her, or harm her, I swear I'll break you in two."

He left the room without another word.

I didn't move or speak, but I turned away, clutching onto Noah's still arm as I heard Jade's fear-filled shrieks a few seconds later. I didn't cry. I felt numb and shaky as I tried desperately not to hear the sickening sucking sound as Matthias fed on the woman's blood. It took all my concentration not to let myself vomit.

Matthias's hand on my shoulder a few minutes later made me jump. I looked up at him expecting his mouth to be bloody, but it wasn't.

"It's okay," he said. "I've taken all I need."

I swallowed. "She stopped screaming."

He looked over his shoulder. "She fainted, but she'll be fine."

"Did it work?"

"I don't know yet. But thank you, Jillian. If it wasn't for you, this wouldn't have happened. I owe you for this."

I nodded, crossing my arms tightly over my chest, feeling sick to my stomach. "Can I take you up on that favor right away?"

He eyed me. "Of course. What do you want?"

I looked down at Noah, who'd only an hour ago been so concerned for my well-being that the idea of me being in pain had upset him. There'd been a couple of times when I thought he was my enemy, someone who'd betray me at a moment's notice, but he wasn't like that. He was a good kid, and he didn't deserve any of this.

And yes, I'd admit it. I still needed him around because of his head for research and his knowledge of all things Nightshade and dhampyr.

Steely resolve filled me, giving me some well-needed strength.

I didn't want to do this. I didn't want to ask for this. But I had no choice.

I looked up at Matthias. "I want you to turn Noah into a vampire."

9

THERE WAS SILENCE AFTER MY REQUEST. FOR A MO-
ment, all I could hear was the rapid pounding of my heart.

Matthias's jaw was clenched. "Noah didn't ask for
this."

"He can't ask for this. And he's going to die any minute
if you don't help him. You said you owed me, and this is
all I want."

He looked down at Noah. "This is exactly what I've
avoided, making more of my kind. I've only sired a hand-
ful of fledglings in four hundred years. A vampire in their
early days is difficult to control and their newfound power
can go to their heads. Their thirst can overwhelm them.
Already weakened like this, he might not survive it. He
might be better off if you just let him die."

My stomach felt like it was tied into knots. "Are you
saying you won't do it?"

"Are you sure of this, Jillian? I warn you, the results
may not be what you're hoping for."

I sniffed and ran my hand under my nose. "In a choice

between life and death, I choose life. For myself and for the people I consider family. Noah's one of them. So yes, I'm sure."

He nodded. "Then wait for me outside."

My eyes widened. "You're going to do it?"

"Yes. Now go before I change my mind."

At that moment I was certain right down to my core that this was the right decision. I cared deeply for Noah and I wanted him to live. I remembered what Meyers had said in the motel parking lot. He'd wanted to be sired by a king so he'd be strong. Matthias was a former king. That was good enough for me.

Noah would be strong. He'd be okay. He'd survive this. There was no other choice.

Declan waited outside the room, past the archway and thirty feet down the long, dim corridor I vaguely remembered being dragged along by one of the vampires who was now just a bad memory. I slowed as I got closer to him. He wasn't looking at me with an ounce of friendliness at the moment. There was grief on his face.

Seeing him displaying noticeable emotions like this was more unsettling than encouraging at the moment.

"You should have stayed in the car," he hissed at me.

Tears burned at my eyes, but I forced them back. "But I didn't."

"No, you didn't."

"It's going to be all right."

"All right," he repeated. "You think this is all right?"

"We found Jade."

"She's insane."

"Well, yeah. There's that."

"And now she's emotionally damaged from seeing her adoptive family murdered before her eyes."

"They were vampires," I reminded him. "And they nearly killed us. I thought you had a problem with vampires and didn't mind when they stopped existing."

"I hate vampires. But seeing that child turn to ash—" He

swallowed hard, flexing his hands into tight fists at his sides. "There was a time when she was really only a kid and didn't have any choice when some fucking monster decided to turn her." He scrubbed his hand over his scalp. "Damn it. The serum isn't working right now. I wish it was."

"It makes things easier for you."

"Yeah." He hissed out a breath and looked back in the direction of the room. "Matthias damn well better not hurt her."

"She'll be fine."

"I can go after Kristoff. I don't care what he said about him being my . . ." His forehead creased. "Even if it's true it won't make any difference. He can't control me. I control myself."

I touched his arm and was half-surprised when he didn't pull away from me. "I don't want you to go after Kristoff and get yourself killed."

He swallowed. "Why? Because you need me?"

"No, because I lov—" I bit off the words and stared at the floor. I wasn't sure where that came from. He was pissed at me right now. Rightfully so. This wasn't the time or place to let him know the depth of my feelings for him. Frankly, I wasn't ready to let myself know, either.

My interrupted sentence didn't escape his attention. "Jill, this is all so fucked up."

I almost laughed. "Tell me something I don't know."

He brushed a lock of black hair off my forehead and I saw that his previously harsh expression had softened. "Why didn't you tell me about my real father?"

I grimaced as guilt skittered through me. "I'm sorry. I should have. I was worried that you'd dealt with so much already after Carson and Dr. Gray were killed. I was afraid how you'd take it."

He didn't say anything for a moment. "You were protecting me."

"Trying to." I bit my bottom lip. I had to tell him about Noah, but I didn't want him running in there and stopping whatever Matthias had to do.

"I should have known this. I need to—" His expression changed so suddenly that it scared me.

"What?"

"Jesus, Jill. You're bleeding again."

"Oh, shit." I reached up and touched my face. It was my nose this time. My fingers trembled as I raised them to look at the reddish black blood.

The pain coiled its way around me. I could see it coming but I couldn't escape it. It tightened its grip and washed over me like an ocean of acid, stripping my flesh away and leaving me raw and screaming. My head felt like it was trapped in a crushing vise.

My legs collapsed from under me and Declan grabbed hold of me.

"It's okay," he said, holding me tightly against him. "It's going to be okay."

He was lying to me. I thought he'd said he wouldn't do that. There was no way anything that felt this bad could possibly be okay.

I didn't remember blacking out this time, but I must have.

When I opened my eyes we weren't in the tunnels under FunTown anymore. I lay on a beige-colored sofa in a beige-colored room. A glass coffee table with several magazines including the *TV Guide* sat three feet away from me.

The pain was gone, but I still felt it like a greedy phantom lurking at the edges of my mind. It would be back for more. The thought made me want to curl up in a ball and cry, but there was no time for tears. I'd have to schedule them in for sometime in my next life.

"You're awake."

I struggled to swallow because my mouth felt dry. I wiped at my nose but there was no blood that I could see, which was an immediate relief. "Where are we?"

"I found us a place to stay temporarily. The owners are out of the country." Declan's deep raspy voice sounded flat again. The control he'd been lacking before was back.

Dealing with him had become like dealing with some-one with a bipolar personality. Hot or cold, nothing in between, and the shift could happen in a split second.

I looked around at the house. It appeared as if the own-ers were related to Ward and June Cleaver. A nice, nor-mal, all-American home meant for a happily married couple with two-point-five children. "How long since we got here?"

"You've been unconscious for a couple of hours." He stood next to the sofa, filling my vision. A tall man with broad shoulders, dressed all in black, with scars and an eye patch. He didn't look as if he belonged in this house.

Maybe this was heaven. Maybe I'd died with my last attack and that had been that. I'd been sent here to the beigest house in the country with Declan continuing to be my guardian angel. I was okay with that.

Too bad it wasn't true.

"Why am I passing out from the pain now? Before I took the fuser I stayed conscious."

"Your body—" he began, but stopped talking for a sec-ond. "Your body can't handle it. For now it knocks you out, but it won't be long before . . ."

"Before what?"

"Before you won't wake up again." His face was stony, but there was a faint flicker of emotion in his gray gaze.

"I'm going to die soon, aren't I?" It was more of a statement of fact than a question.

Whatever it was, Declan ignored it. "I'm going to in-ject you. I'd hoped you'd stay unconscious for this."

I tensed. "You really think the fusing potion makes any difference?"

"Yeah, I do. We'll start doing this weekly to keep things under control. That's how long the fuser lasted be-fore, so that's our timeline."

I was quiet for a moment, but then I nodded. "Okay."

The idea of getting the fuser injected in me every week wasn't a pleasant one, but I knew there wasn't a lot of room for guesswork here. It made me feel like someone being treated regularly for a debilitating disease. It wasn't far from the truth.

"Where's Matthias?" I asked.

"When you collapsed, I left without looking back. I texted him our location."

"I didn't even know he had a cell phone."

"He's a modern-day monster."

I almost smiled, but couldn't manage the expression. "The dhampyr—"

"She's still at the park. I had to leave her behind—with him." He didn't look happy about it.

"But Declan, you wanted to see her. Talk to her."

His shoulders stiffened. "It can wait, and I'll go back later to find her again—although I'm not sure if that will make much of a difference. She seemed crazy. Besides, it can wait until you're well again. Try to relax."

He pushed up the edge of my shirt to bare my stomach and I felt the pinch as the needle slid into my skin just below my belly button. It didn't hurt very much. It was a total breeze compared to everything else.

If it was like last time, I had about fifteen minutes before the potion started working, bonding my blood cells with the Nightshade. It was when they separated that I had problems. My body was trying to reject the poison inside me. I didn't really blame it.

When it started working, I'd know it. The pain I'd felt at the park was only an appetizer.

I didn't understand how the fusing potion worked, but it did. Since it was based on preternatural science, I could only equate it to some sort of earthbound magic. Not the kind that Matthias's old pal Houdini did—sleight of hand and escape tricks. Not hocus-pocus stuff, either. No Harry Potter wizardry here, but there was something truly supernatural involved to account for me still living and breathing with such an unnatural shade of blood. It was that magic that was keeping me alive, that helped to kill a vampire when he or she got a taste of what now ran through my veins.

Declan took my hand in his warm, rough one and squeezed it. I leaned my head against his shoulder and closed my eyes.

It felt like a moment of blissful calm in the center of a hurricane. It felt so strange sitting on a sofa with Declan in the middle of a very normal, very average Los Angeles home. No, not strange. It felt good. I could get used to this. Although, I figured the people who actually owned this home might have a problem with that.

I searched for a subject that didn't involve blood or death. "You said Sara's with the woman who raised you."

"Yeah. Her name's Emily."

"She sounds nice."

He snorted softly. "Sometimes she was. Other times, she was a real bitch. Hard as nails. It was like living with a drill sergeant." The words were harsh, but there was grudging fondness in his voice. "I stayed with her from when I was a baby till I was about ten years old."

"And then what happened?"

"Emily . . . I think I scared her a little. She didn't know about vampires or what I was, so the first time I hurt myself falling out of a tree, she freaked when I healed fast and scarred from it. Got this right here." He touched a small white scar by his right temple. "Apparently I bled so much she thought I was going to die right then and there. She cared about me, but it was too much for her. Carson came and got me."

He said it as if it had happened to somebody else, just a story, not a tale of abandonment.

"Carson got you when you were ten?"

"Yeah. Then we traveled nonstop around the country for the next eight years as I trained to be a hunter."

"That doesn't sound like a lot of fun. Did you go to school?"

"Carson homeschooled me. On the subjects he thought I needed, anyway. I learned what I had to."

"Friends?"

"Kids of other hunters. Nobody close. Let's face it, Jill,

I've always been a bit of a loner. Not exactly a people person, am I?"

I leaned back and looked at him, then touched the scar on his temple lightly before letting my fingertips trail down over his cheek and the rough stubble on his jaw. "You just haven't had much of a chance."

He shrugged. "It doesn't matter anymore."

"Sure it does. That kind of an upbringing can fuck a kid up."

He grinned a little. "That's obvious."

My hand came to rest on his chest. He didn't push me away. "Considering where you came from and how you were treated, I think you turned out pretty damn good."

"Exactly the kind of boy you bring home to meet your parents, right?" he asked dryly.

That did make me laugh. "Well, not exactly."

"What do you think your family would think of me?" His expression shadowed. "I'm sorry. I remember you said your parents passed away."

I nodded. "Five years ago. It was rough. But if they were alive . . . I don't know. They probably wouldn't know what to make of you."

"An ugly brute like me." At my sharp look, "What? It's the truth."

I shook my head. "I never knew you were so vain."

He leaned back into the sofa. "What about admitting I'm ugly is vain?"

I cocked my head to the side. "I think you hold on to your scars to distance yourself from others."

"Is that what I do, Dr. Conrad?" He said it flippantly, but there was a guarded look in his single gray eye. Declan was tough when it came to slicing and dicing vampires, but when it came to quiet moments and conversation like this, he was a bit out of his element. But practice made perfect in many areas he was unfamiliar with.

"For the record? I don't think you're ugly. Or a brute."

He blinked. "Then what am I?"

I leaned forward to whisper in his ear. "Hot as hell."

Laughter rumbled in his chest. "Yeah, right. And I fit so well into your life."

"Maybe not my old life. But screw that. Right now this is the only place I want to be. Here. With you."

"Waiting for the fusing potion to take hold, in a house we're squatting in, sitting next to a scarred up, fucked up dhampyr."

"Pretty much." I snuggled next to him and tried to clear my mind of anything but this moment and enjoy it for as long as I possibly could.

He stroked the hair off my forehead. "I need to go back to the park later and get Noah's body." His voice caught. "Damn it. He was a good kid. Getting shot in the chest was bad enough and now this? It's so fucking unfair."

I tensed. I hadn't told him what I'd asked Matthias to do yet. So much for enjoying the moment.

"Declan—"

"Shh, Jill." He pulled away from me and got up from the sofa, his heavy boots clomping against the hardwood floor. He pulled his silver knife from the sheath at his hip. "Somebody's here."

The next moment the front door swung open and Matthias walked in and scanned the surroundings, stopping when he came to me. "Not perfect, but better than that shoddy motel room."

I gripped the back of the sofa as I forced myself up to my feet. I still felt weak from my attack.

"What did you do to the dhampyr?" Declan demanded.

"She ran away when I was occupied with other matters. I know there are a few members of that clan who didn't die tonight. She'll be fine."

Declan's jaw was tense. "You got your fill of her, did you?"

Matthias smiled. "You know, I've always been a connoisseur of human blood, but now that I've sampled an adult dhampyr's it made me realize that it's a much finer vintage. I'd watch your neck, Declan. I do get thirsty very regularly."

Declan glared at him.

It hadn't worked. I knew it. Noah had been too weak, too drained and he'd died.

"Is Noah's body still at the park?" Declan asked after a moment.

Matthias glanced at me. "His body?"

"Yes, I'll need to bury—" Declan paled visibly as the corpse in question slowly dragged his feet through the open door. My heart raced at the sight of him. He looked like hell. The wound at his throat was still there, although it had stopped bleeding and looked as if it was slowly healing. His face was gaunt, his previously light brown eyes were now black.

"Noah—" I began, and his gaze tracked to me and widened. His lips parted. While I couldn't see fangs yet, his teeth looked sharper than before.

"Blood." It was the one word that spilled from his mouth and it made me freeze with fear. It sounded more like the ragged voice of a monster dhamp than someone I considered a friend.

"Are you sure of this, Jillian? I warn you, the results may not be what you're hoping for."

I'd been warned, but I hadn't listened.

Noah lunged across the room for me, getting close enough that I felt his hand brush against my throat, but Matthias grabbed him by the back of his shirt. With a flick of his arm, he tossed the brand-new vampire backward. Noah flew across the room and hit his head hard against the wall. A framed photo of the unfortunate family who owned this house fell to the floor and smashed. Noah crumpled to the ground unconscious.

I clamped my hand against my mouth so I wouldn't scream.

"My apologies." Matthias looked down at Noah's still form. "It's difficult for me to be close to Jillian; I can only imagine how bad it is for a fledgling."

I barely saw Declan move, but he stormed toward Matthias, grabbing him and slamming him hard against the railing of the stairs leading to the second floor. He pressed his knife against Matthias's chest until I could see a patch of blood appear on his white shirt.

"No, Declan!" I staggered closer to them on weak legs.

"Release me," Matthias hissed.

"You did that to him. You changed him into a blood-sucking monster." Declan's face was red with rage. "I'm going to fucking kill you."

I grabbed his arm. "Declan, stop! Don't hurt him!"

"Don't you see what he did?" There was enough raw emotion in his voice to make me realize that the permanent serum he'd been given was completely worthless. Whatever Declan's dhampyr nature was, and whatever it was evolving into, couldn't be held back by drugs anymore.

The timing couldn't be worse. Emotion-free Declan would have been pissed about this turn of events, but he wouldn't look ready to destroy half of Los Angeles in his quest to sink a silver blade into Matthias's chest.

"Yes, I see." My voice sounded breathless. "Noah's a vampire now. And you need to calm down before some-body gets hurt."

"Why would you do this?" Declan snapped at Matth-ias. "Why would you turn him into a monster like you?"

"Declan—" I began.

His head whipped toward me. "What?"

I met his furious gaze. "He did it because I asked him to."

10

"YOU WHAT?" THE WORDS WEREN'T SO MUCH SPO-
ken as hurled at me.

I wrung my hands. "He couldn't die, Declan. He just *couldn't*. This was the only option."

He stared at me like I was a complete stranger to him—as if we hadn't spent the last two weeks together, sometimes nonstop in each other's company. Declan hated vampires. He cared about Noah. Now Noah was a vampire. The two components couldn't fit together for him.

I'd asked Matthias to do this because I'd truly believed it was the right decision. I hadn't faltered, hadn't had second thoughts. Until now.

I couldn't keep a job because I didn't follow the rules. I'd tried my best, but it rarely felt right to me. The proper rule according to Declan would have meant I let Noah die earlier tonight. Since I'd broken it, I now had to answer for my actions.

Declan pulled the blade away from Matthias's chest.

Matthias glared at him as if he wanted to tear Declan's head off his body and use it as a paperweight. Pulling a knife on a former king didn't show a great deal of respect.

My throat felt strained, but I had to make him understand. "Please try to see that this is for the best."

"Noah's a monster now, and it's your fault."

I flinched. My confidence in my decision was fading fast. I wished I could argue with him, but at the moment I couldn't. I hadn't expected a dead-eyed zombie who only looked like Noah to walk through the door.

Declan turned to look at Matthias. "What's in it for you? Why would you do this?"

"Jillian asked me to save her friend. I agreed."

"Out of the goodness of your heart."

"Is that so hard for you to believe?"

"Yeah, I'm afraid it is. Especially when I see the results." Declan shot a look toward the unconscious fledgling vampire and swore under his breath.

"He likely won't be like that forever," Matthias said.

"You don't sound entirely convinced of that."

"Fledglings either take to being a vampire within a day, or they—don't. Noah was in bad shape, weakened and drained. I do hope for the best."

"That's just not good enough."

"There are more pressing matters to deal with right now." Matthias didn't sound the least bit friendly or compassionate. "My brother has been awakened. Your *father*."

Declan's shoulders stiffened. "Where is he right now?"

"I don't know. Through our bond, I felt everything, saw everything, and then it vanished from my mind. However, the moment I find out where he is, he needs to be dealt with."

"I can't handle this bullshit right now. I need to find Jade again." He pressed his fingers to his temples. "I feel the violence inside me raging right now like a storm. It's getting worse by the second. I have to figure out how to control this or something very bad is going to happen."

He reached for the handle of the front door.

"Declan—" I ran toward him and grabbed his tense arm. "Don't go. Please, I know you're pissed off, but you have to understand why I—"

"Don't touch me." He grabbed my wrist so hard I let out a shriek of pain. Fury flashed in his gaze as his grip tightened on me. He growled and pushed me away from him so I staggered backward. "Fuck!"

He turned and smashed his fist through the lower rung of the staircase, smashing it in half, then came at me, grabbing me by my upper arms before I could scramble away from him. He pushed me up against the wall hard enough to knock the breath right out of me.

"Declan, no—"

Whatever reasoning and compassion had been in his gaze earlier was only a memory, replaced by fury. It was just like last night just before he'd torn the motel room apart. His violent and out-of-control dhampyr nature had been triggered, and it was focused on me. I was the one who'd made the decision for Noah to be sired. I was the one he blamed for it.

The hate I saw in his cold gray eye froze my insides. This wasn't real. This wasn't Declan. There had to be something I could do, something I could say.

"Let go of me." I tried to sound strong and fierce.

"I want to kill you right now," he growled, and his hand closed on my throat. "Damn it. I can't control this."

I shook my head, feeling hot tears streak down my cheeks.

Matthias grabbed Declan's arm tightly, but not enough to completely pull him away. "You're hurting her, dhampyr. I know you don't want to do that. Stop this before I make you."

His voice was surprisingly calm.

Declan's broad chest heaved and his face was red with barely controlled rage. There was a soulless, sour, violent look on his face for a horrible drawn-out moment before he finally released me. I gasped for breath and put a hand to my tender throat.

Regret slid behind his gaze. "I'm sorry. I—I need to get away from you. Now."

He turned and left the house, slamming the door behind him.

Matthias looked at me. "Let him go, Jillian."

I would, but that would be following the rules.

I ran after Declan and caught up with him at the end of the driveway. "Wait!"

He stopped walking and looked over his shoulder at me. "Why are you following me after what I did in there?"

I swallowed hard and wiped at my face. "That wasn't you."

"It was me. And I'm still feeling it, Jill. Stay back from me. I don't want to hurt you." There was pain in his voice to replace the rage I'd heard before.

"Please, Declan, come back inside and we can deal with this."

"I have to find Jade. I have to get to the bottom of what's happening to me before it's too late. And then I have to deal with this on my own."

I crossed my arms over my chest. "You'll be back in a couple of hours though, right?"

He didn't speak for a moment, then shook his head. "I'm not coming back."

My breath caught. "What? You can't say that."

"The only reason I've stayed with you is to protect you from everything that could hurt you. Don't you see that I can't protect you from me? The way I felt in there, the way I'm still feeling." His face was hard and tense. "I'm dangerous. To you. And I won't stick around and see what happens next. I have enough blood on my hands without adding yours to the list."

I was finding it difficult to breathe. "That's the only reason you've stayed with me? To protect me?"

"It's better this way, trust me. I'm better on my own and so are you."

I shook my head, panic swirling inside me. "There has to be another way."

"There isn't."

"Declan—"

His jaw clenched. "You told that fucking vampire to sire Noah and you saw the result. And you won't even admit it was a shitty decision."

"I did what I thought was best. It doesn't mean you have to leave."

"That was only the final push I needed to come to my senses." There was no hesitation or any other indication that he was having a difficult time with this decision. "Don't make this harder on yourself."

I finally felt a spark of anger ignite inside me. He was being irrational and reactive, wanting to run away with his tail between his legs the moment he felt something he couldn't control. "Fine. Go. I can take care of myself. You only wanted to protect me because you knew all of this is your fault." I twisted the words to try to hurt him as much as he was trying to hurt me. "Well, I only stayed with you so you would protect me. And I don't need you anymore when you're like this. I have Matthias now."

His lips twitched into a humorless smile. "There's the spirit. I had a feeling you were hot for the vampire after I found out what happened between you two. Can't blame you that much. He's everything I'm not. Go ahead and fuck his brains out. I don't really give a shit anymore."

His words, way crueler than mine could ever be, made my heart break. "I thought you said you were leaving?"

"I've been gone for a while, Jill. You just haven't realized it yet." He walked to the car, got in, and drove away.

I just stood there feeling bruised and shaken. He'd promised not to leave me, but he was gone and he wasn't coming back. I touched the tears sliding down my cheeks to make sure they weren't made of blood. They weren't. Real tears.

I went back into the house and looked at Matthias, whose expression was unreadable. He was crouched next to Noah as if he'd been checking to make sure he was all right.

"He's gone?" he asked.

I nodded.

And then the fusing potion kicked in, bringing me to my knees with an agonizing pain I hadn't had a chance to prepare myself for. It didn't even do me the courtesy of knocking me out this time. At least when I was unconscious, I couldn't feel anything. It was a small thing to hope for.

This time I suffered. And part of me knew I deserved it.

I WAS DYING. I HAD TO BE. THE PAIN WASN'T GOING away. It froze everything out of my head—no images of Declan as he left me standing on the driveway alone. No worries about Kristoff rising up and taking over the world. No concern for Noah's newly destroyed existence. Just pain.

It wasn't long—minutes, hours, I didn't know—until I began to pray for death.

"Please . . ." I writhed around, clutching the bedsheets. Matthias had helped me upstairs to the bedroom where I was now. It was dark and cool in there but it didn't make any difference.

He grabbed my face. "Open your eyes, Jillian."

I whimpered and tried to do as he asked. Tears blurred my vision but I could see enough to realize he looked grim.

"Can you survive this?" he asked.

I shook my head. "No. It's too much. Kill me . . . please kill me."

His jaw tightened and he swore under his breath. "That's not an option."

Then he was gone, leaving me there alone. The pain came in waves, I was either screaming or I was in shallow recovery for a few seconds before it crashed over me again.

Then I felt his hand at the back of my head, lifting me up. "Look at me, Jillian."

He wiped at my eyes with a tissue so I could see him clearer.

"Can you make the pain go away?" I asked.

"Yes. But I need to influence you."

I just nodded and felt his gaze deepen as if he was reaching right inside of me. It was a strange drawing sensation deep in my gut and it made the pain intensify to a white-hot peak.

"No—what are you doing?" I clutched at him, unable to look away from his gray eyes, hearing pathetic sputtering noises coming from myself.

"It's all right, Jillian. It's going to be all right. I won't let you die. Not like this."

"But, why—"

"This will help you. Drink." He pressed a glass to my lips and tilted it back. I coughed and choked but managed to swallow a few mouthfuls. "Now rest. I'll check on you later."

He finally broke the influence he'd had over me, which didn't feel as if it had helped at all. I watched him walk out of the room, glass in hand. A moment after I heard the click of the door closing behind him, my vision closed in on either side of me and I finally slipped into blissful unconsciousness.

WHEN I WOKE THE PAIN WAS GONE. AT LEAST, THE searing agony caused by the fusing potion was. I still felt the emotional pain from watching Declan leave with a promise to never come back.

It was over. He'd had his say. I never realized how he felt about this situation. I'd fooled myself into believing there was more between us than a bodyguard and his current charge. He managed to set me straight about that.

Still, I fought it, trying to rationalize things that made no sense. According to his last words to me, Declan didn't care what I did or who I did it with.

Fine. So be it.

He hadn't been here when I'd been close to death. He hadn't held my hand while I plunged face-first through the worst pain I'd felt to date. That had been Matthias. His influence, or whatever he'd done to me, had helped a great deal. For that I'd be grateful to him for pretty much forever.

Declan said he'd never leave me. Well, here I was alone. He'd lied to me after promising not to do that. I was on my own and I had to make this work. Since it looked as if I was still breathing, I'd have to find a way to make sure I continued to do that now and into the future.

I was going to see my sister again. I set an image of her in my head, clear as the last time I'd seen her. She looked a lot like me—the old me. Blond, blue-eyed, smiling. She was my goal. When I saw Cathy again, I could finally breathe a sigh of relief and know for certain I'd managed to survive this. Until that moment, I had to keep fighting.

A glance at the clock told me it was nearly noon, meaning I'd slept for more than twelve hours. I brushed my teeth and showered, relishing the feel of the hot water beating into my aching body. My brain worked much better when I wasn't covered in blood. From my tote bag I retrieved my one change of clean clothes—thin black yoga pants and a canary yellow tank top. My stomach growled and I braced myself for more pain, but nothing came. It only indicated that I was hungry.

Downstairs I cringed as I saw Noah sitting on the ceramic tiles of the foyer. Matthias had tied his wrists firmly to the staircase railing. He stared at me as I passed by, giving him a wide berth. He didn't pull at his bindings or struggle to free himself, but I knew he could smell me. The veins I recognized as a sign of a vampire's hunger were a visible web over his entire face and grew darker when I got closer to him.

His breathing was rapid, panting, almost like a dog's. His eyes were still black and vacant.

Was this normal for a fledgling? Matthias said something like that last night. I scanned the downstairs to see if Matthias was around to ask him more about it, but I didn't see him anywhere.

Kristoff wanted to create many fledgling vampires in his quest to take over humanity. There would be thousands, millions, of fledglings that would have the same control as Noah did right now. Vampires who couldn't be reasoned with, who only wanted to feed, not much better than monster dhamps.

The thought scared the shit out of me and only made everything more real.

It made my heart ache to know I'd made the decision that changed Noah into this thing that wore his face, but was nothing like the Noah I'd come to know.

"Noah," I said quietly. "Are you in there? Please, tell me if you are."

Those black eyes moved to my face. He sniffed the air and his veins grew darker. He finally strained against his bindings as he tried to reach for me. *"Blood."*

I covered my mouth with my hand and choked back a sob. This was a mistake. I never should have done this to somebody I claimed to care about. If I'd known what it would do—

"Jill . . ." It was a softer spoken word this time. Noah's brows had drawn together as if he was feeling some pain of his own.

I inhaled and it sounded very shaky. "Noah, is that really you?"

He gave me a small nod. "Wh-where's Declan?"

"He's gone." It was all I said, and I forced myself to twist my pain into anger again. I'd have to do that every time I thought of him from now on or I was seriously going to lose it.

Noah moaned and it sounded broken. "He hates vampires. He hates me now."

"No, don't say that. He doesn't."

"He's going to kill me."

"I won't let him."

He let out a quiet shaky laugh. "I'd like to see you try to stop him."

I took a couple steps closer to him.

"Stay back," Matthias warned from behind me. I wasn't sure where he'd come from, but it was inside the house since I knew he couldn't go out during daylight hours. Vampires didn't burn up from letting sunlight hit their skin, but the sun did fry their eyes and make them go blind. Dark sunglasses allegedly made no difference at all.

I crossed my arms. I felt uncomfortable and awkward and scared as well as feeling a strange welling of gratitude toward him for helping me last night. I did my best to hide all of the above since none of it was the least bit helpful.

"Why, Jill?" Noah asked. The veins faded a little. He didn't have to elaborate on what he meant.

"Because—" I bit my bottom lip. "Because I didn't want you to die. I was selfish and stupid and seeing you bleeding so badly after that vampire attacked you was killing me."

Another barely audible snort. "You're such a softy."

"That's me."

He grimaced. "You have no idea what you smell like to me now, do you?"

I shook my head. "You need to control it, Noah. I know you can do it. If you bite me—"

"I'll die. Got that."

"So . . ." I sniffed and wiped my hand under my nose. "Just suck it up and deal with this. We need you to not flake out on us."

"Bitch."

"That's right."

He looked up at me balefully, and those black eyes were freaking me out. "Well, on the plus side I won't age a day over twenty-four. It's my birthday today."

I pressed my lips together for a moment as I tried not to break down right in front of him. "Happy birthday."

He laughed a little louder at that. "Wish I could say I

craved some birthday cake. I had no idea that the scent of blood was like fucking crack."

I forced myself to turn away from him and started up the stairs. "I'm sorry, Noah."

"Don't be sorry. Just . . . be careful when you're around me, okay? I don't know how well I can handle this." He sounded scared and worried.

I nodded. "Careful's my middle name."

He smiled, which looked more like a grimace, and squeezed his eyes shut. I took that as a good exit line and quickly made my way up the stairs, running by the time I got to the top.

He was going to be fine. He was. I refused to believe otherwise.

11

UPSTAIRS I STARED OUT OF THE BEDROOM WINDOW that faced the street. I wasn't sure what I was expecting to see.

Declan didn't come back.

I hated waiting. It was one of my least favorite things in the world. And yet everything was a wait. Standing in line to buy coffee in the morning, commuting to work in rush-hour traffic, waiting for a table in a busy restaurant. I wasn't the most patient person ever born, that was for sure. But no matter how long I waited right now, I knew he wasn't coming back. I'd crossed a line with him that I hadn't even known was there. His anger over it had triggered his uncontrollable dhampyr rage. And he'd left because of it, both to protect me and to get the hell away from me.

When my parents had died, the pain I felt had twisted into something darker that eventually made me want to hurt myself in order to make that pain end. I hadn't known how to deal with the depth of my grief after losing them in the plane crash. So fast, so unexpected.

This was the closest I'd come to feeling like that again. Lost and alone.

I stared in the bathroom mirror and pushed my black hair behind my ears. I'd always been a blonde until the Nightshade took over. My hair had been platinum when I was born, and darkened over time, but I kept it light thanks to regular trips to the salon. I lived in California; it was practically required of me to be beach blond if I could be. The black hair didn't suit me that well. I thought it made me look too pale and gaunt.

It had the same silky texture as before, though, and fell long and straight to the middle of my back. It smelled the same—at least to me. But apparently it was now infused with the scent of Nightshade and helped lure vampires to me as it triggered their hungers.

It was dangerous to have hair like this, especially around Noah. He couldn't control himself right now so I had to help him any way I could.

Frantically, I began to forage through the medicine cabinet until I found a pair of scissors. I held a lock of hair between the blades then squeezed them together. A long piece of black hair fell to the sink. It was satisfying to see it laying there.

Just before I started hacking the rest of my hair off a hand came over mine, stopping me.

"That's not necessary," Matthias said. He'd surprised me. I hadn't seen him enter the bathroom. He did have a reflection in the mirror—vampires not having reflections was only a myth—but it was dark in here with the shades drawn over the tiny window and he was very stealthy.

Sneaky was more like it.

My knuckles whitened on the scissors. "I need to cut it off."

"No you don't." He took them completely out of my hands. "I like your hair just as it is."

I wiped my tears away and glared at him. "Why can't you leave me alone?"

"If I'd left you alone last night you would have died."

I faltered. I knew he was right about that. "Whatever you did helped me last long enough for the fuser to start working properly. Thank you." I tried to slow my breathing after I'd been close to breaking down just now. It took me a minute. "A vampire's influence, it's like hypnosis."

"A lot like that. Only different."

I snorted a little. "Houdini would be jealous."

"Oh, he was."

Something else to focus on right now was a good thing. "You don't do much magic other than the occasional death-defying act?"

He raised an eyebrow. "I could produce a quarter from your ear if I was so inclined, but I don't think either of us is in much of a mood for tricks at the moment. You're feeling better now, I hope?"

I went still and silent for a moment, trying to sense any aches and pains or warnings that this was just the lull before another storm. But there was nothing. "Much. It's kind of strange. I feel better than I have in a long time. There's usually a cloud over me, an achiness, even with the fuser working properly. But that's lifted."

"Good."

I raked a hand through my freshly washed hair that he'd stopped me from chopping off. "Declan's gone."

"It was the right thing for him to do. Violent outbursts like what happened earlier will become the norm for him soon."

I chewed my bottom lip. "You said that you knew how to help him."

"He's gone. It doesn't matter anymore."

"Were you lying just to find out where Sara is, or is there really a way? You said I wouldn't like the answer, but I still want to know."

The line of his jaw tightened. "He never would have agreed to it. Not after seeing Noah like this."

I frowned, trying to understand. But then I did, and the thought chilled me. "The only way to save him is for him to become a vampire, isn't it?"

Matthias nodded.

I squeezed my eyes shut. I'd hoped for a potion or a drug. Anything but that.

"He'd never agree to it," Matthias said, voicing my thoughts.

I opened my eyes. "No, he wouldn't."

"He despises vampires."

"More than anything."

"Sorry I couldn't win him over with my charming ways. He hated me even more than the others, I think. I figured it was jealousy since it's so obvious that you desire me."

I remembered what Declan said before he left. He'd believed the same thing. "I'm not even going to justify that with a response."

"Why do you deny it, Jillian? It grows tiresome."

This was the absolute last thing I wanted to think about or discuss right now. I'd denied it ever since what happened between us in his chambers. It hadn't been real. It hadn't been anything more than vampiric hypnosis. And yet, standing here with the man who'd taken away my pain after Declan had left me all alone, my arguments seemed to be futile.

He approached so he stood directly behind me, so close it made me more nervous than I already was. "I must admit, I'm a little surprised."

I looked at him cautiously in the reflection. "About what?"

"I could have sworn the dhampyr cared about you."

I blinked hard and looked down at the lock of my hair in the sink. My throat thickened. "I guess you were wrong."

I jumped when I felt him brush the long hair back off my shoulder. "What are you doing?"

"Testing myself."

That immediately got my guard up again. I turned around to face him, but he didn't step back to give me space, making me press back against the counter so I wouldn't be touching him. If he had noticeable body heat I'd be able to feel it sinking into me by now.

"Why do you want to test yourself?"

"Why wouldn't I?"

"I'm not in the mood for games right now, Matthias."

"Me neither." He tangled his fingers into my hair. His eyes had darkened and the thin, dark veins appeared along his cheeks and jaw. I didn't think he was going to bite me. He was the only vampire I knew who had self-control around me. It gave me a chance to study his hunger closer up. It was just as scary as it looked at a distance.

"Bite me and you know what's going to happen," I warned. "You're not immortal anymore."

"I know."

My hands gripped the cool edge of the counter. "Then why are you doing this?"

"You mean, why do I let myself get so close to you?"

"Yes."

"Like I said, I'm testing myself."

I swallowed hard. "I remember the last time you tested yourself. It didn't go so well."

His lips curled. "I'd have to disagree with you there. The taste of your body is a memory I find difficult to forget."

My cheeks heated at the reminder. "You forced me to desire you."

"Desire can't be forced. Acquiescence is another matter altogether. But since you specifically remember desiring me, I'll take that as a compliment."

His words only worked to worry me more than I already was. I wanted to deny this pull I felt toward Matthias. But it was there and it felt stronger than ever at the moment. It scared me that he brought out a part of me that did want him despite my better judgment.

"I heard what he said to you outside. My hearing's very good. Hope you don't mind that I was listening."

"What Declan said?"

"He doesn't care what happens between us. Knowing your ex-lover won't be jealous if we're together must give you some freedom of choice."

I inhaled sharply. "I'm not in love with you, if that's what you're thinking."

He bent over a little and brought his face close to mine. "Humans always obsess about love—but it's a very unstable emotion. If you'd lived as long as I have, you'd see things much more practically. It helps in making decisions to know that nothing is permanent. Everything—partnerships, friendships, lovers, even family—is in a constant state of flux."

There was the slight scent of roses to Matthias's skin. I hadn't noticed it before. I'd rarely gotten this close to him and still had my wits about me. "That's not a very romantic outlook."

"No, it isn't. Two things are constant, though. It's what governs all human behavior—and even the behavior of those who aren't human."

"What are they?"

"Pleasure and pain. One will seek out pleasure and attempt to avoid pain. It's the base reason for every decision we make from the moment we wake to the moment we go to sleep."

It was true about pain—I knew that for a fact. When I'd been experiencing it, I would have done anything to escape from it. "Do you have a point?"

He smiled, and I saw the edge of his sharp fangs. "It's why I keep trying to get close to you, Jillian. Because your body—your blood." He brought his face close enough that his lips brushed against my ear. "It gave me so much pleasure when I got the chance to taste it. At least, for the blissful moment before the pain ripped it away. You have absolutely no idea what I went through for the week it took me to recover enough to find you again. Only the thought of my daughter's safety and the need to destroy Kristoff helped me keep my hold on life. You'd think I'd try to avoid you to make sure I didn't feel that way again. And yet, here I am."

I was breathing faster now, my heart pounding hard in my chest. His words were describing something horrible, but his tone had turned extremely sensual. Being this close to him did strange and unwelcome things to me. It made me feel things I didn't want to feel. The memory of being in his bed as he explored every inch of my body slid through my mind and a mirror of the desire I'd felt then twisted through me now.

"You're fucking with my mind again, aren't you?" I whispered and turned back toward the mirror, hoping that would be enough to break his spell over me.

"No, I'm not fucking with your mind." His gaze moved down the front of me reflected in the mirror, pausing at my hard nipples jutting against the thin material of my tank top. I instinctively crossed my arms to cover myself.

"Why do you fight it, Jillian?" he asked, reaching around me to pull my hands away from my body.

"Go ahead and fuck his brains out. I don't really give a shit."

I grimaced at what Declan had said to me just before he'd left. He'd seen that I had feelings for Matthias, even when I was trying to ignore them. And I would have ignored them forever if only he'd stayed with me.

But he hadn't. He'd practically pushed me at the former vampire king in his attempt to get away from me—a man who'd had more lovers than I could count. A man who didn't believe in love and romance, only pleasure and pain.

"I'm not forcing you to do anything," Matthias whispered. "The dhampyr didn't want you. But I'm here and I want you. Let me show you how much."

His hands slid around to my stomach.

I needed to stop this, collect my thoughts, which were fluttering all over the place like a swarm of butterflies. My pain was gone, I currently felt better than I had since I'd first been injected with the Nightshade. There were too many other things to think about. I didn't need this distraction.

I didn't love Matthias, I knew that for sure.

Declan left me. He didn't want to stay with me. He

wouldn't let me help him and he hated what I'd done to Noah.

Matthias was here. He had taken away my pain. And now he wanted to give me pleasure.

He pressed against my back and the feel of his arousal made me shiver. The mirror's reflection showed his eyes were still black with hunger as his cool hands slowly slid under the bottom edge of my tank top, up over my stomach, until he fully cupped my bare breasts. I let out a tiny moan as he squeezed my nipples.

I wanted him. He wasn't influencing me to feel that way. This was real, no illusion, no tricks. And it was something I never would have considered only yesterday. Funny how things could change so quickly.

I'd lusted after Matthias since practically the moment we met, and the dreams I'd had about him during the last week had only confirmed it. He was handsome and powerful and dangerous—a heady mix. It didn't change how I felt about Declan—or rather, how I'd *felt* about him until he'd left and practically pushed me into the arms of another man by saying he didn't give a shit. Not a terribly healthy relationship there, even aside from the dhampyr rage.

However, this wasn't all that healthy, either.

"Isn't this torture for you?" I managed. He still showed the visible signs of his hunger for my blood.

He smiled against the side of my face. "It's unlike anything I've ever experienced. Before, I thought being close to you was an interesting test for myself. But now I know if I lose control with you, I'll die from it."

I licked my lips. "And you're just sick enough that that excites you, doesn't it?"

"Being so close to the only thing truly capable of killing me? Yes, it excites me like nothing else."

He roughly pulled my shirt up over my breasts so I could watch him boldly caress my body without me doing a damn thing to stop him. His hands then moved under the waist of my yoga pants. He slowly slid his hand down between my legs. I gasped out loud and my knuckles whitened on the edge of the bathroom counter as his fingers moved over me.

"Yes." He smiled. "I knew you wanted me. I can feel it. You can't deny it any longer or blame this on tricks of the mind. Say you want me, Jillian."

I forced myself to turn around in his arms so I could look right into his eyes. This was wrong and I hated myself for feeling anything at all for this vampire. But I did. It took me a while to speak. "You win."

Then I pulled his face to mine and kissed him. His lips were cool but not cold against mine. He groaned low in his throat when I slid my tongue into his mouth, feeling the sharp edge of his fangs for a second before he pulled back from me.

He wasn't smiling. "You are pleasure and pain all at once, Jillian."

I didn't want to think about this. I just needed to forget everything. Live in the moment and give in to pleasure. I unbuttoned his shirt and pulled it over his shoulders, then slid my hands over his smooth chest, down his abdomen that I'd seen sliced open just the other night. No scars remained, just perfect smooth skin over hard muscle. My hands went to his waistband and I unzipped him, sliding his pants down over his hips before drawing his face close to mine again to kiss him.

"Just make me forget, Matthias," I whispered. "Make me forget everything."

He didn't say anything for a moment. "Make you forget *him*."

I nodded. "Please."

His jaw tightened. "You think it's that easy? If I take you right now, you think you can just forget about the dhampyr. Like magic?"

"You're the magician, not me."

"I'm not a magician. Knowing a few tricks is not true magic."

I slid my hands down his chest and would have kept going lower if he didn't catch my wrists.

"What are you waiting for?" I asked.

"You want me to make you forget him."

"Yes." My throat was thick and I felt on the verge of more tears. Damn it. I hated this. I hated that Declan had walked away and hadn't let me try to help him. I hated that he said he didn't care if I slept with Matthias.

"It would be so easy to take what's already mine." He hissed out a breath. "But I think you have me mistaken with someone who doesn't mind being used to make a woman forget who she really wants to be with."

He stepped back from me and did up his pants and shirt.

My face felt hot and I quickly pulled myself together and put my clothes back into place.

His face was expressionless. "The dhampyr pushed you toward me in order to make it easier on the both of you. However, I have no doubt he'll come back for you eventually, when he comes to his senses."

My chest tightened. "Matthias . . ."

"We're going to visit the house where my daughter's staying come nightfall. Please be ready." Without another glance, he left me there alone.

If I didn't know any differently, I'd say I bruised his ego.

—— 12

WHEN I CAME DOWNSTAIRS AFTER SPENDING THE afternoon sequestered in the bedroom, the ropes that tied Noah to the staircase were loose on the floor and he was gone.

I froze.

"He's coming with us," Matthias said. I turned slowly to see him standing between me and the front door. "It'll be a good test for him. You know how much I like my tests."

Yes, I did. All too well.

I finally spotted Noah, crouched in the corner, rocking back and forth like a mental patient.

"I don't know," Noah mumbled. "Jill's blood . . . it—it's too hard for me to resist. I'm not strong enough."

"You can resist it. It's mind over matter."

"Right. If I don't mind, it doesn't matter." Noah groaned. "But that's the problem. I mind. I mind a lot."

"What the hell are you doing, Matthias?" My voice came out pitchy.

"What you saw last night is typical behavior for a brand-new fledgling. But it's been nearly twenty-four hours now and his control is improving. His body is adjusting to being a vampire. There have been no accidents so far, which is a good sign."

"Other than trying to attack me last night."

"All fledglings within the first day are mindlessly hungry and violent like that. But he was stopped before anything could happen. Although it will take him months to settle in completely, he should be able to function nearly as well as he ever did. Better, even."

That didn't really set my mind at ease. "And if he doesn't function as well?"

Matthias glanced at Noah. "If he bites you, he'll die. And the problem he presents will be solved. I'm hoping his desire to live will trump his need to taste your blood."

"Oh, my God," Noah groaned. "This sucks so bad."

My hands curled into fists at my sides. "More games."

Matthias blinked. "No. I'm being practical."

"You want to take a fledgling vampire to see your daughter. And that's being practical?"

"If he makes one move to harm Sara, I'll rip his heart out from his chest. Do you hear me, Noah?"

Noah cleared his throat nervously. "Loud and clear."

I didn't feel good about this, but I didn't have a lot of choice here. I wanted to see Sara, too. I'd been worried about her ever since Declan took her away and refused to tell me where she was. I didn't miss the diapers, constant feeding, and the throwing up, but I did care about the baby's well-being. Knowing she was with someone like Emily, even though I'd never met her before, helped ease my mind a lot.

We left the house without another word spoken between the three of us. After what happened earlier between me and Matthias, I felt awkward and embarrassed. What had seemed like the means to help me forget about Declan, now seemed indulgent and irresponsible. To say the least. I didn't hate the former vampire king—I wasn't sure now if I ever had—but sleeping with him was not a wise choice, despite my attraction to him. When I was with someone, I wanted it to be because I loved him. My libido had gotten me in trouble a few times in my life, but I was older and wiser now. I learned from my mistakes. Matthias would have been a mistake.

He could have had sex with me anyway, but he didn't. He'd stopped just in time. I guess I should thank him for that.

Maybe someday.

We headed for Toluca Woods, a middle-class neighborhood in Burbank. It was warm out tonight, but not hot, and there was a nice breeze in the air. Emily's house was at the end of a cul-de-sac, a redbricked, back split bungalow with a cypress tree out front and a rock garden instead of a grass lawn. Matthias pulled the car alongside the curb and parked there.

Noah sat quietly in the backseat and I was keenly aware of his presence the entire half-hour drive over. He pressed up against the driver's side door, his arms crossed so tightly over his chest it looked painful.

Entering this neighborhood made a sudden and surprisingly large amount of emotion well inside of me. It reminded me of where my sister and my nieces lived, which wasn't very far away from here. My throat closed, making it difficult to swallow.

I had to call her. I'd waffled about this so many times that I'd lost count, but I always came back to what felt right to me. A quick phone call wouldn't put her in jeopardy. It might stress her out, but it would take a weight off her mind that I was still alive. I had to do that. A couple minutes and that was it. Maybe just the sound of her voice would be enough to give me some well-needed strength.

Yes, it felt right to me. The knot of tension I had in my gut loosened a little just thinking about it. I was going to call Cathy. Right now.

"Go on in," I told Matthias and Noah. "I'll be there in a minute."

Matthias eyed me. "All right."

He didn't grill me about why, which was nice. They got

out of the car, Noah a bit reluctantly, and I sat there for a long moment as I tried to gain enough confidence to do what I should have done a week ago.

I had Noah's cell phone in hand. I slowly keyed in the phone number and held it to my ear.

This might be the last time I ever spoke to Cathy. I'd wanted to see her again, to know at that moment everything was back to normal. But I might not have that chance. If my blood killed me—or, rather, *when* my blood killed me—at least I'd die knowing I'd said good-bye. Just because I felt good today compared to how I'd felt before didn't really mean anything in the long run. I knew I was living on borrowed time.

For a moment I thought it would go through to voice mail like last time, but it didn't.

"Hello?" It was my sister's voice.

I found I couldn't speak. The words caught in my throat and I swallowed hard.

"Who's there?" Cathy asked after a moment of silence.

"It's . . ." I licked my lips. "It's me, Cathy."

"Jill? Oh, my God! Is it really you?"

Tears stung my eyes and I felt a wash of relief at hearing her voice. "Yeah, it's me."

"Are you all right?" She sounded surprisingly calm. Eerily so, actually.

I frowned. "I'm fine. Are . . . are *you* okay?"

"Yes."

"And the girls? Meg and Julie? How are they?" Cathy's kids. My nieces—ages eight and six. I wasn't sure why cold dread began to slide through me.

There was a pause. "Don't you know already?"

My grip tightened on the small phone. "Know what?"

"He was very nice, Jill. Such beautiful eyes. I think I could have stared into them forever."

Even though the car window was open, I felt the hot air closing in around me. "Who are you talking about?"

"He was here a little while ago with some of his friends. He said everything would be all right, and I believe him.

He told me that you were alive, but you hadn't been feeling very well, and that you were looking forward to seeing Meg and Julie again. I've been so worried about you for the last two weeks, but I'm so relieved everything's going to turn out okay after all."

I could barely breathe. Fear ate at the edges of my mind. "Who was he, Cathy? Please, please try to concentrate. Tell me."

She was quiet for a moment. "He didn't introduce himself formally, but one of his friends called him Chris—*Chris* something."

"Kristoff?" The name caught in my throat.

"Yes, that was it."

Kristoff had gone to my sister's home and taken my nieces. I didn't know how he'd even known they existed. I'd never met him.

"They're going to be fine." I forced the words out.

"Of course they will be."

Cathy had been mentally influenced. There was no way she would normally be acting like this, so calm and undisturbed by the fact her children had been taken away from her. One look in Kristoff's eyes and he'd made her believe that everything was okay. It was the only reason she wouldn't have phoned the police already and had an Amber alert spreading across the state.

I felt physically ill. "I need to go. It's going to be okay, Cathy. I swear it will. I—I'll be in touch as soon as I can."

I ended the call. My hands were shaking so hard I had a difficult time finding the disconnect button.

Kristoff kidnapped my sister's children and said that he knew about me. I didn't know how that was possible.

There was a rumor about me that a lot of vampires seemed to know about—the woman with the poisoned blood. My reputation preceded me. But I didn't think they knew my name. Most of them wouldn't know my face. Kristoff had only been awakened yesterday. This didn't make any damn sense.

Matthias.

I covered my mouth with my hand. Matthias was psychically connected to his brother—they had a bond, that was what Matthias had called it. I remembered Matthias reacting with intense pain when Kristoff was awakened. He said he could see into his mind, know everything he was thinking, feel everything that he was feeling. And that Kristoff could do the same with him.

He said it had shut off soon after and he hadn't made any other mention of it. Matthias didn't know where Kristoff was. He was waiting for his brother to make the first move once he'd regained his strength. To find Matthias so he could extract his revenge on him for locking Kristoff away for three decades.

In that moment both of their minds were open to each other, Kristoff must have seen everything about me. Who I was. What threat I posed to him. My name. And he'd used that to hunt down my only living relatives. And he'd taken my nieces to use them against me. Matthias knew about my sister from the newspaper article. He'd found out about my nieces easily. They were my family, the people I cared about. The thought made me feel even sicker and fear raced through me.

If he'd gone after my nieces, there was no way Sara would be safe.

My eyes widened. If Kristoff had found out about my family through peering into Matthias's head, then he'd know all about her, too. And considering how much he would hate his brother right now, that was dangerous information.

A baby. A girl. A dhampyr. The daughter of the brother who'd stolen his throne.

I scrambled for the car door and got out so fast I nearly went over on my ankle. I ran to the house to find the front door ajar. The house was dark and quiet.

"Matthias?" I whispered, afraid to shout. "Noah? Where are you?"

I reached the end of the front hallway. As I edged around the corner into the kitchen I stifled a gasp of horror.

A gray-haired woman in her midsixties lay on the ceramic tiled floor in a large puddle of blood coming from her slit throat. Her lifeless eyes were open and glassy as she stared at the ceiling.

"Emily." Fear and pain sliced through me at the sight of the dead woman.

Declan wanted to keep this location a secret from Matthias, thinking that he would be the one we'd have to worry about. I knew Matthias wouldn't hurt Sara and it was my opinion that helped Declan decide to tell Matthias where she was staying.

He couldn't have known this was how it would turn out. That the woman who'd helped to raise him would lie dead in her kitchen now for what she'd agreed to do out of the goodness of her heart.

Grief for a woman I'd never met slid though me, but there was no time to stop.

I made it to the stairs and went up, clutching tightly at the banister. The house was so quiet. The nursery was at the end of the hallway on the second floor.

A little relief spread through me when I saw Matthias standing there, holding the side of the crib, his shoulders tense. It was so dark in the nursery, the only light was coming through the window from the moon. I walked quickly to his side and looked with dread down at the blankets and stuffed toys.

Sara wasn't there.

A sob caught in my throat. "He was here, wasn't he? He killed Emily downstairs."

"This is all my brother's fault."

I tried to think, tried to figure out what to do next. "My sister—I spoke to her on the phone just now. She says he was there, too. He took my nieces and mentally influenced her not to panic—to think everything's okay when it's anything but. And now he's taken Sara." My hands were shaking. "It's because he could see into your mind. That's where he got the information. Everything that you know—*everything*—he could see it and he wants to use it against us."

He pulled me against him tightly. I didn't resist. I felt numb. His daughter whom he'd sworn to protect had been taken before he'd even had a chance to see her face. I couldn't help but felt his pain. I felt it, too.

"We have to find him, Matthias. There's no time to waste."

He pulled back a little from me, stroking the black hair off my face and tucking it behind my ears. "There's only one problem with that plan, Jillian."

I looked up at him. "What is it?"

He cupped my face in his hands. "I'm not Matthias."

13

TERROR RIPPED THROUGH ME. I STAGGERED BACK from him until my foot hit something. I looked down to see it was Matthias—the real one—unconscious on the floor.

"Your other friend is downstairs." He cocked his head to the left. "But, don't worry. He's not dead."

Kristoff was identical to Matthias right down to the last detail. Now that I was paying attention I saw he was wearing different clothes, but it was dark in here and I hadn't been concentrating when I'd ran in.

"Cat got your tongue?" he asked after a moment.

"What have you done with my sister's children?" My voice was hoarse. "Where's Sara?"

He pulled a small stuffed lamb out of the crib and looked down at it. "The children are fine."

Kristoff had been a looming threat, something that stayed in the distance to be dealt with by someone else. I hadn't expected to meet him face-to-face. My mind felt numb with panic.

He closed his eyes and inhaled, his nostrils flaring. The hunger pattern branched around his mouth and eyes. Even that was identical to Matthias. I'd thought it was like a fingerprint, something that each vampire showed differently, but it seemed as if twins shared that as well as their appearance.

Through my fear, it reminded me that this vampire wasn't without an Achilles' heel. He would be affected by my blood. If he bit me he would lose his immortality much as Matthias had and there would be the chance to kill him. I'd volunteered for this. Funny how it had seemed like a reasonable idea before he was right here in front of me. Now it seemed to be a dangerous and deadly idea. But there was no going back now.

If I could get him to drink my blood, he was one wooden or silver stake away from complete destruction.

I forced myself not to cringe away from him as he drew closer.

"Your scent is just as tempting as they say it is." He swept my hair off my throat and leaned closer. I tensed as I felt the cool brush of his lips against my neck before the sharpness of his fangs scraped against my skin. My heart thundered in my chest. He was going to do it.

But I couldn't let him. The thought crashed over me. I couldn't let him bite me, not yet. I didn't know where the children were.

I didn't have to worry. He pulled away with a small smile on his lips. It looked exactly like Matthias's smile.

"You don't have to be afraid, Jillian. I know, despite your enhancements, you're only human. You're not an assassin. You're an innocent in all of this. I've seen you in his mind—someone who might seem so dangerous to us, but in reality needs to be protected. One who is as fragile as she is deadly. I see why he's so intrigued by you."

Matthias saw me as fragile and deadly. A delicate flower with an unfortunate aftertaste. I wasn't sure I entirely agreed with him. I wasn't that fragile, but maybe that was just wishful thinking. Maybe the vampire knew me better than I thought he did.

I grappled for something to say. "It's torture for him to be near me. You must have seen that through your bond with him. Standing this close to me is risky for you."

"I saw everything, Jillian. All I needed were a few moments with his mind open to me and I saw everything I needed to know. Your scent *is* torture. And I know you're a risk to me." He walked a slow circle around me, his gaze taking in every inch as I stood there with my arms crossed tightly over my chest, afraid to move. Afraid to breathe.

I watched him warily. "You're not going to kill me."

He raised an eyebrow. "I'm not?"

I shook my head. "You never would have gone to the trouble of kidnapping my nieces if you were just going to kill me. You want to use me for something. And you think I'll behave if you threaten the people I love."

"Jillian." His smile didn't waver. "You're spoiling my surprise."

"What do you want from me?"

"All in good time."

His cool demeanor wasn't helping me to relax even a fraction. In fact, it was scaring me much more than if he'd been a raving lunatic.

There were footsteps in the hallway outside the nursery and I looked over my shoulder to see three men standing there. One I recognized as Meyers, Matthias's former blood servant who'd brutally cut the key from his body.

"Your majesty?" he said, his eyes widening slightly at the sight of me.

"Take her and the others." One of the men came toward me and grabbed my arm so tightly I gasped with pain. "But please be gentle with her. I don't want her bruised."

They stuck a piece of duct tape over my mouth and forcibly dragged me out of the room, down the stairs, and shoved me into the back of a van in the driveway leaving me undamaged but shaken. A few moments later, the unconscious bodies of Matthias and Noah joined me.

My mind was a blur but I forced myself to remain calm and not to lose hope. I was alive. That meant there was still a chance to find a way out of this. I seemed to lose hope when there were lulls, when I had too much time to think about the poison in my veins and what it meant for the future. When I was in danger, that was when my hope rose up inside of me ready to fight for the chance to live another day.

I didn't have to be strong just for myself. I had to be strong for my nieces, for Sara, and for Matthias and Noah.

Kristoff wanted me to live. For now. And he thought, through what he'd seen in Matthias's mind, that I was no danger to him, apart from my blood. I could work with that.

The van didn't have windows so I couldn't see where I was going. We drove for nearly an hour before the van came to an abrupt stop and the back door opened. The first thing I saw was the ocean, black and expansive with the moon reflected overhead. To my left was a huge luxury home with no close neighbors. It was the type of home a movie star might own. One of the A-listers who had tens of millions of dollars to burn on a nice piece of oceanside real estate.

The thugs pushed me forward toward the door, which opened before we even reached it. A thin girl with mousy blond hair stood there with a baby in her arms—Sara. My chest tightened and I tried to go to her, but the thug kept me firmly in his grip so I couldn't move where he didn't want me to. The girl smiled at us and I saw her fangs.

"My brother's child is fine, as you can see," Kristoff said from a bit behind me as I was pushed through the doorway and into the foyer of the house. "And the other children are in there."

I looked to my right to see an open door leading into a huge room. Meg and Julie were inside the room, seated in front of a large flat-screen television that was showing *Finding Nemo*. They looked unharmed, and were watching the movie with undivided attention. I wasn't sure if I should have felt sick or relieved when I heard them laugh.

They were having fun. They had no idea where they were or what this meant.

Kristoff was in front of me when I turned around. "Let me take care of this for you." He reached forward and ripped the tape off my mouth. It hurt like hell.

"You need to let them go. Please. I'll do what you want without any duress."

"Come." He turned and continued walking through the home to the other side, away from the kids, until we reached a large room that looked like a banquet hall with a massive chandelier hanging from the ceiling. Large and expensive-looking oil paintings of landscapes adorned the walls that were painted a burgundy color. The crown molding was gold.

The room was empty apart from a large red chair with gold arms and legs near the back. It was a throne room in Malibu.

"Welcome to my home," Kristoff said, following my gaze as I took in my surroundings. "It's so good to be back close to the ocean again. My brother chose to live underground. I am not my brother. I like the fresh air and the smell of the ocean."

My mouth was dry. "Please, we need to—"

He held up a hand. "Just a moment, Jillian. There's something else I have to deal with first."

Matthias was shoved across the room. The vampire behind him pushed him so hard that he fell to his knees on the hardwood floor. Dread slithered through me at how powerless he looked at the moment. He'd drank Jade's blood in order to regain his strength so he could face off against his brother. It looked as if that was in vain.

They looked so much alike. Except one was sprawled on the ground and the other now sat on a throne looking down at him.

Kristoff's face held concern, which I hadn't expected. "You're unwell."

Matthias glared up at him. "I'm fine."

"I'd sensed you were weakened. This is more than I expected."

"Do you feel sorry for me?" Matthias pushed himself up to his feet. "It's so nice of you to care."

"Your tongue's grown sharper in thirty years. Unfortunately for you, it's not much of a weapon."

"I assume you want to kill me." Matthias said it bluntly, and it worried me that he'd already given up hope at the thought he was outmatched.

"How can I kill somebody who's immortal?" Kristoff asked, watching Matthias carefully for his response.

Matthias exchanged a glance with me. "The ritual."

"I know it worked, just as I said it would. You doubted me. You shouldn't have." He glanced at my disgusted expression at the mention of the immortality ritual. "You told her about it, didn't you?"

"It's disgusting," I said, unable to hold my tongue.

"What is?"

He wanted me to say it out loud. "You murdered your own child so you could have the chance to live forever."

I felt a shove at my back that made me fall forward onto my knees, hard enough to bruise.

The vampire behind me hissed. "Watch your mouth, you worthless human bitch. The only reason you're not dead yet is because the king allows you to live."

Kristoff inhaled slowly and released it. "I thought I asked that Jillian not be harmed?"

The vampire's fierce expression wavered. "But your majesty—"

"Please take him away and deal with him. Now."

A glance over my shoulder showed the vampire who'd shoved me was being dragged out of the room by one of the five vampires with us. The king spoke and his subjects obeyed. The thought didn't ease my mind.

Kristoff's gray eyes got a faraway look in them. "What I had to sacrifice for the ritual was not something I took lightly. Being king means one must make difficult choices that not everyone understands. You also made a difficult choice recently. You chose to have your friend Noah sired rather than let him die."

"How do you know that?" Matthias demanded. "You were only in my mind the once and it was before that happened."

"Thirty years of slumber didn't weaken me as you might have thought. It strengthened me. You're weak. Therefore, I can read you without you even realizing it."

"Forget about mind reading." I swallowed bitterly. "If you're comparing what happened with Noah to what you did to your daughter, it's not even in the same universe. Don't you feel the least bit guilty? She was your daughter."

"Of course I feel guilty, Jillian." A serious expression now creased his brow. "It weighs on my conscience to this very day."

I was surprised to see his pain, but it didn't change anything. "Do you regret it?"

"Would that make a difference to you?"

"Probably not."

"Blood sacrifices are necessary for all dark magic like what was used in the immortality ritual. All this time I never knew for sure if it worked as it was supposed to or if my daughter gave her life for nothing."

There was no friendliness in the look in Matthias's eyes. "It worked. If you know everything, then you also know that I drank Jillian's blood. What kills all other vampires didn't kill me."

"I do know that."

Matthias hissed out a breath. "You forced me to participate in that ritual. You made me a monster just like you, never satisfied with what you already had."

Kristoff sighed. "You're such a noble man, aren't you? Or so you'd like everyone to believe."

There were two vampires guarding the archway leading into this room and I knew another two were still standing by the front doors. This place was like a vault. I had no idea how I was supposed to escape with the children, but I had to figure it out as soon as possible. "If you forced him to drink the blood in that ritual, I can't really blame him."

Kristoff paced to the other side of the room before returning. There was stress and old disappointment in his expression. "All of Matthias's protests were in vain. Once he got a taste of the blood he eventually had to be pulled away from her still body. Matthias is the one who killed my daughter and yet he still blames her death on me."

I looked at Matthias with horror that deepened with every word Kristoff spoke.

His brow was deeply furrowed and he stared at the ground. "You set me up to end her life against my will—to use my guilt against me. It was another form of manipulation to keep me in line and away from thoughts of becoming king."

This was an ancient power struggle between brothers. A rivalry that spanned centuries. I felt it—whatever love they'd had for each other in the past had soured and turned black with hate. It made me think of Cain and Abel—one bad, one good—whose deep-seated rivalry led to the very first murder.

Kristoff stood from his seat and walked over to face his brother. "We were so close for so long. We thought alike, we acted alike. This is the unfortunate event that finally drove us apart. I thought it would be just the opposite— that I was willing to share my discovery with you. I wanted you to live forever just like me and not have to fear death. Instead it prompted you to steal my throne, thinking that you knew best. And what has it gotten you?"

"A chance to do things my way for once."

His gray gaze flicked to me. "You believe you're no longer immortal because of Jillian's blood."

There was an edge of despair in Matthias's eyes then. Kristoff did know everything in his mind. If there were no secrets then there was no way Kristoff would ever drink my blood knowing what the consequences were.

Kristoff studied his face. "It's true, isn't it? You believe a stake through your heart will end your life."

"Why do you ask if you already know how I feel?"

"Good point. So a little poison is all it takes to wash away everything we did, everything that was sacrificed." Kristoff drew close enough to whisper in his ear. "Let's see if you're right."

There was a silver dagger in his right hand. I saw it only a moment before Kristoff sliced it into his brother's heart.

14

I SCREAMED.

Matthias staggered backward. The knife protruded from his chest. His *heart*. He pulled it out with effort and it clattered to the floor. He fell to his knees.

"No—Matthias!" I couldn't breathe, couldn't think. He was going to die right in front of me. There was pain and anger in his eyes as they locked with mine. I braced myself to watch him explode into ash and fire, gone forever.

But nothing happened.

Instead, Matthias fell forward onto his hands and knees. Blood dripped from his chest, forming a small pool. He didn't die. He didn't disappear. He was still here, long past the time when he should have been destroyed. A silver blade through his heart—Kristoff hadn't been playing around. He'd been aiming to kill. Matthias looked dead, but he wasn't.

Kristoff picked up the dagger from the floor and wiped the blade clean on a cloth. "Looks like you were wrong. You're still immortal, just like me."

My eyes widened as I fully understood what I'd just

witnessed. Whatever pain he'd faced, whatever weakness he'd felt after drinking my poisoned blood—it hadn't been nearly enough to strip away his immortality.

I didn't know how much damage he could take before he'd actually die. Maybe there was no limit. Maybe he couldn't die at all. Ever. Suddenly the thought of living an eternity was infinitely scarier than dying young.

I went to his side and touched his face. There was a flicker of life in his eyes, but other than that he didn't move. I forced myself to look at Kristoff, feeling fear toward this man who seemed very reasonable in the way he spoke, but was able to inflict pain or death on others without a second thought.

"That wasn't necessary." The words felt thick in my mouth.

He sat down on his throne again. "He thought he was vulnerable now and I wasn't sure either way. There was only one way to find out. Consider it an experiment. My daughter's unfortunate death has given both of us the chance to live forever."

Icy fear surged through me as I thought about Sara. "That's why you took his daughter. Are you planning on giving her to the Amarantos Society so they can follow in your footsteps?"

His brows drew together. "What kind of a monster do you take me for?"

"That's a loaded question."

"The Amarantos Society aren't on my side and have proven this by letting me stay trapped, comatose, locked away in a coffin for three decades. I owe them nothing." He glanced over my shoulder. "Bring her in."

I thought he was talking about Sara, but someone else I wasn't expecting came into the room. Her red hair was the first thing I saw.

Jade, the dhampyr. She was now dressed only in a black bra and panties, her body much thinner than I would have guessed from the first time I'd seen her. She didn't fight against the vampires who held her.

I gasped out loud at the sight of her unclothed. Unlike Declan, who'd received many scars from fighting vampires and getting injured, stabbed, and shot over the years, Jade's scars were up and down her arms and thighs, small white puncture marks from where she'd been fed upon all of her life. It made my heart twist for her pain—a different pain from what Declan had experienced, but no less traumatic. I wondered then how much of her insanity had been caused simply by being a dhampyr and how much was from the horrors she'd had to face.

My sympathy quickly turned to alarm.

Declan had been on his way to find her when he left last night. It would have been his first stop. Maybe she was already gone by the time he reached the amusement park again.

"You have her here so you can drink from her," I said quietly. "You saw in Matthias's mind how he planned to use her blood to regain his strength."

"Yes, I did. And I will drink from her, but I haven't yet. I feel quite well at the moment, but it's a good thing to have a backup plan." He waved his hand toward Matthias and the thugs brought Jade toward him where he lay on the floor. "Her blood will help him regain his strength from this new injury. It's the least I can do."

I eyed him warily, but stayed silent. That was it? No more suffering for the person responsible for imprisoning him all these years?

Kristoff took his dagger out again. The men held Jade still as he drew the sharp tip over her inner forearm and blood welled up immediately.

"Don't hurt her," I managed to say.

Kristoff flicked a glance at me. "I wouldn't dream of it. She's too valuable to harm. Just like you are."

This didn't set my mind at ease one tiny bit.

Jade was forced to bring her bleeding arm down to Matthias's mouth. Jade didn't make a single sound this time and it worried me that she'd lost her will to fight.

I hadn't. Not yet.

"Okay, Kristoff. What do you want me to do?" I asked point-blank.

"Patience, Jillian."

"I'm fresh out of patience. Here's the problem—whatever you want to do with me, you don't have much time. I'm dying. The Nightshade—the poison in me—it's killing me."

He didn't react to this other than templing his fingers and studying me. "I didn't read that in Matthias's mind."

"I guess he doesn't give my mortality a lot of thought. All I know is I don't have a lot of time left. So whatever you want me for, whatever will help me get my nieces safely back home, you better speak up now."

He was silent for so long that I began to worry I'd gone too far, broken too many rules, said too much. I was overvaluing myself, thinking he wanted me to live when really all he'd done was ask his thugs not to give me any more bruises.

I couldn't believe my original plan was to march in front of him and get him to bite me. This was not a man who lacked control. He had it to spare. Standing within six feet of me—the usual distance it took to get a good sniff of the Nightshade—he showed no sign that my scent affected him at all. He'd never be weak enough to bite me. He'd never lose that much of his control knowing what he did about my blood.

And it wouldn't really make any difference if he did. He'd still be immortal.

This was a hopeless situation and I didn't know what I could say or do to make it turn out any differently. I wasn't the type of woman who relished the thought of a man swinging in to save me when I'd gotten myself into trouble, but I desperately wished that Declan would storm in here, guns blazing, and save us all.

He didn't.

"Well?" I asked after a long moment had passed. "Are you going to tell me what your big plan for me is? Why you kidnapped my nieces?"

"I'm surprised it isn't obvious." He leaned forward a little. "There's someone I want you to kill."

I blanched. "I'm not a killer."

"I know." He smiled. "Which is why it will prove to be an interesting experiment."

Matthias had his tests. Kristoff had his experiments.

I licked my dry lips. "Who is it?"

"The leader of the Amarantos Society you spoke about earlier. He's an enemy of mine whom I anticipate will try to stand in my way now that I'm back. I want him dead, and I want to see if you can do it for me. You will retrieve the ring he wears as proof of his death. In return, your nieces will be released safely with no idea that anything happened other than a fun night of movies and games in a distant relative's big house."

"I get him to bite me and that's that."

"Yes."

"What's the catch?" Although it sounded horrible and dangerous and not something I wanted to be a part of, it was fairly straightforward.

"The catch is that I'm not entirely convinced you can do it, based on what I've seen of you in my brother's mind." He reached forward to touch my cheek and I tried not to flinch away from him. "You're too soft. Too sweet."

I looked down at the vampire seated on the floor, a large patch of blood on his chest. He looked pale and gaunt and near death. His gaze met mine weakly.

"Soft and sweet?" I asked him.

"You are," he replied.

"I can help give you the strength you'll need. Look at me," Kristoff said and the moment I turned back to him he locked gazes with me. My heart sank as I expected to immediately be taken under by his mental influence. I hated to think what he could make me do when I had no choice in the matter. He looked deeply into my eyes and I waited to feel the warm wash flow over me as he took control of my mind, but it didn't happen. His pale brows knit together.

"I can't—" Kristoff frowned before clarity entered his light gray eyes. "Oh Matthias, what have you done now?"

"Only what I had to." Matthias had fully sat up, his hand pressed against the wound in his chest. I wondered how long it would take to heal or if being stabbed through his heart was the same as anything else he'd been through. It seemed more severe to me, but I wasn't an expert on vampiric injuries. His face was paler than normal and coated with a sheen of perspiration.

Jade sat next to him, her knees pulled up to her chest, her head down. She rocked gently back and forth and she was mumbling something, but I couldn't make out what it was.

Kristoff put a hand under my chin and forced me to look at him again. "My brother continues to surprise me. I didn't see this. It must be very new."

I pulled back from him. "What are you talking about?"

"Matthias has claimed you."

I shook my head. "I don't understand."

"Only once in a vampire's existence can we claim a human. Claiming is typically reserved for a favored blood servant or a human lover who refuses to be sired. It's a bond that can be broken only with death—his or yours. And since he can't die, it's an eternal bond."

I stared at him with growing shock. He wasn't fucking with me—his expression held only sincerity. This was real. "How did this—when did this—"

"Last night," Matthias said wearily.

I looked down at him still kneeling on the floor. "Why would you do that?"

"Yes, I'm curious, too." Kristoff slid his dagger back into a sheath that hung from his belt. "Are you in love with her?"

I held my breath even though I already knew the answer to that. He didn't love me. So what the hell was this?

"She was dying. She wouldn't have survived the night. I saw the life leaving her right in front of my eyes. It was a rash decision on my part to save her. I bonded our minds and she drank my blood to seal the deal."

I was about to argue that I never did anything of the sort when I remembered the glass he held to my lips. I was so out of it I didn't even register what I was drinking. After that, the pain disappeared.

Clarity rapidly set in. "Are you saying that because of what you did I'm not going to die because of the Nightshade?"

Matthias studied me for a long moment. "You can still be killed. But you won't die from the poison inside you or from any other human disease or weakness. And no other vampire apart from me can influence you anymore."

"Only you." I swallowed.

"Yes."

"That still sounds dangerous to me." I stared at him, stunned by all of this. He'd claimed me so I wouldn't die. I was bonded with him eternally. I didn't know how I felt about that. Angry that he hadn't told me or asked my permission to do something so major, but—also grateful that he'd given so much in order to let me keep breathing. I needed time to let this all settle in. Unfortunately, time was a luxury I didn't have.

Matthias slowly pushed himself up to his feet, and I could tell it caused him great pain. Even after drinking the dhampyr's blood again—and I didn't know how much he'd had—he was going to need a lot more recovery time.

Kristoff watched him, his brow creased with concentration. "I think I understand why you really did this. You saved her because of what she is and what she can do. You thought you could use her to destroy me. If she was dead she'd be no use to you. That's it, isn't it?"

Matthias glared at him. "I can't hide anything from you."

"You're right, you can't."

Of course that was why he'd done this. I'm surprised I hadn't thought of it myself.

I wanted to feel used, but I was still filled with a strange gratitude toward him that he'd use up his entire wild card on me. It was a generous gift with dubious motivation behind the giving. And in the end, it hadn't helped at all.

"We're through here," Kristoff said, nodding at his thugs who moved in. "Take my brother away."

They grabbed Matthias and dragged him out of the room.

I clenched my fists at my sides. "What are they going to do to him?"

He raked a hand through his dark blond hair as he watched his brother's departure. "Don't worry about Matthias. He'll be fine."

I wasn't convinced of that. Kristoff had spent thirty years locked away somewhere. An ineffective knife through the heart didn't seem like it was nearly enough to even the scales. Matthias was in trouble.

"You didn't say yes to my request," Kristoff said. "Unfortunately, since Matthias has claimed you I can't give you any extra influence to help in the task. But it still needs to be done."

"You think I'll fail."

"I'm hoping you'll give it your best shot."

He made it sound like a piano rehearsal rather than premeditated murder.

I crossed my arms tightly. "And if I don't agree to this, you'll kill Meg and Julie."

He looked at me as if I'd grown another head. "I don't kill children, Jillian."

Frustration rose inside me. "I don't want them to get hurt."

"All I'm threatening with your nieces is to keep them away from their mother. They're in no danger here. I love children. And if you're making these assumptions based on what you know about the immortality ritual—"

"I am."

"I told you that it was Matthias who was the one responsible for that death."

"I don't blame him for what happened." Tears burned at my eyes. I had to stay strong, but I felt off balance and extremely vulnerable. "He was forced into a situation he never would have chosen for himself and bad things happened."

He cocked his head. "You care about him, don't you?"

"I care about a lot of people."

"Like Declan."

I froze. "What?"

"When I saw him in Matthias's mind, it was a surprise. I never knew Monica was pregnant. Then again, I didn't have much of a chance to know of it before I was locked away without blood for all those years."

Fear pushed away every other emotion I was fighting against. "Where is he?"

"He's been here since last night."

It felt as if someone had clutched my heart and squeezed. "What have you done to him?"

"He's very dangerous, Jillian. You know that, don't you?"

I shook my head. "He's not."

"Yes, he is. He was in a rage when he was brought here to see me. Uncontrollable. His dhampyr nature has taken hold of him very quickly and can't be reversed. My men wanted to kill him outright, but I told them not to. I knew you'd want to see him."

Declan was here. I hadn't wanted to believe he'd been with Jade when she'd been taken, but that was what had happened. I felt sick at the thought that he'd been here all this time and I hadn't known it.

"Come with me. There isn't much time." Kristoff walked out of the room, leaving me standing there, stunned. I had to run to catch up to him. A couple thugs fell in behind me along a hallway and down a flight of stairs to the basement that had cold cement walls and no luxurious décor like upstairs. A large iron door stood in front of me and one of the vampires opened it up so Kristoff could walk through.

It led into a large room that looked like a hospital room—all white and steel, sterile and cold. Declan lay on a narrow bed, restrained, with his arms and legs strapped down. There was a leather strap across his bare chest and neck. An IV unit was next to the bed and a clear liquid dripped into the tube attached to his arm. His eye was closed.

I ran to his side. My hand shook as I touched his face. "What is this? What happened to him?"

Kristoff's jaw tightened. "As I said, he was difficult to control. He had to be subdued before he could do damage to himself or to others."

"Declan . . ." I whispered. "Can you hear me?"

After a moment his eye opened slowly and he looked up at me. "Jill . . . you're here . . ."

"I'm here. It's okay now."

"This isn't okay."

I almost smiled, I was so relieved to see he was still alive. "Maybe you're right."

"I know I was an asshole leaving you last night, but seeing Noah like that . . ."

"I understand." I did. I'd felt hurt and betrayed and that combination had messed my mind up and almost pushed me into Matthias's arms completely, but now everything seemed so much clearer.

"No, it was wrong. I shouldn't have left, but I was afraid I'd hurt you. It's inside me, this rage. I can't control it anymore. I never could have lived with myself if anything happened to you."

"So instead you ran off to meet—" I glanced over my shoulder at Kristoff, looking so eerily like Matthias that it continued to throw me off. He watched us from the doorway.

"My father," Declan said.

My attention returned to Declan's face. "For the record, you look nothing like him."

"You're right. He has fewer scars." His glimmer of a smile faded. "He told me he won't hurt you."

"So the rumor goes. Who would have thought that he'd be such a friendly neighborhood vampire king?"

He laughed a little humorlessly. "I don't think friendliness has much to do with it. I had to agree to something first."

I felt myself tense. "What did you agree to?"

"Jill, it's my fault you were dragged into all of this in the first place. If I hadn't shown up the minute you were in the lobby, Anderson never would have grabbed you. I pushed him too far and he reacted."

"I thought we were over this. It happened. Shit happens and we deal."

He swallowed and I slid my hand over the leather strap across his chest. It was tight and strong. He wasn't going anywhere. I didn't understand why this was necessary. He seemed fine. No violence. He wasn't going to hurt anyone.

"Declan only wants the best for you, Jillian," Kristoff said. "So we were able to come to an understanding."

My guard went up. "And what understanding is that?"

"He is extremely self-aware for his stage of dhampyrism. It's likely due to the serum his adoptive father kept him on for so long. It's delayed this necessary step."

My gaze moved to the IV that I'd assumed was some sort of medicine. "What are you giving him? What is that?"

Declan looked up at me, his brow creased. "It's poison."

15

WITHOUT THINKING, I MOVED TOWARD THE IV, KNOW-
ing I had to get it out of his arm. Before I could touch it,
Kristoff's men pulled me back. I fought, but one was all it
took to hold me in place.

Kristoff looked grim. "Declan agreed to this."

"He agreed to let you poison him?" My throat hurt as
panic raced through me.

"Yes. The most humane way to deal with a dhampyr is
to euthanize them. Declan is a danger to everyone around
him now, and there's no going back. In return for your
safety, he agreed not to fight me on this. I could have let
my men kill him last night. It would have been faster, but
much more painful and there would have been no guaran-
tees when it came to you."

I felt as if I was going to be physically ill. My entire
body went cold and still and I felt the blood drain from my
face. "Declan, is that true?"

He turned his head toward me. "There's no other way,
Jill."

"There's always another way."

His jaw tightened. "No other way I'm willing to accept."

He knew. What Matthias told me about how to save a dhampyr was something Declan already knew from his research.

"Declan, no. Please." I shook my head so hard it hurt my neck. "Don't do this."

"It's already done."

"You can't leave me again. Not like this."

His expression grew pained. "Kristoff said he'll release you. He won't hurt you."

"And you believed him? You know who he is. You took him at his word?"

His eye closed before he could say anything else. I heard someone let out a ragged sob and realized it was me.

"He wanted to say good-bye to you, Jillian," Kristoff said softly. "It was the least I could do for him."

I shook my head. "He's not going to die."

"The poison will only take a couple more minutes to work."

"No. No, it's not going to happen. Declan's *not* going to die. I can't believe he'd agree to this, for what? Just thinking he was saving me? It doesn't make sense."

"If you'd seen him last night—there was no reasoning there. He was a raging beast who wanted to destroy. His mind isn't working as it should. This is the only way to deal with a dhampyr like that."

The vampire behind me held me firm in his viselike grip. A glance at him showed that the signs of hunger were readily visible on his strained face, but he didn't even attempt to bite me.

I felt like I wanted to give up, but part of me knew I had to keep fighting. I was in deep trouble, in the house of a vampire king who was putting his dhampyr son down like a rabid dog. And the rabid dog had agreed to it.

He didn't think he deserved to live. He didn't want to hurt me.

This hurt.

There was one thing I believed in, apart from everything else. I'd just never realized how strong my belief was. I wasn't religious. I wasn't spiritual. I basically lived one day at a time, grateful for any day I didn't wallow in the depression I'd felt that made me take a razor blade to my wrist five years ago.

I believed in one thing, and that was life. If I was breathing then there was still hope for everything to turn out okay. Death was forever and there was no coming back from it. Life meant there was still a chance.

I believed in life. That was my religion.

Kristoff might want me to believe that he was a nice guy—one who didn't deserve the bad rep Matthias had given him. It would be easier if I did believe that. But he didn't fool me. He was self-involved, power-hungry, and willing to kill to get what he wanted, even if it meant he had to slit the throat of a harmless sixty-year-old woman in her kitchen. A smile and a kind word afterward didn't mean shit to me.

But I needed him right now. More than anyone else.

"You want me to go kill this enemy of yours," I said. "This leader of the Amarantos Society who wants to take you down."

"That's right."

"I'll do it. And I'll succeed at it."

He raised an eyebrow. I saw it out of the corner of my eye even though I hadn't taken my attention away from Declan for a moment. "You really think you can?"

"Yes, I do. But you have to do something for me."

"I'll release your nieces if you're successful."

"You'll definitely do that." I swallowed. "But I want something else."

He nodded at his thug. "Let her go."

Only a second later, the vampire let go of me. He watched me warily as if expecting me to launch myself at Declan's IV again, but I stayed right where I was.

"What do you want?" Kristoff asked.

I licked my dry lips and finally looked directly at him. "I want you to sire Declan."

Surprise slid behind his gray gaze. "That's impossible."
My heart sank. "Why is it impossible?"

"Dhampyrs are too unpredictable and prone to turn more monstrous and violent if they're sired. It's against vampire law to take that chance, both for the safety of the dhampyr and for everyone else."

"Who made that law?"

He raised an eyebrow. "I did."

"Then you can break it."

"My son hates vampires, I've seen how much through my brother's mind. He kills them whenever possible. You'd have him made into something that he despises? You'd take the chance this act will turn him into more of a monster than he was to begin with?"

Declan had freaked out at my decision to have Noah turned into a vampire to save his life. If he found out I made the same decision for him—

Kristoff approached me and pressed his hand against my cheek. For a moment he looked so much like Matthias I almost forgot who he really was. "Jillian?"

Declan would choose death over becoming a vampire without a second thought—in fact, it looked like he already had. My overlapping thoughts and dark pain inside of me at the rush of information became too much. I tried to breathe, tried to figure this out.

He'd hate me for doing this to him. If he'd been furious with what I'd decided with Noah, it would pale in comparison to how he'd feel about it happening to himself, especially if this backfired and he became even more violent.

He'd be a vampire who wanted to rip out my throat. And for the rest of his life or mine, one taste of my blood would be able to kill him in seconds.

"There's not much time left before he's gone," Kristoff said very seriously. "What do you want me to do?"

I looked up at him and a hot tear slid down my cheek. "Sire him."

— 16

I DIDN'T SEE WHAT HAPPENED NEXT. I WAS TAKEN out of the room and back upstairs feeling stunned and ill by what just happened.

I was eternally bonded to a former vampire king.

I'd asked Kristoff to turn Declan into a vampire.

In return, I'd agreed to assassinate the leader of the Amarantos Society.

And to think, it was only ten o'clock.

Meyers was there and he knew what to do to get me ready. It involved a short black dress, stiletto heels, a case of makeup, and about a half an hour, twenty minutes of which I simply paced back and forth in the ensuite bathroom of a large bedroom they'd locked me in like a rat in a luxurious cage.

I tried not to think, but that was impossible.

My decision about Declan had been a hasty one, I knew that. And I'd made it selfishly and without much thought to how he'd feel about it. But I couldn't let him die. Not like that. When he'd agreed to let Kristoff euthanize him, he hadn't been thinking right. Jade was insane from being a dhampyr of her age. It was possible Declan wasn't dealing only with the violence, but the beginning stages of insanity as well.

I tried to justify my actions any way I could, but I knew there would be consequences.

I got dressed and pulled myself together as much as I could. I applied the makeup as if I was going out to a club with some girlfriends, going heavier with the eyeliner than when I was a blonde. When I was satisfied with the results, I knocked on the bedroom door.

"I'm ready."

When the door opened I was surprised by who was waiting for me. Noah stood there in the hallway, his arms crossed over his chest.

"Oh shit!" He clamped his hand over his nose as veins branched over his cheeks.

I tensed. "Good to see you, too."

"They want me to go with you." His words were now muffled.

"You?" I swallowed hard and looked over at Meyers, who stood patiently to the side, leaning against the wall. "Why him?"

Meyers shrugged. "Kristoff wants to do an experiment. See if Noah has any worth to him as an assistant. If he can't handle being with you, then it's decided."

Noah looked dismayed. "It's a job interview."

"Great." More complications for me to deal with. The thought that being near a hungry fledgling was the least of my worries at the moment didn't help much.

Noah's eyes were black. "You look kind of hot right now in that dress. You smell even better."

"Is that going to be a problem for you?"

"Oh, yeah."

I slipped into the high heels and eyed him cautiously. "Is it a problem you're going to be able to handle?"

"I don't know."

"That's not a very good answer."

His face showed his stress. "Even though I know it'll kill me, all I want to do is drink your blood."

"That's even less of a good answer."

This was what Declan would be like—but worse, much worse. Noah wasn't angry with me, he didn't hate me, and he hadn't been a dhampyr to start with. And he *still* wanted to bite me. I shuddered to think what was in Declan's immediate future. All I remembered was how Noah was in the beginning—zombielike, uncontrollable, and ravenous.

I'd made a horrible mistake. But there was no going back now, only forward.

Noah drew closer, closing his eyes and inhaling. "Holy hell. I'm so fucking hungry." His lips curled back from his fangs and I felt his breath on my skin.

I slapped him. "Stop it."

He held his hand against his face. "Shit. That hurt."

"I don't want you to die. I need you too much."

His brows drew together. "You do?"

I nodded. "Declan's being sired."

"Oh, shit. Really? Why? How? Who?"

"I asked Kristoff to do it." At Noah's look of shock, "There was no choice. He was dying—being poisoned. It was the only answer."

His mouth fell open. "He hates vampires."

"I know."

"He's going to kill you."

I cringed. The reminder only made things worse.

"I mean . . . uh, he might not even *want* to kill you, but I'd stay about a million miles away from him until he gets his shit together. As a dhampyr to start with—" He grimaced.

"What?"

"I wouldn't want to be in the same room with him. And I'm already a vampire."

I didn't think my stomach could sink any lower than it already was, but I was wrong.

"And Kristoff's going to do it himself?" Noah asked. "You know what that means, right?"

I looked at him with concern. "No. What does it mean?"

"As both Declan's father *and* his sire, he'll have total control over him. They'll have the ultimate blood bond. No wonder Kristoff agreed to do this. After all, it's against vampire law to turn a dhampyr."

Noah was a wealth of knowledge about all things vampire, especially now that he was one.

I felt ill. Kristoff had agreed pretty quickly to this, considering he was the one who'd created the law in the first place. Kristoff saw the benefits, and it was similar to what Carson had done with Declan, only much worse. Over six feet of mindless muscle who obeyed every order. The ultimate bodyguard to protect the new vampire king from those who might not share his vision. I was just surprised he hadn't thought of it himself.

All I knew for sure was that whether Declan had died or was turned into a vampire . . . he was now lost to me forever. It hurt worse than I ever would have thought, but I had to put it out of my mind and focus on my task tonight. Doing the exact thing I'd tried to avoid from the beginning—kill someone purposefully with my blood. The safety of my nieces depended on me succeeding. Kristoff could say he loved children and that they were in no danger, but I didn't trust him. Actions spoke much louder than words.

I shook my head and tried to ignore the pain in my heart. "I'll deal with all of this later. Right now I have to do something and it looks like you're coming with me."

He looked grim. "They already told me all about it. You agreed to this? Really?"

"I had no choice."

Instead of questioning me more about it, he just nodded. "Okay, then let's go. There's a car waiting outside."

Meyers watched me as we passed him, a small smile twisting at his mouth. "Good luck, Jillian."

I smiled back at him. "Fuck you."

I had to take my frustrations out on someone.

THE DRIVER TOOK US TO A NIGHTCLUB CALLED THE Silver Cross that was an hour away from Kristoff's home.

"Man, I've heard of this place. Really? This is it?" Noah looked up at the sign.

I eyed the exterior guardedly. "What have you heard? That the leader of a secret vampire society owns it?"

"Actually, that didn't come up. It's a sex club. Very elite. Only for the richest and horniest in Southern California."

Kristoff better not be messing me with me right now by sending us here. "But you heard nothing about vampires being here?"

"I think I would have remembered something like that."

I couldn't say I was all that surprised. Vampires enjoyed mixing blood and sex, and where better to feed off both desires than a sex club?

Be strong, Jill, I told myself when I found it difficult to force myself toward the front doors. I couldn't lose it now, I had to stay strong. For the kids. For Noah. For . . . Declan.

Even for Matthias—wherever he'd been taken. I'd be more worried about him if I didn't know he was immortal. He wouldn't be killed only because he *couldn't* be killed. It didn't set my mind at ease very much. There were many things Kristoff could do to his brother that didn't include murder.

Our life forces were bound together. Maybe I'd know if something happened to him. All I knew was that despite my circumstances and stress, I physically felt better than ever. Even better than before I'd been injected with Nightshade in the first place. I felt stronger, more alert, and full of energy. There was no pain. The bruises I'd had yesterday were completely gone. For the first time in two weeks I didn't feel like I was going to die.

He'd given me a second chance at life. But I could still be killed.

"Game plan?" Noah asked, breaking through my thoughts.

I pulled my long hair over my left shoulder. "I'm open to suggestion."

"He's expecting you. He thinks you're a gift from Kristoff."

I grimaced. "I love blind dates."

"You ready?"

I inhaled deeply and exhaled slowly. "Yes."

"Then let's do this."

We approached the front doors to The Silver Cross. The bouncer eyed us.

Noah nodded at me. "This is Jill. Alex is expecting her."

The bouncer's fat face didn't change, but his light gray gaze scanned me and his nostrils flared. I smelled good to him thanks to my *Eau du Nightshade*.

I tried my best to look at ease, as if I was accustomed to being sent from one vampire to another like a slutty blood servant. It was a struggle.

Thanks to my brand-new bond with Matthias, the fang marks on my neck from the last bar I'd been to had faded completely. I was fresh and unblemished meat. I bit my bottom lip, tasting the thick red lipstick there, then adjusted the front of my low-cut dress that barely covered my breasts and left my entire back bare. And I focused on not being afraid.

I didn't think about Declan and how he'd react to becoming the very thing he'd hated all of his life. I didn't think about Matthias and wherever he'd been dragged away to. I didn't think about Sara, the dhampyr baby with very valuable blood who was completely and utterly helpless right now. And I didn't think about my sister's kids, who had no idea they were in horrible danger while their mother had no idea what had really happened.

Or . . . I *tried* not to think of these things.

What I needed to do was focus on Alex, the leader of the Amarantos Society—someone who sounded horrible and greedy and manipulative. He was a vampire who deserved to die and one I would feel no guilt about killing.

The bouncer spoke into his earpiece, then nodded and opened the door for us. Someone else was waiting there— tall, big, bald, and ugly.

"Follow me," he said.

After exchanging a glance with Noah, we followed him. Despite Noah's initial reaction to seeing me again, I was impressed by how in control he seemed right now. His survival instincts had kicked in. Between death and becoming Kristoff's reluctant vampire assistant, he'd chosen door number two.

The interior of the club was dark and loud pounding music assaulted my ears. At first glance, it looked like any other club I'd ever been to. There was a long black bar along one side of the expansive room. A dance floor. Dozens of couches like domino tiles spread in front of me. Silver and black were the main colors, and a sparkle of light from a mirror ball scattered across the faces of the dozens of people here tonight.

At second glance I saw more details of the patrons of The Silver Cross. Varying degrees of nudity, bodies pressed against each other, the smell of sex and sweat, and the heavy cloying scent of perfume.

"Only humans out here," Noah whispered to me.

"How can you tell?"

"I can smell them."

I didn't look too closely at my surroundings. I kept my eyes ahead, focused on a door in front of us marked "VIP Access Only."

Our guide silently eyed us, then pushed the door open to let Noah and me through into the next room.

It was darker in here—so dark I could barely see my hand in front of my face until my eyes adjusted a bit better. Hotter, too—easily over ninety degrees. The room was smaller than the previous one and there was no music playing, apart from the muffled throb that could be heard coming from the previous room.

In here I smelled blood as well as sex. My gut twisted with fear. Out of the corner of my eye I could see the outline of a naked woman, tied to a pole with her arms above her head, a look of bliss on her face. A fully nude man fed from her inner thigh and a half-dressed woman fed on her throat.

"Vampires," Noah said. "Lots of them."

"No shit."

And suddenly, every eye in the house went to me.

"Keep walking," Noah said.

"Trying to." I stumbled on something on the ground and a cool hand reached out to steady me. I didn't see who it belonged to, but it slid up my bare thigh under the edge of my skirt and headed north. I slipped away from whoever it was before they got any friendlier.

"She's for Alex," our guide snapped. "Hands off unless you want it permanently removed from your body."

That helped save me from any more groping, but I still felt the curious stares weighed down with hunger as I moved through the hot room, silent except for the sounds of feeding or grunts and moans of pleasure.

There was a mirrored wall in front of us that reflected the darkly lit Hieronymus Bosch scene behind me. The Silver Cross was my first vampire sex club. I sincerely hoped it would be my last.

My own image was reflected before me—heavy makeup, midnight black hair and eyes, and a tiny tight dress to match. Long bare legs, stiletto heels. I looked like someone who belonged in a place like this. The thought wasn't much of a comfort.

Our vampire guide opened a door hidden in the mirror that led into another dark room. Noah was about to walk through, but was stopped.

"Just the human," the guide said.

"Jill—" Noah began.

"It's okay." I swallowed hard and took a deep breath to steady myself. "Wait out here for me. I'll be fine."

Noah frowned. He might be acting as if he was totally in control, but just being in a place like this had pushed him a little further over the edge. His eyes were black and hunger had branched over his cheekbones.

He nodded. "Try not to die." It might have sounded like a joke if he didn't look so serious.

I stepped through the door and it slowly closed between us. I then realized that the mirror was two-way glass, and from this new room I could see everything that was going on right next door. This was an observation room.

"I was told to expect you."

I stiffened at the smooth, deep voice and fear snaked through me.

Showtime, I thought.

Time to be a killer.

17

THE ROOM WAS LIT WITH CANDLES. HUNDREDS OF them. There was a huge room with an enormous bed to one side. On the bed were several naked bodies—at least three: two men and a woman—tangled in the bloodstained white satin sheets. They weren't moving. I hoped they were only sleeping after a completely consensual threesome.

The rattle of chains to my right grabbed my attention and my head whipped in that direction to see a monster dhampyr straining against its bindings. It was naked, with pale translucent skin, thick pockets of which drooped from its protruding abdomen. It had an alien appearance— slightly human, but mostly not. It was bald, with a large flat face and enormous eyes that were entirely black. Thin white lips peeled back to show ragged, sharp teeth and a thick black tongue. At the end of its long thin arms, each of its tapered fingers was tipped with a razor-sharp talon— the same talons a monster dhamp used to claw its way out of its human mother's body.

I shuddered with fear and disgust at the sight of it.

"Bloooooddd," it moaned in a hoarse whisper. "Waanntt bloooddd."

"Ignore him. He's always hungry."

Be strong, I thought as I pushed down a sob rising in my throat. I found myself frozen in place unable to look away from the monster toward the man who spoke. *This is about survival, nothing else. As soon as you can kill this vampire, the sooner you can get the fuck out of here.*

"Seems like something that's hard to ignore," I said.

"He won't hurt you if you don't get close to him. Come here."

I swallowed hard and finally tore my gaze away from the chained monster to focus on the direction of the vampire's voice. Through the darkness of the room I could see him seated on a metal chair.

A wheelchair.

I forced myself to move toward him, straining to see what awaited me. The high heels pinched my feet. My heart drummed painfully in my chest, and a cool trickle of perspiration slid down my bare back.

"I can smell your fear," Alex said. "Practically taste it."

As I drew closer I stifled my shock as I finally saw what was in front of me. There had been one time when this vampire had been devastatingly attractive. Dark hair brushed his shoulders, his face was akin to a male model's with sensual lips and high cheekbones. Broad shoulders. Square jaw. The works.

But he had no legs. And he had no eyes.

I inhaled sharply.

He smiled. "Kristoff didn't warn you about what I looked like?"

"The subject didn't come up." My voice sounded weak.

"I lost these in a war a very long time ago." He touched his thighs that had nothing below the knee. Then he touched his eyes, sunken and blackened. "And I lost these in a fight a bit more recently than that."

"A fight."

"The sun isn't a friend to my kind."

His eyes had been burned away because he'd gone out into the sunshine. I'd heard about the results of this, but I hadn't seen it for myself. Alex had been blinded and that made him much more vulnerable now.

"I can smell your pity," he said. "Trust me, it's not necessary. My senses are much more acute now than they ever were before."

"I don't pity you."

"Disgust, then?"

"Just surprise, that's all."

He leaned back in his wheelchair. "How do you feel about being given from one vampire to another? Is this your thing?"

"My thing?" My shoes pinched me. It was distracting.

He leaned forward a little. "Are you a whore, Jillian?"

I stiffened. I guess that was what this seemed like— me being sent out from Kristoff like a fruit basket in a tight black dress. "I'm not a whore. I'm a prisoner."

"So you have no choice."

"Pretty much."

"But you're not fighting it. It makes me believe he's blackmailing you in some way—perhaps keeping someone you love captive to make you go along with his plans." He absently played with a large gold ring on his index finger that was set with a huge ruby. It was the ring Kristoff wanted me to take as proof of his death.

I eyed him and the ring warily. "Sounds like you know him."

"It's been a long time since I last spoke with him, but some acquaintances leave a lasting impression. Kristoff is one of them." He cocked his head. "Come closer. Since I can't see you I'll need more evidence that he sent me an acceptable gift."

I wanted to stay hard and focused right now, but I couldn't help the disgust, and, yes, pity I felt for this once handsome and once human man. I cast a glance over my shoulder. The monster dhampyr was silent and watching me, its chest moving in and out. A line of drool slid down the side of its mouth to the floor.

I got close enough that Alex could smell more than just my fear. This time he was the one to inhale sharply. "My God. Your scent . . ."

I tensed. "I'm kind of special."

"He sent word that your blood is ambrosia—food for the gods. That I've never tasted anything like you in my entire existence."

That was an understatement if ever I'd heard one. Kristoff really wanted this guy dead, but for the life of me I couldn't figure out why. He didn't seem to be any threat. He might be the leader of the Amarantos Society, but he couldn't function without assistance. He was blind. He couldn't walk. He was helpless. Why send me to do Kristoff's dirty work when anyone willing to kill would do?

Then again, why not? I already knew Kristoff enjoyed his experiments. I was yet another experiment. He didn't think I could do it and I wasn't entirely convinced of it myself.

"Closer," Alex said.

Any closer and I'd be sitting on his lap.

I forced myself to lean toward him and I willed my sympathy for him to go far, far away. This wasn't a normal veteran of a war who'd sustained serious injuries fighting to keep his country free. This was a vampire who owned a sex club and had three unconscious—possibly *dead*—humans in his bed no more than twenty feet away from us right now, not to mention a monster dhamp chained to his wall. He was a sightless predator on wheels.

Feeling sorry for this guy I had to kill wasn't going to make this any damn easier.

"Yes, you smell good." His lips curved. He placed his cool fingertips on my face and slid them over my forehead, my cheeks, nose, chin, and jaw. One hand slid into my hair, which he brought to his nose so he could inhale its scent. "You're warm, too."

"Ninety-eight point six."

He touched my hands for a moment, my short nails, my palms. His touch wasn't rough, but it did nothing to relax me. Apart from my fear, I didn't like being inspected like a slab of beef to determine my quality. He touched the silky material of my dress, his hands skimming down my sides. I stiffened and he stopped at my waist.

"Nice dress." His smile looked slightly wicked at the edges. I'd assume blood was not the only thing Kristoff had promised from my visit.

"It's borrowed."

"Color?"

"Black."

"What color is your hair?"

"Black."

"How old are you, Jillian?"

"Twenty-eight."

"You're different from what I expected." His hands moved back up to tangle in my hair and he brought my face down level to his.

"Am I?" I felt sick to my stomach. How far was I willing to go to make this work? I would have thought he'd already have bitten me by now, but nothing had happened, only a light groping that I hoped was over. "What were you expecting?"

"I'm not sure." He leaned back in his wheelchair a little, his face tilted up as if he was gazing at me. "Assassins are usually a bit more forward than this."

I froze. "What?"

"I know who you are, Jillian. I know *what* you are."

I shifted back, but he had my hair so tightly in his grip I could barely move. "I don't know what you're talking about."

"You're the woman with the poisoned blood. And Kristoff sent you here to kill me."

Busted. The thought was like a physical blow. I'd expected many things from this encounter, including putting myself directly in harm's way, but I hadn't expected that he'd already know about me. If I ran, I'd never get out of here alive.

I swallowed. "Are you going to kill me?"

His lips thinned. "That depends on how you answer my next question."

I didn't struggle any more. I watched him carefully. "What's the question?"

"Did Kristoff's immortality ritual work? The one he shared with Matthias?"

"I don't know." I didn't trust Alex. He was the leader of the secret society that initiated the ritual in the first place. Sara's safety was in jeopardy if anyone knew about the ritual's effectiveness. I couldn't let that happen.

"I think you do know. Matthias drank your blood. He still lives, doesn't he?"

"It—it's true. At least, the last time I saw him he was still . . . alive."

A look of relief crossed Alex's tense expression. "Good. Kristoff needs to be removed from the throne. He never should have been released from his prison."

"It's a little late for that."

"It's never too late."

I watched the emotions play on his face. This wasn't a subject that held any apathy for him. He was convinced that Kristoff was just as evil as Matthias said he was. "You were expecting him to make an attempt on your life?"

"Of course."

"Why? What are you to him? Just a rival? An enemy?"

He smiled, but it lacked humor. "We have a long history. Kristoff sired me three hundred years ago. He, Matthias, and myself—we had a great deal of fun together for a very long time. But they had much more drive than I did. I was fine with simply existing. They wanted power."

"So they killed the last king." It was a guess more than anything.

"Yes. He was a fool, the old king. Half mad. He was easy to defeat since his subjects were ready for a change.

Matthias and Kristoff agreed to share the power—they were so alike back then. Kristoff is the older by minutes so he was to be first, and after an agreed-to time, he'd hand the throne over to Matthias."

"But he didn't."

"No. He changed his mind. Power had gone to his head, and it affected his and Matthias's relationship. That's when he discovered the immortality ritual. He hoped it would bind him and Matthias together eternally, so he'd be forgiven any of his sins. Matthias felt otherwise."

To say the least. "That was the straw that broke the camel's back. The ritual that killed Kristoff's daughter."

"Yes. But Matthias's distrust and growing abhorrence toward his brother was a long time coming."

"What did you have to do with it? And why does Kristoff hate you so much?"

He sighed and finally let go of my hair. I straightened up but didn't back away. He was speaking quietly, as if afraid someone might overhear us.

"I sided with Matthias. But there was never any doubt about whom I would choose. I chose him over my own sire and Kristoff resented that. Matthias owned my heart and what remained of my soul. Kristoff saw himself and his brother as two sides of the same coin, interchangeable, but there was a difference. Both could be cruel and unforgiving when they had to be, but—" He shook his head. "Matthias was different. Better, in my opinion, than his brother in many ways."

There was something more than simple respect in his voice. "You and Matthias—were together?"

"We were. Although, I was much more"—he smiled wistfully—"*faithful* to him than he ever could be to me. It's something one has to accept when involved with someone like him. His hungers must be satisfied, and jealousy doesn't fit into that equation."

Matthias had hinted that, while he preferred women, he hadn't been all that sexually exclusive over the years. This was the proof. It surprised me, but not as much as I would have thought. "Was it a fight with Kristoff that made you lose your eyes?"

His smile faded. "No. Matthias caused this."

I actually gasped out loud. "Matthias did this to you?"

He touched the edges of his ruined eyes. "Twenty years ago he heard a rumor that I was conspiring to have his brother released from the prison he'd created for him. It was a lie, but he wasn't thinking straight, and sometimes rage makes a man do horrible things. He had his blood servants drag me outside as punishment. I couldn't find shelter. A few minutes I could have healed from, but it was hours before he realized his mistake. By then it was too late."

The thought of this made me feel physically ill. Matthias did this. He'd had Alex dragged outside knowing it would fry the eyes right out of his skull. "I—I'm so sorry."

"Be careful with him, Jillian. He can be . . ." He hesitated. "*Passionate* to a fault. Be wary, especially since I know you're bound to him now."

I forced my nausea away at the picture of melting eyeballs and stupid, enraged vampires out of my head. "How do you know that?"

"The same informant who told me that you would be sent here to kill me tonight said that he'd claimed you to save your life, hoping to use your blood against Kristoff."

"Your informant is full of useful information."

The smile returned. "He is."

"So you hate Matthias."

"No. The contrary. I forgive mistakes, although I must admit it took me a long time. To help atone for this, Matthias bought me this nightclub so I could easily feed off the desire contained inside. It's a nightly feast and I never have to worry about going hungry. In return, I've kept things with the Amarantos as quiet and controlled as possible. This hasn't been accepted by all members. Some are still interested in the immortality ritual. I'm able to keep a lid on this, and any members who are out to make trouble are removed."

I wasn't sure if removed meant their membership was revoked, or if they were removed from being alive. I didn't ask. "Sounds like you're a good leader."

"I've tried to be. I've seen what can happen when the wrong person has power, and that's what I want to avoid at all costs."

I nodded even though he wouldn't be able to see it. "Fair enough."

"If I let you leave here, Jillian, you must promise me something. Will you do that?"

I searched his face for deception, but saw nothing there. What disgust I'd originally felt toward him had faded into something more like admiration. This vampire wasn't one of the bad ones—despite all evidence to the contrary. Over my shoulder I heard a sleepy groan as the occupants of the bed slowly woke. They weren't dead. Just sleeping. The thought was a relief.

Maybe I could get Alex to give me his ring to prove he was dead. It would buy me enough time to get my nieces out of the house and back to my sister. Then I'd tell her to leave the city—get somewhere safe until all of this blew over. It made sense to me. It felt right.

"What do you want me to promise?" I asked.

"You must do everything you can to help Matthias defeat Kristoff."

I drew in a breath. "I think you have me confused with somebody with power."

He looked up in my general direction with his nonexistent eyes. "You're not a victim, Jillian. I feel it. There is strength inside of you and courage as well. Your blood is just as powerful as they say it is. That is your true gift."

"Death is not a gift."

"Depends on how you look at it. Your blood is what makes you different from any other human. It makes you special. And it makes you very dangerous."

"I don't feel all that dangerous."

"You are. Trust me, you are." He sat there for a moment, his arms resting on the sides of the wheelchair. "You haven't promised."

"To help defeat Kristoff? I promise. I'll do whatever I can."

"Good." He nodded. "Now, lastly. Can you give Matthias a message for me?"

That depended on where he was right now, but I couldn't worry about the former vampire king. Not now. One thing at a time. "I'll try."

"Tell him that I forgive him and that I still have faith in everything he does."

I frowned. "You should tell him that your—"

Alex reached forward, his fingers biting into my shoulders, and pulled me down on top of him. He swept my hair back and I felt his mouth press against my throat.

"No—don't do this—" I pushed at him, not knowing what this was or where it came from. He'd been so still a moment ago and he'd just lashed out. Panic gripped me as I felt his fangs sharp against my skin only a moment before they cut into me. I shrieked, but it was the last noise I could make as his bite paralyzed me and I slumped forward against him.

I couldn't move, couldn't speak, but I could hear him drinking my blood, a low groan escaping his throat. It hurt badly; because of my bond with Matthias he couldn't influence me first to dampen the pain. I'd liked him. He'd convinced me he was one of the good guys—as much as a vampire could be, anyway. I couldn't believe he'd just lost control. He'd handled my scent fine up until now.

"So good . . ." he murmured, his breath cool against my raw throat. He finally released me and slid his tongue over his bloody bottom lip. I immediately regained the use of my body and scrambled back from him, my hand at my throat to press against the fresh wound.

I shook my head, my eyes burning with tears. "Why did you do this?"

He raised his face up in the direction of mine. "Because it's the only way."

Then he convulsed and gritted his teeth together before fire consumed him. In seconds the only thing that remained of Alex was a fall of gray ash, snowing down over his wheelchair. The ring he'd worn dropped to the floor next to the chair.

I couldn't move. I just stared at where he'd been seated only moments before. I was in shock. He'd killed himself. Suicide by Nightshade. And I didn't think there were any Houdini-inspired tricks up his sleeve like Matthias had used.

Alex was gone. Three hundred years of existence snuffed out by a woman in a black dress with poisoned blood.

I realized I was crying and I pushed at my tears, more angry than sad. I didn't wait around for long. I grabbed the ring, then turned and walked quickly across the room, coming a bit too close to the monster dhamp as I passed. It reached out toward me with its long arms, a sharp talon slicing shallowly into my upper arm. I jumped back from it and it looked at me with black, hungry eyes.

"Bloooddd," it screeched. "Deeaatthh."

A sob caught in my throat but I swallowed it down. "That's right. My blood is death. Don't forget it."

I expected someone to stop me. After all, I'd just killed their blind, legless leader. I'd been sent as a gift from someone who wanted Alex dead. And even though it hadn't gone remotely as I'd ever imagined it would, I'd done it.

Someone on the bed finally roused, lifting her head up off another's bare thigh.

"What's going on?" she asked groggily. "Where's Alex?"

I looked at her, my vision too blurry to see more than her outline. "He's gone."

I pounded on the door when I found it was locked. A moment later it opened and I pushed through, walking

blindly through the crowd who hadn't stopped their hedo-
nistic activities for a moment since I'd gone in. The world
still rotated. The drinks still flowed. Everything was normal at the vampire sex club ironically called The Silver
Cross. Only its owner was dead because I'd killed him.

I'd wanted him to be bloodthirsty, cruel, and horrible. What I'd got was Matthias's ex-lover, a vampire who
seemed to know right from wrong and had been through
horrible pain in his life. He'd seen me as his chance to
escape that pain once and for all and he'd taken it.

Suddenly, Noah was at my side. I hadn't seen him approach, but my mind was on other things. He still looked
monstrous with the signs of hunger showing on his face,
but otherwise he was the same Noah he'd ever been.

"Well?" he asked.

"It's done." My throat felt thick and it was hard to
swallow.

With a concerned look, he grabbed my hand as if to
remove it from my throat to inspect my wound.

I shook my head. "No. I'm bleeding. You shouldn't
look at it right now."

He grimaced. "Good point."

"Let's get the hell out of here."

"Fine with me."

In my other hand I had Alex's ring clutched so tightly
it would likely leave an imprint behind. I'd killed him.
And I was taking Kristoff the proof of just how deadly I
was.

My unpleasant mission was a success.

And I knew Kristoff was going to kill me anyway.

THE HOUR-LONG DRIVE BACK TO THE HOUSE ONLY
served to fuel my anger. By the time we got back I'd said
good-bye to fear and was ready to confront Kristoff face-
to-face, come what may.

He was waiting for me in his makeshift throne room. I

marched right toward him, but faltered when I saw who he was with. My nieces, tired and rubbing at their eyes, sat cross-legged on the floor. Since it was well after midnight, I wasn't surprised that they looked so weary.

"Welcome back," Kristoff said.

That fear I'd misplaced on the drive here came back in spades. I wondered if Kristoff had predicted my mood and wanted to remind me of what was at stake. If so, he'd succeeded amazingly well.

"Aunt Jill?" Meg, my eight-year-old niece, looked up at me with a frown. "You look really different."

"Yeah?" I twisted a finger into my hair and tried to ignore the hammering of my heart. "Different good or different bad?"

"I don't know." She looked at her sister. They were both blond and blue-eyed like their mom. Like the old me. "Just different. What are you doing here?"

"Your aunt is a friend of mine," Kristoff said. "She's visiting and she wanted to say hi."

"Hi," six-year-old Julie said. She clutched a pink teddy bear to her chest. "We watched movies all night. Past bedtime."

I forced a smile onto my face. "Sounds like fun."

"It was. We're supposed to wait here for mommy to come get us."

I looked at Kristoff who nodded. "She asked me to look after the girls, keep them safe. How could I say no?"

My face felt tight. "You're so generous."

Kristoff smiled. "Okay, kids. It's well past time for bed now. Have a good sleep."

Meg and Julie got up from where they were seated and came toward me to give me a hug. I held on to each of them tightly before reluctantly letting them go.

I looked into their faces, each in turn. "You're going home soon. Promise."

Meg shrugged. "Okay."

If nothing else, their ignorance about where they were

and who held them was a relief. I wasn't going to disturb that for anything.

The girl I'd seen earlier holding Sara was waiting at the entrance to the room and the children went toward her. She must be some sort of vampire nanny Kristoff had on staff. The thought wasn't comforting. I tensed, but didn't make a move to stop them from leaving.

"I just love children," Kristoff said. "They fill my heart with joy."

I turned to glare at him. "I swear, if you hurt them—"

"Why would I hurt them?" His gaze moved to my hand. "You have Alex's ring. I'll assume everything went according to plan."

"He's dead."

"That was the plan. Maybe you're more useful than I thought you'd be." He held out his hand and I drew close enough to give him the ring. He studied it for a moment. "What did he have to say?"

"Not much."

He slipped the ring on his index finger. "I find that hard to believe. If there was one thing I could depend on from Alex, it was that he loved to talk. Too much for his own good sometimes."

"He won't be talking anymore. So you can do as you said and let my nieces go. We had a deal."

He studied my tense expression for a moment. "Tomorrow. Let them sleep now. It's been a long day for all of us. Good night Jillian."

Two of his men took me by my arms and began to direct me out of the room. "Wait. What happened with Declan? Is he okay? Where is he right now?"

Before he could say anything in reply we were out of the room, and the vampires took me down a hallway and up a flight of stairs. They stopped in front of a door and unlocked it, then pushed me into the expansive, dark bedroom. All I saw were shadows and outlines. For a moment I figured this was where I was supposed to sleep for the night, although I'd never felt less tired in my entire life.

I gasped when I felt the rough slide of rope over my wrists.

"What are you doing?" I demanded as they tied me to the bedpost with my arms behind me.

One of the vampires grasped my face tightly. His eyes were black and his jaw was lined with dark veins. "Kristoff wants you to be part of a new experiment. Good luck."

And then they were gone, closing and locking the door behind them.

What the hell?

Any anger I'd felt earlier faded away until fear was the only thing left. I hated to be left alone with my thoughts. The more I had to deal with, the better off I was. But now there was nothing except dread filling my senses. I pulled at my bindings, but it didn't do any good.

Kristoff wanted me put in here, tied up, as some sort of experiment. I didn't know what kind of experiment, though I supposed the options were disturbingly endless.

I stilled, both body and thoughts, and strained to listen.

Someone else was in here with me, only I couldn't see who it was. My eyes adjusted to the darkness.

"Who's here?" I whispered.

I wasn't sure why I asked. I already knew who it was. I craned my neck to see the outline of his body lying against the wall. After a moment, he moved, muscles flexing as he looked across the room toward me. His black eye narrowed and his lips curled back from his teeth enough that I could clearly see his fangs.

Declan's fangs.

18

DECLAN STOOD UP. HIS CHEST WAS BARE AND ALL HE wore were black jeans. His scars were still there, of course, but they seemed to have lightened slightly against his pale skin.

He was a vampire now. Just like his father.

This was the experiment. Kristoff wanted me to be in the same room with Declan now that my blood could kill him. It was a test to see if he was strong enough to resist biting me. Maybe a rite of passage as he'd done with Noah—a job interview.

Bite me and die or resist and live. But Noah had a full day before he'd been given the opportunity to test his strength around me. Declan would have been sired only hours ago. And he already had fangs.

Cold fear slid through me.

"Declan—" I began.

"Shut up." There was pain in his voice.

I pressed my lips together.

"This is your fault," he growled at me.

"That you're still alive?" My voice shook, not sure if I

should be encouraged or terrified that he could form complete sentences. "Yeah, I guess that's all on me."

"I was supposed to die tonight. I agreed to it."

"Well, that's just too fucking bad, isn't it? Suck it up. Noah did. And—and don't come any closer to me."

He ignored my request and drew nearer to where I was tied up like a sacrificial offering. As predicted, six feet away he froze, his nostrils flaring. "Fuck."

"Different now, isn't it?" I cringed as I watched the all-too-familiar spiderweb of veins appear around his eye and eye patch and down to his jawline. His hands were fisted at his sides, his muscles tense.

His face was shadowed, but his single black eye glittered in the near darkness. "Your scent . . . is complete . . . and utter torture."

I pulled at the ropes but they didn't give in the slightest and only cut painfully into my wrists. "It'll be worse if you bite me."

"He's . . . testing me."

"Brilliant deduction." I eyed him warily as he drew closer still. There was dark anger on his face as he glared at me.

"He's sure only one of us will leave this room."

I gasped as he clutched my throat. "You can't bite me."

"No. But there are other ways of dealing with you so you're not a problem for me any longer."

My breath caught. I was right. He was going to kill me. "Let go of me."

He tilted his head as he stared at me. He seemed suddenly as emotionless as he'd ever been, the rage disappearing from his expression completely. He looked like a stone-cold killer. "This relationship can only end in a couple of ways, Jill. My death or yours. I might slip up and bite you now and that's a risk for me. I'm strong—stronger than he thought I'd be when he did this to me. Stronger than Noah was. But I'm not *that* strong. It's hell being this close to you knowing I can't taste you."

I couldn't see the scars on his face for the pattern of

dark lines that showed his hunger. "Noah says my blood is like crack to him now."

His grip on my throat tightened. "*You're* like crack to me."

I struggled to keep the fear out of my eyes. "Such a sweet talker when you're talking about killing me."

He shook his head and grimaced, his lips curling back so I could see those sharp white fangs again. I shuddered. The sight of them made me mourn for the Declan who was now gone forever. He pushed my head to the side so he could see Alex's fangs marks on my neck and hissed out a breath.

"It was only a matter of time. You're too soft, Jill. Too human. You don't have the killer instinct like I do. If Kristoff decides to keep using you as an assassin, you wouldn't last more than a couple days before some vamp snapped your neck."

He believed it, every word. I could see it in his gaze. I was soft, weak, and I needed someone to protect me. Now that he couldn't do it I was on my own—a baby bird that had fallen out of the nest.

I wasn't as weak as he thought I was.

He brought his other hand up to my throat so he would be able to squeeze the life out of me the moment he made the decision to end this conversation. "I don't understand why you'd do it, Jill. Why would you get Kristoff to sire me when you damn well knew I'd never want something like that?"

His grip was nearly too tight for me to speak. I felt a wash of emotion—fear, anger, frustration, despair—as I stared at the vampire in front of me.

"You were dying."

"Why didn't you let me die?"

"Because I needed you to live."

He shook his head. "Why would you have me made into something I hate?"

"I knew you'd want to kill me for this."

"And yet you asked Kristoff to sire me anyway. Why?" His brows drew together.

"Because I wanted you to live, no matter what. I was too selfish and too stubborn to let you die like that."

"Why?" he demanded.

"Because—" My voice caught. "Because I love you."

He didn't move, didn't react, but his hands loosened on me. My heart pounded so fast and hard that I could hear it loudly in my ears. Tears slid down my cheeks.

And then he released me completely and took a step back. The air in the room felt cool on my throat.

He was frowning deeply. "You love me."

I inhaled shakily. "Is—is that really such a big surprise to you?"

"No one has ever—" His jaw tightened.

He didn't finish the sentence. He didn't need to. No one had ever told Declan that they loved him before—probably not even Emily, the woman who'd looked after him as a little boy. Not Carson in all the years he'd raised him. Declan had had no previous girlfriends since he couldn't experience true emotion or desire while on the serum. And his birth mother had never told him the truth, had never loved him a day of his life.

No one had ever loved Declan enough to make a stupid, selfish decision like this on his behalf.

I'd known I loved Declan for a while now, but I'd been afraid to admit it even to myself. Lust was easy. But love was an emotion far more dangerous and unpredictable than the thirstiest vampire.

I licked my dry lips as the silence spread between us. "Matthias said vampires don't love the way humans do. They have detached emotions, I guess. They can see things more objectively. So they can't become emotionally attached to anyone."

His gaze hardened again. "And yet he claimed you."

I cringed. "You say that like it's a bad thing."

"It is."

"It's the only thing keeping the Nightshade from killing me. I feel better than I have for weeks."

His eye widened slightly at the news that my death watch could be called off. "So do I."

"Your serum—"

"Gone. The vampire blood . . . it burned away any remaining serum. And since I'm not a dhampyr anymore, I don't have the mindless rage to deal with, either."

"Just a little bloodlust and an aversion to sunlight." I grimaced. "Sounds like a fair trade."

"I'm not sure about that." Declan pulled his silver blade from the leather sheath at his hip.

So much for my heartfelt admission. It hadn't made any damn difference. He was still going to kill me. "You don't have to do this. You need to untie me, and then we have to find Matthias and get the hell out of here."

"I find it difficult to give a shit what happens to Matthias, actually."

"My connection to him is no different than your connection to Kristoff. A means to an end, that's all."

His eye narrowed. "The only difference is I didn't have to fuck Kristoff for our connection, I just had to drink his blood."

I stared at him. "I didn't have sex with Matthias."

Surprise flickered in his gaze. "I don't believe you."

"It's true."

He pulled back enough that I could see his shadowed face and that fiery look in the black as midnight eye. "I don't know how he can be so close to you and not lose control of himself."

I eyed the sharp knife he held. "Maturity. Practice. Self-denial."

"It was a rhetorical question, but it's great to know you're such a fan of the former vampire king."

Anger burned away anything else I was feeling. "I'm sick of talking, Declan. I've had my say. Do it. Get it over with."

"Okay." He raised the knife.

So much for my bluff. I couldn't die, not before I knew Meg and Julie were okay. "No, wait! You're not the same as the others. You can control yourself. You're not like Noah was last night. And Kristoff has no power over you. He's your father, but that doesn't mean a damn thing. I know you, Declan, and I know I've hurt you, but you don't have to—"

"I'm not going to kill you, Jill. I never was."

I sucked in a mouthful of air so deeply I nearly choked on it as his words registered with me. I glared at him. "Then stop fucking around and untie me."

"Yes, ma'am." He moved behind me to slit the ropes with the knife, freeing my hands. I rubbed my rope-burned wrists gingerly as he sheathed the knife. I didn't move an inch from where I stood. Neither did he.

"Tell me again why you asked Kristoff to sire me," he said softly, raising his gaze from my wrists to my eyes.

I blinked. "Because I need you."

"Why else?"

"Because I didn't want you to die."

"Why else?" He slid his hand down my right cheek and wiped away a tear there.

I touched his hand, still warm unlike Matthias's cool skin—the difference four hundred years as a vampire would make. Relief washed over me. "Because I love you so much I knew I'd die if you did."

He shook his head. "That's your bond with Matthias, not ours."

"Maybe on paper. But not where it counts."

His frown deepened and the dark veins were still there on his face. "He's better-looking than me, richer, more powerful. And he can control himself around you."

"I'm sure you're trying to make a point, but it's lost on me." I flattened my hands on the broad, muscled slabs of his chest. His warmth was more a relief than I thought it was. I guess vampires took time to cool off, since Declan was still hot to the touch.

His expression showed dark hunger as his mouth closed

over mine. I kissed him, pulling him against me. He growled against my lips and it sounded pained and uncertain.

"Fuck," he whispered harshly against my lips. "This is pure torture."

I tried to catch my breath. "You don't have to be this close to me."

"Wrong. I've dreamed about this for days. About you."

My fear from earlier had been replaced with something else, something like cautious optimism and relief. And as he kissed me again, I felt a deep aching need inside me. I wanted him so badly, and I never thought this could happen again between us. Especially not now that he'd been changed.

But he hadn't changed that much. He just had a couple more issues to deal with now.

He grabbed the sides of my black dress and pulled it up over my hips, then hooked his fingers into the sides of my panties and pulled them down over my legs so I was naked from the waist down. He grasped my buttocks and pulled me against him firmly so I could feel his erection straining against the front of his pants. He'd barely stopped kissing me the entire time. He ground himself against me as if he couldn't control himself. The bedpost dug into my back, but I barely felt it. I just felt him. And he felt good.

He pulled back a little to look into my eyes. "Jill . . . this isn't easy for me . . ."

"I know."

"I want to taste you."

Panic fluttered in my chest. "You can't. Declan . . . maybe this is a mistake. It's too soon—"

"Do you want me to stop?" His face was so tense for a moment.

"No." I slid my hand from his shoulders up over his face, tracing one of the dark veins. It was flat against his skin and looked like a tattoo this close up. "I just don't want you to lose control and bite me."

"I'll try."

"That's not good enough."

"I won't bite you."

I smiled. "That's better."

He swallowed, his Adam's apple shifting as I brushed my lips over his throat. "Tell me what you want, Jill."

"Other than you not biting me?" I kissed his mouth again. "I want you inside of me."

That blunt request made him swear harshly under his breath.

I slid my hands down his broad chest, over the hard ridges of his abdomen, to the waistband of his pants. I unbuttoned and unzipped and slid my hand inside, wrapping my fingers around his length while I worked his pants down over his hips. His breathing became more erratic as I began to stroke him.

He swore under his breath as my mouth met his again, nearly hard enough to bruise, and a low groan escaped his throat.

Moving a little away from the bedpost, he leaned me back on the waiting bed, pulling my dress off over my head, breaking the kiss only long enough to do so.

Maybe this was only a dream. When I'd asked Kristoff to turn Declan into a vampire to save his life, I was convinced he'd be different, more monstrous, only interested in feeding and filled with rage that I'd made this decision for him. He'd been confused, of course. He didn't know my motivation. He knew it now. I loved him, fangs or no fangs.

Being a dhampyr must make the transition easier. Some dhampyrs got worse, more violent and uncontrollable, as Kristoff said—but maybe he was just saying that to scare me. Or maybe Declan was the exception. He'd been sired by a king—a centuries-old vampire who'd been conserving his strength for thirty years. Declan had been sired by his real father. That had to make a huge difference.

I moaned as I felt Declan's weight cover me, his hands stroking my inner thighs as he spread my legs. I fumbled to grasp his thick cock and guide it against me. He growled, his lips curling back to show his fangs, and he grasped my wrist to pull my hand away from him, bringing both of my arms up over my head.

"It'll be over too soon if you keep touching me like that."

I grinned a little, but it faded as I felt him push against me, stretching me as he guided himself inside slowly . . . so slowly. He released my wrists so I could grip his shoulders as he filled me.

I held his face between my hands and stared up at him. We stayed exactly like this, unmoving, just feeling—skin to skin, his body deeply inside of mine—for a few moments before he began to rock his hips against mine.

I gasped. "Declan . . ."

"You have no idea how this feels." His voice was raw and ragged against my ear. "Pleasure and pain."

"Fifty-fifty?"

He brushed his mouth against mine. "Sixty-forty."

"Better."

I was shocked at how this night had ended up. I half expected a fit of rage to take him over like last time, but nothing happened except for the exquisite sensation of his body sliding in and out of mine.

"Just . . . don't . . . bite me," I managed to whisper against his lips.

He made a broken sound and it could have been a laugh. "I'll try my best."

I groaned as he suddenly pulled completely out of me. "What are you doing? Is something wrong?"

His mouth was on my throat, kissing me there. I tensed so I grabbed his face and brought him up a little so I could look into his eye. He looked serious and his breathing was labored.

"What?"

"I thought you were lost to me."

"When?"

"Kristoff told me about Matthias's claim on you." He

pressed his lips to my collarbone before moving his hands and mouth to my breasts. I felt the sharp edge of his brand-new fangs against my left nipple and it made me jump.

"Be careful," I warned.

"Careful . . ." He slid his tongue between my breasts and down to my belly button, leaving a damp circle behind, as he moved even lower on my body. "Not sure I want to be."

Worry mixed with the pleasure he was giving me. "Promise me you'll never bite me."

"I won't bite you." He kissed my inner thigh. "But I can still taste you."

I felt the rasp of his stubble a moment before the hot, wet slide of his tongue against me. I arched my back and cried out. His mouth on me was enough to send me right over the edge. It didn't take long before the pleasure was too intense and my orgasm crashed over me, leaving me moaning and crying his name over and over. The world appeared to grow dark around the edges and I thought for a second I was going to black out.

Declan gathered me into his arms, pulling me up off the bed so I was seated on his lap and I felt him slide into me again. I felt boneless and liquid and I clung to him as his thrusts became deeper and harder.

"Jill . . . fuck . . . so good . . ." He kissed me, open-mouthed and ravenous, and I tasted myself on his tongue. I'd forgotten everything apart from this moment. Nothing else mattered. I forgot that he was a vampire now, that he couldn't bite me, that anyone had ever touched me before except him. It was his touch that burned. It was his touch that made me crave more.

I hadn't lied. I loved Declan no matter who or what he was—or even what the consequences might be.

The last vestige of control left him as he approached his own climax. His lips curled back from his fangs and he dove for my throat. I feared for the worst, bracing for the pain, but he didn't try to taste my blood. He roared against my skin as he came deep inside of me.

I held him tightly, stroking his back, his face, wanting this moment to last forever, even though I knew it couldn't.

"I claim you, Jill," he whispered hoarsely against my lips. "You're mine."

He kissed me again—the dark web of hunger had never left his face for one moment while we'd been together. At that moment I *was* his, body and soul. But I knew he could never claim me completely.

After all, another vampire had already gotten there first.

19

THERE WASN'T MUCH TIME FOR AN AFTERGLOW.

"I need to get you out of here," Declan said, handing me my dress. I grabbed it from him as well as my panties from the ground and put them back on.

I eyed him as he pulled his pants over his legs. "Love 'em and leave 'em, huh?"

He smiled, but he looked worried. "Kristoff was sure I'd kill you or you'd kill me. Not sure he expected that."

"And yet he put us in a bedroom. I think your father is smarter than you give him credit for."

"He's not my father." His expression shadowed. "Nothing there except biology and that doesn't count in my books."

"He had me kill Alex, the leader of the Amarantos." The memory was painful and I still didn't fully understand why Alex would bite me, knowing what would happen.

He touched my throat gently. "The marks are already fading. You heal up faster because of your bond with Matthias."

I looked at my arm where the monster dhamp had scratched me earlier. It was only a faint pink line now. "Holy shit."

"What did he say to you before he bit you?" he asked, his thumb moving over the fading wound. "Did he tell you anything important?"

"He wanted me to promise to help Matthias defeat Kristoff. He was definitely anti-Kristoff as king. Convinced he was evil incarnate. And then he just bit me knowing it was going to kill him."

"He knew and he still did it?"

I nodded. "It was so strange. The guy had a death wish. He also wanted me to tell Matthias that he forgives him for . . . some bad shit that happened between them." I paced to the other side of the dark room before I turned to look at Declan again. "We need to find Matthias. Then we need to get Sara and my nieces and get the hell out of here so we can figure out what to do next. It's too dangerous to stay here."

Declan frowned. "Sara's here? How is that possible?"

I swallowed. "Emily's . . . I'm sorry, but she—she's dead. Kristoff found out where she was—"

"How?" There was pain in his expression.

"He has a mental bond with Matthias. He saw everything. Matthias knew where Sara was being looked after so that meant his brother knew it as well."

He rubbed his hand over his scalp and grief crossed his expression. "Fuck. I knew I shouldn't have told him. I knew it." He exhaled a long breath. "It's too late to change anything. It's done and there's no going back, only forward. I'm going to assume you're not willing to negotiate about leaving Matthias behind."

"No, I'm not. I don't know what they've done to him. He was dragged away after being stabbed."

"Still alive."

I nodded. "He's immortal even though he doubted it. It's proven now. The ritual worked exactly the way Kristoff wanted it to."

Declan went silent for a moment, his eye shifting back and forth as he thought it through. "Then Sara's in more danger than I thought she was."

"She is. Alex controlled the Amarantos, but now that he's gone—I don't know what will happen."

He nodded and raised his gaze to mine. "Then we need to find her father and get them both the hell out of here."

I almost smiled. "Sounds like a plan. There's a problem, though. I have no idea where he is right now."

"Sure you do."

I frowned. "I do?"

"You can use your bond to find him." There was a thickness to his voice, an unpleasantness that sounded like jealousy. His gaze hardened and he drew closer to press his hand against my chest. "You can find him because your soul is bound to his now."

I gaped at him. "You make it sound like we're soul mates."

"You are."

So that was what claiming actually meant. Even though I wasn't in love with him, Matthias was my official soul mate in the least romantic way possible. There couldn't be that many soul mates who became so because one wanted to use the other one for their blood. "I don't feel any differently."

"You do. You said so yourself. You're stronger. Healthier. And the poison doesn't affect you any longer even though it still runs through your veins. Trust me, I know for a fact it does because your smell is . . . painfully tempting." I watched as the veins slowly disappeared from his face and his eye returned to gray, although it was a shade lighter than it used to be when he was only a dhampyr.

I chewed my bottom lip, feeling awkward again. "You don't have to be jealous about the bond between me and Matthias."

"I'm not jealous. I'm concerned." He hissed out a breath. "There's no time for this. If you concentrate you'll be able to locate him pretty much anywhere in the world."

"And he could do the same for me."

"Yeah."

"Forever."

"Pretty much."

While I appreciated the fact I wasn't dying because of the Nightshade, this claiming felt much too permanent and intimate. He'd claimed me without asking me if I wanted it. I guess it was similar to what I'd done to Declan—I'd asked that he be sired even though I knew he'd have a harsh adjustment becoming the same thing he'd always hated. The same thing he'd hunted. Matthias had claimed me without asking me and he would have had to know I wouldn't be entirely thrilled about this situation. No choice. No vote. Just a permanent change to my life.

One thing at a time.

I closed my eyes and thought about him, remembering how he'd looked when Kristoff stabbed him through his heart. He'd believed he was going to die, I'd seen it on his face. But he didn't. He was immortal. And he was bound to me until the day I died.

Matthias, where are you?

There was nothing for at least a minute, but I tried to concentrate as hard as I could. I felt it then, like a thin, sinuous rope attached to me. I mentally grabbed hold of it and followed it into the darkness. I couldn't see him, but I felt him on the other end of it. I drew closer.

There he was. Matthias's face was strained and furious, his hands pressed against a barrier only inches from his body. He was in pain, constrained in a tight space from which he couldn't break free. I felt claustrophobic, desperate to escape this place. *He* was desperate to escape from it. It was an effort for me to keep him clear in my head.

He stilled as if he sensed me.

He was in horrible pain, in the darkness all alone. I felt his fear—for his daughter, for himself.

"Jillian." My name was barely audible, but it confirmed that he knew I was there with him on some level. Shame replaced his fear. He didn't want me to know he was afraid.

"I see you," I whispered. "It's going to be okay."

And then I felt myself pulled upward back along the rope until I opened my eyes and gasped for breath. Declan stood in front of me holding my arms.

"You saw where he is?"

I nodded. "I know where to find him."

His expression was unreadable. "Your bond is stronger than I thought it was."

I didn't have a chance to reply to that. Declan grasped my wrist and pulled me toward the door. He banged on it and it opened a moment later.

"Finally finished with the—" the guard asked before Declan grabbed him by the front of his shirt, pulled him into the room, and sliced his dagger upward into his heart. The vampire's ashes scattered before he even had the chance to scream.

Another guard stared at him with shock, reaching for the gun at his side. "You're one of us now—you can't be a hunter, too."

"Wrong." Declan slashed his throat and thrust the blade into his chest as well. A moment later, he crouched down and grabbed the guard's gun from the pile of burning ash and inspected it. "Silver bullets. Nice."

I was frozen in place, trying to process two kills in less than thirty seconds. "They didn't seem all that prepared for you."

He grinned. "They thought I'd lose my mind the moment I smelled you." He slid the gun into his waistband. "They were right."

"Your mind seems fine to me."

"I'm putting up a good front. Right now, I'd much rather throw you back on that bed and devour you than go find Matthias."

"Devour me."

His gaze slid to my mouth. "Yes."

"No fangs involved."

"No fangs."

A shiver of pleasure at the reminder of what just happened between us moved over my skin. "I can work with that."

He kissed me quickly before pulling back. His eye had turned black again and he swore under his breath and grimaced as the veins appeared then quickly disappeared. "You're very dangerous to me now, Jill."

"I wish it was different."

"It isn't. So let's go get your soul mate."

I grimaced. "Let's agree not to call him that, okay?"

"Fine with me." He scanned the empty hallway. "There are fifteen vampires here and three blood servants. I just took care of two of them. Lots more where they came from."

"We just need the right incentive."

"I have it. I want to get you the hell out of here before it's too late. Being with you—" He hesitated and his arm tensed under my touch. "It reminded me what's important and who I need to protect."

"The troublemaking human with the poisonous blood."

"Yeah, her."

I faltered. "The one whose decision made you into a vampire."

He pulled me closer for a moment. "You chose right."

I was surprised. "What?"

"If I was dead, I couldn't protect you."

"If you'd taught me how to kick some ass, I wouldn't need so much protection," I countered.

"You're not a killer."

"And yet I seem to be proving you wrong time and time again."

He shook his head. "Being the reluctant cause of death doesn't make you a killer."

I eyed the weapon he had tucked into his pants. "I'd still like to know how to use a gun."

His lips twitched into a slight grin. "We get out of this alive and I promise I'll teach you everything I know."

That sounded like something worth waiting for. A lesson in firearms from Declan Reyes, ex-dhampyr turned vampire. "It's a deal."

"Let's move. Lead the way."

We walked swiftly down the hall and descended the stairs. I knew Matthias was in the basement in a room with a green metal door.

We went down the stairs to the basement. It was dark and cool and dry and as we walked it led to a far room with cement walls and no furniture.

I put my hand up against the wall, feeling confused. "No. This can't be all there is. He's deeper than this."

Declan looked around. "Then there must be a door in here somewhere. We just need to find it."

Quickly would be good. My nerves were fried, and I was afraid someone would come after us when they found the empty room sprinkled with dead vampire ashes upstairs. I scanned our surroundings but it was difficult to see and I couldn't find a light switch anywhere. The only decoration in the entire room was a throw rug on the dirty floor. And it didn't exactly look as if it belonged here.

I grabbed the corner of it and pulled it to the side.

"You mean something like this?" I pointed down at the outline of the trapdoor hidden underneath.

Declan raised an eyebrow. "That looks about right."

He grabbed the rusty handle and lifted up, swinging the door back, and it landed with a thud, leaving a three-foot by three-foot opening that led into more darkness. Hanging from the side was a rope ladder that didn't look very sturdy.

At the bottom, somewhere down there, was Matthias. And the sooner we found him, the sooner we could get the hell out of here.

"I'll go first." Declan didn't hesitate and grabbed hold of the ladder, swinging his legs into the opening as he began to make his way downward.

I wasn't quite as gung ho as that. I didn't like heights on a good day, but especially not when I was descending into complete darkness. But I swallowed my fear, kicked off my shoes, and held on to the rope so tightly it burned my palms. And I started climbing down one rung at a time.

Declan's heavy boots hit the ground not long after, and I felt him grab hold of me for the last few feet of my climb. I tried to get my bearings. It was lit down here with the occasional overhead lamp set into the low ceiling.

"This isn't just a basement," I said. "There are tunnels down here."

"Most vampires have some sort of underground community. I think this is the one Kristoff used when he was in power. It's abandoned now. Most vamps who didn't turn rogue went to live with Matthias's clan."

The tunnel appeared to be cut right out of rock and led as far as my eye could see to the left and to the right with more tunnels branching off from that. It was an underground maze underneath a high-end Malibu beach house.

"Which way?" he asked.

I'd be lost if I didn't have my internal compass that tied me to Matthias. "Left."

If I knew where Matthias was, didn't that mean Kristoff would know where Declan was? No, of course not. He hadn't claimed Declan, he'd sired him. It was a different thing altogether. We were okay, at least for the rest of the night. We had to escape from here while it was still dark out. Matthias couldn't be out in the sunlight . . . and now, neither could Declan.

It pained me to think he'd never see daylight again. A flash of Alex's gouged eyes, as if someone had gone in with a blowtorch and burned them out right of his head, haunted me. Declan had already lost one eye. I didn't want him to lose the other.

Being a vampire definitely came with its limitations.

"Here," I whispered after it felt as if we'd gone a mile. There was a green metal door to the left side of the passageway, just as I'd seen in my mind's eye. No guards. Declan tried the handle, pushing against the door, but it was locked.

"Do you think you can—" I began.

Declan thrust his weight against it, shoulder-first. I heard something splinter.

I raised my eyebrows. "I'll take that as a yes."

He glared at the door. "It's an almost. You're sure this is the right spot?"

"Positive."

He threw himself at the door again. More splintering. The next time he kicked it, landing his heavy boot right in the center of it, and the door swung inward.

It was a small room—maybe ten feet square. Empty apart from a black coffin up on a ledge along the right side. A bare lightbulb hung from the ceiling.

"He's inside." I found it difficult to breathe. I'd seen this in my mind. This was the confined space Matthias was trapped in.

Declan eyed it. "No one would normally check a coffin looking for a living being inside. It's good camouflage, especially after the vampire starves enough to go into his sleeping state."

I went to it and grabbed hold of the padlock. "Not many coffins are locked shut, though."

"No, they aren't. Stand back." Declan pulled out the gun and held it to the lock. The sound of the shot made me jump. It was so loud, it had to alert someone to our location if there was anyone down here in the tunnels.

Declan fumbled with the lock until it fell to the ground, then he swung open the coffin.

Matthias's pale white hand slowly reached over the side. He moaned—it sounded a bit like my name—but he didn't say anything else.

I was at his side in an instant. He looked horrible, pale, gaunt, the dark, nearly black circles were under his eyes again. The irises of his eyes were so pale they looked almost white. He opened his mouth but nothing came out.

"Matthias, can you move? What's wrong with you?"

"Fuck." Declan stood next to me, staring down at the vampire. "I didn't expect this."

"What?"

He reached into the coffin and spread Matthias's shirt. The blood there wasn't just remaining from when he'd been staked earlier.

"Oh shit." I covered my mouth with my hand as my stomach lurched. For a moment I thought I'd vomit until I gained control over myself again. "Matthias. What did they do to you?"

His chest had been cut open, leaving behind a mess of congealed blood and torn flesh that hadn't healed.

"His heart is gone," Declan said grimly.

I gasped. "His heart? How—how is this possible?"

"It's only possible because he's immortal. Otherwise this would have killed him instantly. But he can't function until he gets his heart back. He's not healing because this is a major injury—his body has stopped regenerating itself since it's now missing a major organ."

"You are fucking kidding me."

Declan didn't look like he was kidding. "I had a feeling he'd given his heart away. I didn't know it was to someone other than you."

I gaped at him. "And this is the time you decide to get funny?"

He shrugged a little. He wasn't nearly as upset about this situation as I was. "We'll have to find his heart."

I forced myself to look at Matthias's bloody chest again. "And what? Just shove it back inside him?"

"That should do it."

If I'd had any doubt about what kind of a monster Kristoff was, I didn't any longer. No wonder I'd sensed so much pain from Matthias. He wasn't healing. He was missing his heart. And yet he was still alive. And he would have stayed like this, in agony, until I found him again.

The thought made me sick to my stomach.

Kristoff likely found this to be a nice ironic way of dealing with the brother he hated, by punishing him the same way Matthias punished rogue vampires—by tearing his heart from his chest. The difference was that the rogues would have felt pain for only a few seconds before they turned to ash. Matthias didn't have that promise of relief.

I touched Matthias's hair, stroking it back off his forehead, compassion and worry spilling over inside of me for this troublesome vampire who'd bonded me to him eternally. "I'll find it. I swear I will. And I'll be back as soon as I can."

He gave me an almost imperceptible nod, and I saw the pain in his eyes as I closed the lid.

This was a roadblock and we had to get around it before we could get the hell out of here. "Declan, put the lock back on. It's busted now, but if anyone glances in here they won't suspect anything right away."

"You just want to leave him here like that?"

I looked at him. "Unless you were planning to piggyback a vampire with a gaping chest wound up that rope ladder . . ."

"That might be a bit tricky."

"Exactly."

He crossed his arms, his brow lowering. "We could leave him here tonight. Get Sara and your nieces. Get the fuck out of here before sunrise and come back later."

I only had to think about it briefly. "I can't leave him here like this. And it has nothing to do with him claiming me or whatever you think our special soul-mate bond is now. I wouldn't let anyone suffer like that any longer than they had to. He doesn't deserve this."

"That's debatable."

"Declan," I said sharply. "Are you with me on this or not?"

He was quiet for a moment. "Fine. I'm with you. We need to find his heart as soon as possible. Pray that Kristoff didn't burn it."

I grimaced. "Pray for a vampire's heart. I can do that."

"I figure the only reason he's still conscious is because of his bond with you. He's drawing on your energy right now to maintain his."

Our bond. I felt a little weaker than I had before, now

218   MICHELLE ROWEN

that he mentioned it, but I'd figured it was because it had been a long, stressful day. My weariness wasn't much, but it was enough to notice. I remembered that metaphysical rope that tied me and Matthias together that I'd used to find him down here. It was entirely possible he could use that rope to access my life force.

Shit. This was seriously messed up. But if it was true then it meant that the more injured Matthias was, the weaker I'd become. I hadn't signed up for this, but I needed to deal with it. And I needed to find his heart so he could heal himself again.

The thought that Kristoff could have burned the heart filled me with a fresh wash of panic. Perhaps that was the only way to destroy an immortal vampire—fire. But if so, then that wouldn't make them truly immortal. They had to be invulnerable. But we were still working with the laws of nature on some level. Vampires were a living entity—although very different from humans. Their hearts barely beat, but they still needed them, as evidenced by Matthias's inability to function without his. Their body temperatures were lower, but, as I've learned, fledglings didn't become cooler to the touch immediately. Days. Months. Years. I didn't know how long it would take before Declan's temperature lowered to what Matthias's was.

All I knew was if we couldn't find the heart, Matthias would be in this state for a very long time—possibly forever. That would be hell. I didn't think his sanity would last very long trapped in a coffin with an empty chest.

I tried to climb the rope ladder quickly, but it was unstable and my hands were shaking. The faster I tried to be, the slower I actually went. My hands and feet, plus just about every other muscle in my body hurt by the time I reached the top. A glance behind me confirmed that Declan wasn't even breaking a sweat. I couldn't express how happy and relieved I was that he was helping me. I couldn't do this without him.

I got to the top first and pulled myself up.

Five vampires including Kristoff waited for us there. I

stopped breathing, eyes widening with shock at the sight of them. Then despair crashed over me.

Shit.

Declan pulled himself through the trapdoor and slowly got to his feet. His muscles were tense as he scanned the faces of the vampires standing there.

I expected him to immediately leap forward, slashing his silver blade though their hearts. Or use his new gun with the silver bullets to take them out one by one. There were too many of them, though. He couldn't possibly take them on without getting hurt or killed in the process.

"Please, Declan," I whispered. "Don't fight them."

He stayed in one place, his hands at his sides. Kristoff drew closer to him.

"Well?" he asked.

"You were right," Declan said evenly. "Matthias isn't going anywhere in his current condition."

I stared at him. "Declan . . ."

Kristoff crossed his arms. "So you're able to control yourself around her."

Declan nodded. "Yeah. I'll admit it's a struggle, but I'm glad I asked for the opportunity to test myself. Now I know for sure."

"Were you tempted?"

"Of course I was. Her blood is an incredibly powerful weapon against vampires, more than I even realized."

Kristoff looked pleased. "Well done. Dhampyrs make the strongest vampires—always have. It's one of the reasons I created the law preventing their siring and destroyed those already made before my rule. But I'm glad I made an exception for you, my son. You will be a great asset to me now."

"Alex was against you, just as you thought. Jill told me he asked her to help Matthias to defeat you."

I felt the color draining from my face with every word he spoke, and disappointment cut into my chest as sharply as a stake.

Declan finally glanced at me and I saw nothing on his

face to indicate what the hell was going on. Then again, I didn't really think I needed a program to know the players in this particular game.

The son of the vampire king had been tested. And he'd passed with flying colors.

20

I NOW KNEW HOW MATTHIAS FELT. MY HEART HAD been ripped out of my chest, too.

I'd believed. Maybe a little too quickly. Declan sired from dhampyr to vampire and, other than a bit of initial surliness, he was exactly the same as before. Better even. His dhampyr rage was gone. He was able to resist my blood. He no longer had the side effects of the serum that dampened his emotions and desire.

It had been the best of both worlds. Or so I'd foolishly thought.

When Kristoff's men grabbed me, I used what little energy I had left to fight against them, but it was in vain. They subdued me easily. My blood was the only dangerous thing about me.

I'd trusted him completely. I hadn't even questioned whether or not I should.

My mistake.

I'd been used. And I'd gone along for the ride one hundred percent, all too willing to believe he couldn't be changed or coerced just because he'd grown a set of fangs.

"See you later, Jill," Declan said as the vampires began to drag me out of the basement.

"Eat me, you bastard," I snapped, feeling the anger rise up past my initial stunned reaction.

"Been there, done that. You can go down on me next time to keep things fair." He smiled, and it chilled me to see how cold it was.

"In your dreams."

His smile held. "Or yours."

The vampires dragging me away laughed at this fantastic hilarity as we moved up the two sets of stairs leading back to the bedroom I'd been in before with the ashes on the floor. Declan had taken those two vampires out, sacrificing them so I'd believe he was trying to help me escape. I was shoved inside and the door locked behind me.

As I stood there in the darkness, my bottom lip quivered but I refused to cry. My heart was broken, but it was still beating. I was still alive. Which meant only one thing—they still needed me. I'd proven that I could kill a VIP vampire. My usefulness outweighed me being a liability to them.

Declan . . .

No, I couldn't dwell on him. He'd always said he hated vampires. I guess that changed the moment he became one. I still couldn't believe he'd accept Kristoff so readily after everything Matthias had told us about him. Kristoff was dangerous to humanity—a vampire with a deadly widespread agenda.

And Declan was okay with that? Would stand by his father's side?

Carson had been a horrible father, but his morals were in the right place, generally speaking. The man saw things as strictly black or white, but he knew the difference between good and evil and he'd ingrained that in his adopted son. He'd taught Declan that vampires were evil right across the board.

I'd wanted to see the good in Noah. In Matthias. In . . . Declan. But maybe there wasn't any good to see. Maybe I was trying to fill in the blanks when they should remain blank.

Matthias hadn't claimed me because he was madly in love with me and wanted me to stay alive despite the Nightshade in my blood. No, he'd wanted to use me in a failed attempt to defeat his newly awakened brother. Noah was confused right now, trying to get a grasp on what it means to be a vampire. But would he stop himself when it came to killing someone when his new thirst overwhelmed him? I wanted to believe he could, but I wasn't sure.

And Declan. He hadn't been given any choice in the matter. I'd decided for him and that decision had turned him into the monster I'd just met downstairs. Cool, calculated, willing to lie to get what he wanted. So different from the rage he'd had to deal with as a dhampyr—the exact opposite, actually.

It had felt so real between us earlier. I'd even told him I loved him.

But he hadn't said it in return.

I was on my own. Again. And I had to get the hell out of here before it was too late. I figured I had two choices: become Kristoff's assassin or try to escape.

Escaping sounded good to me. But I also had to think about my nieces and Sara. I hadn't signed up to be Mother Goose, but my instincts kicked in. The children were my main concern. I had to get them safely out of here.

I paced back and forth for what felt like forever, but no good plan came to me. I had no idea what time it was but it was late. Or, possibly, early. We'd returned from the vampire club after midnight and that already felt like hours ago. Sunrise couldn't be that far off.

A plan came to me, but it was far from being a good one. Unfortunately I didn't have enough time to think too much about it; I had to act now while there was still a chance to get out of here. I looked around the dim room until I saw something that might be able to help me. A lamp.

I unscrewed the lightbulb, then smashed it against the

ground. I stared at the broken glass for several minutes, willing myself to find the courage to do this.

My sister's face came to mind. I wondered if she was sleeping right now or if the mental influence had worn off and she was beside herself with worry about Meg and Julie. She'd never understand what was happening. Kristoff said he'd release them, but I didn't believe him. Putting that much power in his hands—the lives of my nieces—without question was not something I wanted to do. Ever.

Using this thought as my strength, I sliced the edge of the broken lightbulb over my wrist. The act made me flash back to another time when I'd done something similar. In my bathroom, staring at my red-eyed reflection in the mirror. Things had seemed pretty damn bleak that evening. Had I really wanted to die when I pressed that razor blade to my wrist and watched the bright red blood spill into the sink?

Maybe for a moment. But, thankfully, that moment passed.

It was just the opposite tonight. I was slitting my wrist because I wanted to live.

The dark red blood felt hot on my skin as I watched it well up from the wound I'd made.

I waited another moment before I dropped the broken glass and went to the door. I pounded my fist against it.

"Please help me," I shouted. "I'm hurt."

There was somebody waiting on the other side of the door. Guarding me. Watching for any trouble.

They'd come to the right place.

A minute later the door creaked open and a pasty-faced guard peered inside.

"What?" he snapped.

I held my wrist out to him. "I'm bleeding."

His nostrils flared and I could practically see the drool as the scent of my blood hit him like a two-by-four. I wasn't sure if he already knew who I was and what my blood could do. Maybe Kristoff hadn't shared my secret with everyone yet. Actually, I was counting on it.

The guard's eyes narrowed. "Hasn't anyone ever told you that it's not healthy to offer your blood to a vampire?"

"I cut myself on a piece of glass."

"I see that." His eyes were black and hunger branched across his face.

Blood dripped from my wrist to the floor as I held it aloft and tried to ignore the stinging pain. "Will you please help me?"

It was as close as I could get to tearing my clothes off and begging him to take me. Desire snaked over his expression. I had no idea who he was, where he came from, if he was a nice guy once, or if anyone might miss him if he died.

He'd been the one to open the door. Game on. I tried desperately to look like a sexy, bleeding victim in waiting.

"They warned me about you," he whispered as he drew closer, his gaze locked on my wrist.

That was worrying. "What did they say about little ol' me?"

"That you're dangerous."

"Me?" I tried to look innocent. "Dangerous? That's crazy talk. I'm just a weak little human trapped in a house full of thirsty vampires. Are you thirsty right now?"

It was too dark in the room for him to notice my blood was an unusual shade of red. Or maybe he was color-blind.

"Damn, you smell so good." He took my arm and brought it to his lips, before sliding his cool tongue over my wound. "You taste so good."

I felt a mix of disgust, regret, and victory. They didn't blend well together. "I've been told that before."

He began to suck on the wound, drawing more blood into his mouth. I didn't try to stop him.

"I see why Matthias claimed you. Your blood is—" He gasped and looked at me with wide eyes.

"Very bad for vampires with no self-control." I nodded. "Bye now."

He opened his mouth to scream, but the flames took him over before he had a chance. I stepped away so I wouldn't be burned and batted at the bits of ash that fell down and caught in my hair.

Without waiting a moment longer, I grabbed the door handle and swung it open.

Declan stood there blocking my way. I felt surprise and painful defeat. I'd been so close. He wore a shirt now, a long-sleeved black one stretched tight across his muscular chest. It looked borrowed from someone smaller than him.

His gaze moved to my bleeding wrist and he hissed. "Cover that."

"Or what?" I snapped. "You'll be tempted to have a taste?" I held my arm up toward him and he flinched away from me. I didn't think I'd ever seen Declan flinch before. He'd been affected by my blood as a dhampyr enough to be drawn to it; to me. I could only imagine how much harder it was for him now. "Why are you here? To kill me? To drag me in front of daddy dearest? How could you do this?"

His jaw tightened, the tattoolike spiderweb appearing on his face only making him look scarier. "Maybe you should have let me die when you had the chance."

Frustration spilled over inside of me. "Why, Declan? Do you hate me so much that you'd string me along like a fool? Just to try to get some answers about Alex and Matthias?"

He glared at me. "In case you haven't realized it, my real father is also my sire. Do you know how powerful that combination is? He does. He controls me now."

"So what does that mean? You need to do what he says?"

"Yes. I'm compelled to follow his orders, no matter what they are."

I faltered. "So he ordered you to sleep with me?"

"It was a test on whether or not I could resist your blood. I agreed to it. In fact, I requested it."

"You resisted."

"Yeah, I did."

My eyes narrowed. "Just like Matthias's test. He resisted me, too, when he had me naked and vulnerable. Only he didn't follow through and fuck me when his heart wasn't really in it. Even though—just an FYI—I would have let him."

His lips curled back from his fangs and his expression darkened. "I guess he's way more of a saint than I am, isn't he?"

"Get the fuck out of my way, Declan." I sounded so much stronger than I felt. In reality I was ready to give up. But I couldn't.

"Or what? You'll bleed in my general direction?"

"The guard couldn't resist me."

"I'm not some stupid fucking guard. My whole life I was taught self-denial. This is no different."

"What did Kristoff send you here for right now? Let's just say I'm not feeling very friendly at the moment if you were looking for another quick lay."

He glared at me. "You're not going to beg me to help you? Rely on my fondness for you to help you escape?"

"Fondness? I wouldn't know if you felt anything at all for me. You're not exactly the expressive type. Not much with the flowers and chocolate."

He was silent for a moment. "You're wrong. I've brought you a gift. It's the reason I came here. No one knows where I am right now."

"Keep it. I don't want anything from you."

"I think you'll want this." He held out a glass jar to me. "Take it."

My mouth dropped open. Inside it looked like something from a medical lab—a bloody, fleshy organ the size of a fist. I knew exactly what it was. Mine had been broken only a few hours ago down in the basement. "That's—"

"Matthias's heart. I stole it from Kristoff's room. It won't be long before he realizes it's gone."

I looked at him with so much shock that it made it difficult to speak. "Why are you doing this?"

"Why do you think?"

"Before, you—and Kristoff—when we came up from downstairs—"

He grabbed my hand and placed the cool jar containing the bloody organ in it. "As my sire and father, I can't disobey him. But it doesn't mean I agree with what he's making me do."

I couldn't believe what I was hearing. "Are you trying to tell me that you're not . . ." I didn't know how to say it.

"Not evil?" His lips twitched.

"That's what I—I don't know what's going on, Declan. I don't understand any of this."

"Kristoff expects me to be one way with him now. That's what I showed him downstairs. He thinks I've changed." His expression was tight. "I have changed. But not the way he thinks. This is the one chance I've got to get to you, to give you this so you can get Matthias and get the hell out of here. He'll protect you now."

I grabbed on to his arm. "You're coming with me."

He shook his head. "I can't leave. Kristoff will find me—our bond isn't the same as yours and Matthias's, but there are some similarities. If he can find me, he'll find you." He watched my confusion for a moment as everything pieced together in my head, his brow creasing. "You really thought I'd betray you like that? You didn't even give me the benefit of a doubt after everything we've been through together?"

I was overwhelmed by all of this. "I didn't know for sure. You're—you're a vampire now."

"Yeah, thanks for the reminder. But other than an unnatural thirst for blood"—his teeth clenched—"*your* blood in particular—I don't feel much different than before. Maybe that'll come over time, but not yet."

I *had* thought the worst of him. I'd been too afraid to even hope for anything other than total betrayal. That was messed up and I was ashamed of it, but it protected me from any paralyzing disappointment that would have made me curl up in a ball somewhere, unable to help my nieces get out of here.

"You have to come with me," I said. "We'll deal with Kristoff later."

"I can't."

"Please, I don't think I can do this by myself."

"That's not true. You can do it. You're stronger than you think you are. Just go, get Matthias, help him—and he'll help you." He looked over his shoulder. "I can't stay. Go now while there's time and leave here as fast as you can."

I reached for him, but he was already gone.

21

MY GRIP TIGHTENED ON THE JAR CONTAINING MAT-thias's heart and I felt frozen in place, afraid of failing and afraid of dying.

Nothing new there.

I left the room and retraced my steps, keeping close to the wall and freezing whenever I heard a sound. I figured even the vampires had to be headed for bed by now. Sunrise couldn't be that far off.

I quickly crept down the stairs to the basement, then pulled up the trapdoor.

"Hey, where are you going?" a familiar voice said.

I nearly dropped the jar when I jumped. I whipped around to see Noah looking at me sheepishly. "Sorry, did I scare you?"

I tensed. "Why are you following me?"

"Caught a whiff in the hallway, figured it was you." He grimaced and crossed his arms tightly over his T-shirt. "You know, the more I expose myself to it, the easier it is to resist. And by easier I mean fractionally not as difficult.

Still, the scent of the Nightshade seems to trigger my saliva glands like nothing else I've ever experienced. It's very interesting, actually." His gaze moved to the jar. "Is that a human heart you've got there?"

Being near Noah didn't set my mind at ease. It got my back up now that I wasn't sure about vampires again. I wouldn't recover from Declan's act in front of his father for a while. But it was an act just to fool him, to keep Kristoff from realizing Declan was still helping me. He'd been trying to avoid a direct order that he wouldn't have been able to ignore.

Maybe the stronger the vampire that made you, the more control you had. Weaker vampires sired weaker fledglings that had the most problems with control—the ones who couldn't help themselves when they were near me, like the guard. Like several others I'd come across since meeting the syringe full of Nightshade.

It was a theory. And according to this theory, Noah should be one of the stronger ones, like Declan was. Only Declan had a better head start being a dhampyr to begin with. He'd already been halfway there.

"Uh, the heart?" Noah said. "Is there an answer or are you just wandering around looking for Frankenstein's lab?"

I looked at the organ. It was hard to believe it was over four hundred years old, but I was no expert. "It's Matthias's."

Noah blinked. "Never seen a vampire's heart. Shouldn't it be ash by now?" His face whitened. "Matthias is immortal. Holy shit, he's still alive without that in his chest. He must be in agony right now."

"And that brings you up to speed on the exciting night I've had."

Noah whistled. "Damn. Remind me not to drink any baby's blood in any secret-society rituals."

I eyed him. "If I need to remind you about something like that I think we have a serious problem."

"Good point. So, need some help?"

I glanced behind us at the empty basement, not nearly ready to let my guard down yet. "So they just let you wander around freely?"

"Are you kidding? I slipped out of the room they'd locked me in and I was about to take off, but I felt all guilty about leaving everyone behind. And there you were, lurking around in the basement." He glanced at the rope ladder. "So what are we waiting for? Let's go shove that bloody thing back in his chest."

Sounded about right to me.

If I thought climbing the rope ladder was difficult before, I hadn't tried it while carrying something breakable. I ended up shoving the jar down the front of my dress and praying that it wouldn't fall out. I went down the ladder so quickly that I burned my hands on the rope, but I touched down to solid ground with everything intact. Noah made it down easily as if he'd climbed rope ladders all of his life.

"This way." I started heading left along the humid, musty underground tunnels until I finally came to the green metal door that was slightly ajar after Declan had broken it off its hinges. "Here it is."

I half expected someone to stop us. After all, Kristoff and some of his men knew where we'd been before, knew that we'd seen Matthias in his makeshift coffin. But after Declan's "betrayal," and my being thrown into a locked room, it was likely that Kristoff thought I was safely and soundly tucked away for the rest of the night.

While Noah seemed able to be around me without digging his fangs into my skin, he didn't try to get too close, keeping several feet of air between us at all times.

"Open it up," I told him, and he pushed up the lid of the coffin after undoing the broken padlock. Even in the near darkness of the room that was lit by only one bare light-bulb, Matthias looked so pale he nearly glowed in the dark.

I felt immediately relieved that he was still alive. Despite the promise of immortality, I wasn't sure. "See? I told you I'd be back."

He just stared up at me. I felt wearier than I had before, which told me he was pulling energy from me to stay conscious. If he passed out, I figured there would have to be a full awakening like what had been done with Kristoff. Matthias said it had involved the blood of a dozen human sacrifices. I'd really like to avoid that at all costs for too many reasons to list.

"Are you trained in first aid?" Noah asked nervously, looking around the empty room and ending at Matthias's pale and sickly form.

I shook my head. "Afraid not. You?"

"A little. But this is your show, Jill. I'm not going near that heart. It disturbs me how delicious it looks."

I cringed. "That is disturbing."

"Should you wash your hands first?"

"With what?"

"Right. That's another excellent point. This place isn't decked out with a full commode, is it?"

I didn't exactly have a game plan here. Matthias must have seen the trepidation in my gaze.

"It's . . . okay . . ." His voice was so quiet I barely heard it.

I felt weak suddenly with the prospect of what I had to do. "There's nothing okay about this. This is going to hurt you, and I don't even know if it'll work. Plus, I think I might throw up."

His forehead was creased and he let out a small sound that may have been a laugh.

I glared at him. "This isn't even remotely funny."

"You'll . . . be fine. Just . . ." He paused and swallowed thickly. "Take it . . . shove it into my chest . . ."

Shove the vampire's severed heart into his bloody chest. This wasn't happening. This was a horror movie I'd fallen into and couldn't get out of.

"What do you want me to do?" Noah asked.

I tried to breathe. "Catch me if I pass out."

"Will do."

I unscrewed the lid of the jar and placed it on the ground. Then I forced myself to reach into the glass container and wrap my fingers around the cool, slippery heart. My own heart beat so wildly in my chest it made me dizzy. Matthias's heart didn't currently beat. It felt cold and dead, like meat you might buy from the deli section of the grocery store.

I faltered. Maybe I couldn't do this. I'd failed biology in high school and never dreamed about being a nurse or a doctor when I grew up. This was a million miles outside of my comfort zone. "I don't want to hurt you."

"Then . . . do it . . . quickly."

I nodded. "Uh, Noah?"

"Yeah."

"Which way is up?"

He drew a bit closer. "You have it upside down."

"Okay." I adjusted it.

I gripped it tightly and pushed apart Matthias's bloody ruined shirt so I could clearly see the gaping wound in his chest. I gagged. Couldn't help it. If nothing else, at least it hadn't healed over yet. That would have meant I would have had to cut him open again.

Not a good thought. None of this was good. But if it worked, then it was worth it. I'd chalk the inevitable nightmares up to a successful learning experience.

I looked in his pale eyes, this vampire who'd claimed me so he could use my blood to destroy his brother. His brother who'd tried to gain vengeance on him by tearing out his heart and locking him away in a coffin to let him suffer.

He'd saved my life. I wasn't saving his—he'd live even if his heart was destroyed. But this wasn't living.

My soul mate. The other end of my metaphysical rope. The leech on my energy. The reason I wasn't going to die because of the Nightshade.

"Do it . . ." Matthias whispered.

Before I could second-guess myself, I shoved the heart into his chest.

He arched his back and cried out in pain as my hand

disappeared deep into his flesh and up under his rib cage where the original wound had been.

I gagged again at the feel of the inside of Matthias's body. Vampires were warmer on the inside than I would have expected. Not regular human body temperature, but warmer than room temperature. I forced the heart in as far as it could go, then pulled my hand out. It made a disgusting, wet smacking sound.

I tried not to think. I pressed down on the wound that started to ooze blood again. My right hand and arm were now red and slick with blood up to my elbow.

"Okay, I'm a vampire now, and that was still pretty fucking gross to watch," Noah said, the disgust naked in his voice. "Wow."

Matthias writhed under my touch, his face contorted with pain.

"Shit, Noah—" I'd begun to feel more panicky with every passing moment. "I don't think it's working. He's not healing."

I heard a creak and my head whipped in the direction of the door expecting to see we'd been discovered and Kristoff's men would drag me away from Matthias before he'd recovered.

Jade peered in at us. She wore a long blue dress printed with sunflowers and her red hair was back in a ponytail.

Relief mixed with annoyance. The last thing I needed to deal with right now was an insane dhampyr. She entered a little more, her gaze moving over each of us in turn and ending with Matthias. By the look on her face, I knew she recognized him. He was the vampire who'd forced her to give him blood to help heal his internal damage from drinking my blood. The same vampire she'd been forced to feed earlier tonight when he'd been staked.

It had helped him both times. Her blood healed. My blood killed.

Life and death, Jade and me were. Like two sides of a coin.

"Jade," I whispered fiercely. "What are you doing down here?"

Her expression was distant but there was concern there. "He's evil, you know. And there is so much blood. An ocean to wade in and a sunrise beyond. It scares me."

I frowned. "Who's evil?"

"The man who looks like this one." She nodded at Matthias. "He wants to kill my baby."

"Your baby." I remembered what Isaiah said before he was killed, that Jade had a child who died years ago, which was likely why she fixated on the child vampire Patricia so much. "Do you mean . . . Sara?"

She nodded. "Yes, my baby. How could anyone want to hurt her?"

"Who wants to hurt her?" Kristoff said she wasn't in danger. I wasn't surprised he'd lied about that, too. I kept my hands pressed firmly against Matthias's bleeding chest. He suffered in silence now, but I knew the pain hadn't lessened for him. I blamed that knowledge on our brand-new bond.

Jade leaned against the doorframe. "I heard the blond man talking on the telephone. He said they could have her and use her blood however they wanted. He told them to come immediately to take her away. Amore, amar—"

"Amarantos," I finished for her, stunned. "He said he's going to give Sara to the Amarantos?"

"I don't want Sara to be hurt." Tears streaked down her cheeks.

My head hurt as I thought it through as quickly as I could. "Do you know how you can save your baby, Jade?"

"How?" she asked eagerly, drawing closer to me.

"You need to give Matthias some of your blood. He can stop Kristoff."

She looked down at the badly injured vampire. "He can?"

I nodded. "I swear he can. If you can help him, he can help Sara. I promise."

It wasn't a lie. I believed Matthias had the motivation

and the ability to stop his brother. However, I didn't know for sure that he'd be successful, especially not after going through all of this.

Jade frowned deeply. "They all drink from me. I should be used to it, I suppose, but I never am. It hurts so much. They give me gifts and let me ride on the Ferris wheel, but it doesn't make it better."

Maybe her insanity was a blessing more than a curse. It helped her escape into a world where her baby was still alive and all was well with the world of amusement-park rides and family dinners. "I'm sorry."

I eyed Matthias with deepening concern. He looked close to death, struggling to breathe, struggling to deal with whatever pain he felt right now. And the only relief I could get for him was in the form of a crazy dhampyr with some major maternal instincts.

There wasn't enough time to try to convince Jade to help the easy way. The hard way would have to do. "Do you want to help Sara or do you want her to die a horrible death at the hands of greedy, child-killing monsters?"

She visibly flinched.

"They'll tear her apart, drink her blood, and throw her tiny body away like garbage." I forced the words out, twisting like a knife to get the reaction I needed. "Is that what you want? Or do you want her to live?"

She drew in a shaky breath. "I want my baby to live."

"Then give Matthias your blood now, Jade. *Now.*"

She stared at me in silence for so long I was sure she was going to run away. I'd been too harsh. Pushed too hard.

But instead, she nodded.

I held my breath as she moved closer to the coffin and extended her arm over Matthias's mouth.

"Drink from me," she said.

His pained gaze flicked to mine for a moment, before he slowly reached up to grip her arm and brought it to his lips. I saw her wince as he bit into her wrist and the slide of red blood down the corner of his mouth as he began to feed, his eyes blackening, and hunger branched along his cheeks.

Noah watched with rapt attention. "Damn, I'm so thirsty right now."

It was as if all of my coiled up energy disappeared and I stumbled backward until I felt the solid stone wall behind me. It helped to keep me on my feet. I didn't think it had anything to do with Matthias and my bond this time. I'd just been so tense for so long that something had to give. What gave was my ability to keep myself upright at the moment. I wiped my right hand and arm off on the skirt of the black dress I wore until only my fingernails were stained with Matthias's blood.

Matthias fed for a while. Finally Jade staggered back a few steps and sat down on the floor, holding her arm to her chest. She looked at me and I hated to see the pain and confusion on her pale face, but I wasn't sorry I got her to agree to this. I pushed away from the wall and went to Matthias's side. His eyes were closed and there was blood on his lips. I thought for a moment that it hadn't worked, but then I looked down at his wound. It was still bloody, but it had begun to heal. I let out an audible sigh of relief.

"Go," I said to Noah. "Get to the kids upstairs. We'll be up as soon as we can and then we're leaving."

He nodded and helped the dhampyr to her feet. He closed the broken door as best he could behind him.

A couple minutes later Matthias's eyelids fluttered open and he immediately focused on me. His wound had healed over, although it wasn't completely gone—a thick, raised pink line remained. Maybe this injury would actually leave a scar this time.

I pressed my hand against his cool forehead. "How are you feeling right now?"

He looked up at me. "I'm improving."

I let out a breath I hadn't realized I'd been holding. "Kristoff ripped out your heart and stuffed you in a coffin."

"My brother doesn't forgive easily."

"No shit."

He blinked. His eyes had returned to their normal pale gray color. The dark patches under his eyes were fading. "You saved me."

I couldn't help but smile a little at that. "If you call stuffing your heart back in your chest and hoping like hell that it worked, then I guess I did."

"Others would have left me right where I lay."

"I couldn't do that." His intense gaze was making me nervous. "And it has nothing to do with our bond, if that's what you're thinking."

"I never said it did."

"Honestly Matthias, you should have told me you were going to do that to me."

He swallowed, then reached down to touch where his wound had been. "You weren't well after Declan injected you with the fusing potion. I was certain you'd die."

"But I didn't."

"That's right, you didn't." His meaning was clear. I would have died if he hadn't claimed me right then and right there.

"I'm not saying I'm sorry you did it. I want to live. But—but maybe you should have saved it and used it on someone who wanted to be bound to you for all eternity. Declan says this makes us soul mates."

He didn't reply. I'd take that as a confirmation.

I sighed. "Fabulous. And now I can find you—that's how I found you down here. I sensed where you were like a rope that ties us together. I'm guessing you can do the same for me."

"Yes."

"Anything else?"

"It's a good metaphor—the rope. Your life is tied to mine. You're still human and can be hurt or killed. But it will take a great deal more effort. You will also be stronger—as strong as a dhampyr. Along with your blood it will be a lethal combination."

I thought it through. "How can it be reversed?"

"It can't be." He didn't look upset by this, there was the slight glimmer of amusement in his eyes now, which was nothing but infuriating considering the topic of conversation. "I know you'd prefer to be bound to Declan."

"I'm not sure I want to be bound to anyone. Not this much."

"He's a vampire now."

I gripped the edge of the coffin. "I guess I'm a sucker for men who like the nightlife."

Matthias was silent for a moment, then he struggled to sit up so we were at eye level to each other. "I can make you forget him if you want."

I frowned. "What?"

"No other vampire can ever influence you again, except for me. Let me show you. Look at me, Jillian."

The moment I looked at him everything else suddenly flew away from me. Every stressful thought, every worry, every single problem. There was only Matthias.

He had complete and total power over me.

He'd influenced me before just after I'd first met him. Influenced me into his bed and made me desire him even though I knew on some level that it was wrong and unnatural and not how I truly felt. My emotions weren't involved then, just my body.

But now everything had changed.

I loved him. I knew for certain that he was the only man I wanted to be with. I'd do anything for him. I craved his touch, his kiss, his caress. I wanted to be at his side forever. In his bed every night.

I touched his face, trying to memorize every feature, every line. My fingers trailed over his cheek, his jaw, his mouth.

"What do you want, Jillian?" he whispered.

"You." I brushed my lips against his, my hand moving to tangle into his hair.

I needed his body against me, filling me. It was a desperate need that I couldn't—

Suddenly, the feeling vanished as if I'd just had a bucket of cold water thrown at me.

"See what I mean?" he said, amusement sliding behind his gray eyes.

I slapped him so hard across his face that my hand stung.

"Don't do that," I snapped.

He shrugged. "It worked though, didn't it?"

"It wasn't real. Stop fucking with my mind."

He raised a pale eyebrow. "What's real? If every one of your senses tells you something is real, then why can't it be?"

"I'm not in love with you."

He studied my face. "In the beginning I could only increase the desire you already felt for me, but now it sounds like there are more interesting emotions to play with. Let me know when you want me to make it permanent."

I tried to slap him again but he caught my wrist.

"I'll take that as a polite no?" he said.

"You can take it as a hell no."

Matthias scared me and this was just another example of why. He had too much power over me. If he chose to exert that power again and not take it away, I knew he could make me do whatever he wanted and I'd follow him around happily like an adoring pet. It seemed so real, if only for a moment. That was almost scarier than anything Kristoff could do.

He eased himself out of the coffin. "Enough of this. I'm better now and I need to find my daughter."

"Nice to know we agree on something." I crossed my arms tightly over my chest. "And by the way, Matthias? Influence me like that again and next time I'll rip your heart out myself."

I could have sworn I saw him grin at me, but I turned my back and exited the room.

Maybe I should have left him locked in the coffin after all.

22

MY ANGER AT HAVING MY EMOTIONS SHAMELESSLY manipulated faded quickly. As soon as we left the room Matthias had been imprisoned in, I got my priorities straight again. Also memories of what happened earlier at The Silver Cross and what Alex wanted me to tell Matthias kept replaying in my head.

"I need to tell you something," I said as we quickly moved down the tunnel toward the rope ladder leading back to the basement. "It's about . . . Alex."

Matthias stopped walking. "I know what Kristoff wanted you to do. He saw Alex as a threat now that he's been awakened."

I nodded. "Kristoff sent me to his nightclub earlier tonight."

His expression tensed. "Is he dead?"

I clasped my hands in front of me to stop them from shaking and nodded. Matthias needed to know this. Maybe this wasn't exactly the ideal time to tell him, but if something went wrong I was afraid there might not be another time. "He knew why I was there—someone tipped him off about my blood, but . . . but he bit me anyway. I—I tried to stop him. I'm so sorry."

He didn't speak for a moment.

A big part of me worried about how he'd take this news. My blood had killed someone Matthias had cared deeply for at one time, someone he likely felt a great deal of guilt about. I wondered if he'd been there when Alex was dragged out into the sunshine, watching from a safe, dark place as he extracted his vengeance.

I'd seen many sides of Matthias. It was very possible he could be that cruel if he felt justified in what he was doing due to a perceived betrayal.

"I hadn't seen him in years," he said quietly.

"He—he wanted me to tell you something."

Matthias looked at me, his expression grim. "What?"

"That he forgives you. And that he still has faith in everything you do." I didn't elaborate. I think Matthias would know all too well what was being forgiven.

Matthias squeezed his eyes shut for a moment. "There are very few things I regret in my long life, Jillian. What happened between me and Alex is one of those things. A dying man's forgiveness doesn't ease my guilt very much about the choices I've had to make then or now. Sometimes there's only one path that can be traveled, even if it's a rocky one."

He started walking again. I wasn't going to make him keep talking about Alex. I wasn't that cruel.

No one stopped us. It felt as if the entire house was abandoned. It was eerie, but I pushed aside my uneasiness enough to get this done.

"It's nearly sunrise," Matthias said. "You'll have to leave without me. Take Sara and I'll meet up with you when I can."

There was no room for argument in his voice. You couldn't argue with sunlight.

I nodded. "All right."

"We need to remove her from this house before Kristoff has the opportunity to hand her over to the new leader of the Amarantos."

I looked at him with surprise. "That has to be Kristoff's goal in killing Alex. Getting a new leader in place who doesn't hate his guts."

"I'm sure he has someone positioned to take over. And what better way to buy his allegiance than with a bribe of immortality?"

I really didn't like the sound of that.

I scanned the hallways looking for Jade and Noah, but didn't see them. We kept moving. Finding the room Sara was being kept in took a few tries, but the crib in a small room near the front of the expansive house was a good tip-off. The vampire nanny snoozed in a chair by the door. As we opened it, she woke, leaping to her feet to stand in our way and baring her fangs.

"The baby's sleeping," she hissed. "And you're not Kristoff."

Matthias frowned. "How can you tell?"

"Kristoff isn't wearing a blood-drenched shirt tonight."

Matthias looked down at himself. "Good point."

She launched herself at him, but he easily knocked her to the side. She hit her head on the wall and fell to a heap on the floor.

I eyed him. "You do look exactly like him. It's freaky."

His lips curved. "One thing I can never fault Kristoff for is his good looks."

"Right. Or his brother's extreme vanity." I moved toward the crib and was immediately relieved to see Sara sleeping there safe and sound, wrapped in a thin yellow blanket. I carefully picked her up and held her against my chest.

"Here she is," I whispered. "You can finally take a look at your daughter."

Matthias sent another fervent glance out the open door as I drew closer to him. Finally he gazed down at the face of his daughter, and he drew in a breath. It was the most honest reaction I think I'd ever witnessed from him.

"She's as beautiful as I'd imagined she'd be."

"She'll be a heartbreaker one day."

He smiled and touched my arm. "Please keep her safe for me. I'll be able to find both of you through our bond."

I nodded. "I'll have to stock up on baby formula and diapers again. Walmart here I come."

She opened her pale gray eyes and yawned. So adorable. And to think, I'd never really given much thought to having children before, but she was pretty darn—

Just then, Sara screwed up her face and started to cry, a sharp sound that cut through the silence of the dark house like a knife.

I winced at the earsplitting noise. Babies weren't cut out to be stealthy escape artists.

"Go now," Matthias commanded.

I didn't argue. With a last look at him and the painful knowledge that we were running out of time to escape undetected, I hurried down the hall and then another. I had to find the room my nieces were in. I couldn't just walk out the door with Sara and leave them behind.

They were nowhere to be found. My chest tightened and I tried to hold back the panic and frustration overflowing in me.

"Where are they?" I whispered, trying to will the baby in my arms to stop crying.

All I had to do was find Meg and Julie and I was marching out that front door into the early morning light. I passed a grandfather clock that confirmed it was a quarter to six. The morning after what was, quite possibly, the longest night of my life.

So close to being free again I could taste it.

I turned a corner to find Declan standing there.

I gulped a mouthful of air, and tried to stop my heart from beating so wildly in my chest. "Oh, thank God. Declan, you have to help me find the girls."

He looked frustrated. "You should have tried to be quieter, Jill."

I looked down at Sara. "Babies don't take direction very well."

Out of the corner of my eye I saw Jade approach from the far end of the hallway, her arms stretched in front of her. "There's my baby. Darling baby."

I turned my attention from the crazy baby-loving dhampyr to Declan. "I have to get out of here before Kristoff knows—"

"He already knows everything. He commanded me to bring you to see him for a private meeting." His face was expressionless.

"He *commanded* you," I repeated, feeling sick.

"I told you what that means."

All too well, I was afraid. "You said you can't disobey him."

"That's right."

I looked over my shoulder.

"Looking for your soul mate?" Declan asked dryly. "I easily knocked him out a minute ago and the guards took him away. There is a hidden camera in the tunnels downstairs. Kristoff saw everything."

This wasn't happening. I'd been so close to getting out of here. Declan couldn't be the one to stop me—he was supposed to help me. "Did you know there was a camera there?"

"I do now."

I looked into his face, desperately searching for some sort of signal that he was just faking this like he'd done earlier. "No, Declan. Please. You have to fight this."

He shook his head, his expression bleak. "I can't. I have to do what he says. He asked me to bring you to him and I'm compelled to obey. Give the baby to Jade."

"Your father wants to give this baby to the new leader of the Amarantos Society. And you're just going to let him do that?" My words twisted into anger.

He grasped my upper arm so tightly I flinched. "Hand

Jade the baby or you might drop her. I know you don't want that to happen."

Of course I didn't. Reluctantly, I handed her the baby. Jade cooed at her and rocked her gently in her arms. The next moment, Sara finally stopped crying.

Maternal instinct. Sara seemed to like the crazy dhampyr. Go figure.

Declan wasn't quite as gentle as he dragged me down the hall to see the vampire king.

— 23

"I KNOW YOU DON'T UNDERSTAND," DECLAN HISSED at me as I continued to fight him. "You don't know what it's like to be compelled to do something when you know it's wrong."

He knew what he was doing was wrong, and yet he did it anyway. There had to be a way he could fight this. If not, then there was no way I could get away from him. He was too strong. "You don't realize just how much of a hold Matthias has on me."

His lips thinned. "Wrong. I do know. I watched you give him back his heart. I saw the way you looked at him. And I saw you kiss him."

My stomach sank. "That was mind manipulation."

"You didn't seem to resist very much."

"Neither do you."

"It's not the same."

Kristoff was waiting in his throne room, the same one in which he'd originally stabbed Matthias in the chest shortly after our arrival. He sat in his high-backed red and gold chair with his fingertips pressed to each other as Declan pulled me closer.

"Good morning, Jillian," Kristoff said. "You've had an interesting night, haven't you?"

The nanny was right. Except for the bloody shirt, he could be Matthias. "I think my reply to that is 'fuck you.' As will be my reply to pretty much anything you have to say."

"You don't know how generous I can be with those who don't constantly defy me."

I glared at him, trying to fight the fear and despair growing inside me. "Where's Matthias?"

"He's restrained in the next room." He nodded toward his left. "I'm thinking I might set him outside so he can watch the sunrise. I know he approves of that as another method of punishment to those who cross him. I think you saw the proof of that last night."

A shiver raced down my spine at that pleasant-sounding threat to blind Matthias. "You ripped his heart out of his chest."

"Yes, I did. It was an experiment to see what would happen. Turns out, nothing did, and he will recover completely in a few days." He leaned back in his seat. "And I didn't thank you very well earlier for your help with Alex. Very impressive."

I glanced over my shoulder to see Declan standing there, his arms at his sides, staring straight forward like a soldier awaiting orders. "I'm not really sure why you even wanted him dead. He couldn't have been that much of a threat to you."

"You think because of his disabilities he was helpless?" He shook his head. "You underestimated him. He was a vicious creature in his time."

"I guess it goes with the territory." I tried to clear my mind of any panic I was feeling. I had to figure a way out of this, but it was looking pretty bleak. Declan was compelled to help Kristoff. Matthias was weakened and restrained. I was in deep shit.

"Alex had to die so a new friend of mine could step up

to the plate as leader of the Amarantos. He has been waiting for years for such an opportunity and he didn't want to delay."

The hardwood floor felt cold against my bare feet, but the sensation helped me to concentrate. "A new friend."

"Alex would have opposed me now that I'm back. I couldn't have that. I knew there was no time to waste. In fact, it was an excellent chance to kill two birds with one stone because I wanted to show you off to Stephen. He was impressed."

Stephen—the new leader of the Amarantos and Kristoff's buddy. He was the one Kristoff planned to give Sara to. My stomach lurched.

"It's nice to have friends in high places," I said.

"He's here. He arrived just before sunrise."

Shit. He was going to sacrifice Sara this morning so his "friend" could live forever. I tried to think of a way out of this, but came up blank. But there had to be something I could do, something I could say to stop this from happening.

There were too many obstacles at the moment and, even though I allegedly had strength equivalent to a dhampyr now, I was still technically only human. Kristoff was an immortal vampire with a bloody agenda and a small army to back him up—including Declan.

I tried to remain as calm as possible—or at least appear that way. "Sounds like you have everything under control. Why did you want to see me?"

"Why do you think?"

"My first guess is that you hate my guts and want to kill me."

He studied me for a long moment and I began to feel more hopeless than I did to begin with. "All of these vampires who are irresistibly drawn to you—compelled to taste your blood. That must be exciting for you."

I blanched. "Not exciting. Scary and painful, yes. Exciting, no."

"And you have the affection of both my son and my brother."

"*Affection* is a debatable choice of words."

"My brother claims you, a natural enemy to vampires everywhere, after four hundred years of claiming no one. He is bound to you for the rest of your now-extended life."

I looked up into his pale gray eyes, identical to Matthias's. "I didn't ask him to do that."

"I know you didn't. I just find it interesting. And then there's my son, who seems entirely smitten with you, so much so that he fights my influence over him even as we speak."

I didn't risk a look at the silent Declan to see if I could notice any fighting. After all, he hadn't hesitated to drag me here in the first place. And smitten? I couldn't really imagine Declan being smitten by anything—including me.

"Are you going to force him to kill me?" The words sounded horrible leaving my mouth, but I had to ask.

He cocked his head. "You presume that my solution to every problem is death. I don't fully understand why you feel that way toward me."

"I guess we just don't see eye to eye on your plans for the future."

"Such as?"

"Such as giving Sara to your new Amarantos friend as a gift so he won't stop you from creating more vampires to rise up against the human world."

He raised his eyebrows. "Sounds like I'm going to be very busy. My true aim is to make the world a better place. And I could debate this issue with you for hours, Jillian, but I have a feeling that we will never see eye to eye on this."

I hissed out a long sigh. My hands were clenched so tightly that my short fingernails bit painfully into my skin. I was desperate to figure out a way out of this. I couldn't save the world, but I had to save the kids. One goal at a time.

"Please, Kristoff," I didn't like the pleading tone to my voice. "Do whatever you want with me, but you can't hurt my nieces. And you can't give Sara away to someone who's going to hurt her. It's not right. You have to see that."

He looked down at the ring that used to belong to Alex.

"How did you escape the room you were in to go to my brother's side earlier?"

I stared at him. "Pardon me?"

"I told the guards to keep you in your room, but you managed to get out. I don't have security cameras up there."

"I cut myself." I held up my arm to show him, but the wound was almost healed by now. "And lured the guard in. He bit me."

His gaze moved over the faint pink line. "And you say you're not an assassin."

"I had no choice." I hated that I felt the least bit guilty about killing the guard, but I did.

"The problem with that story is that Declan was also guarding your room. And yet he's still standing."

My breath caught in my chest. He'd helped me against Kristoff's wishes and that likely wouldn't be acceptable. "He wasn't there. Maybe he'd gone on a break."

"My brother's bond with you makes it impossible to coax the truth from your lips." Kristoff appeared mildly frustrated with me, the first emotion I'd seen on his face during this uncomfortable conversation. "Declan, you helped Jillian escape and you also stole the heart from my chambers so she could return it to my brother. Is that right?"

"Yes," Declan said, and I cringed at his automatic and unavoidably truthful answer.

"Why? I asked you to guard her."

Declan's gaze didn't move to me; he stared straight forward. "To guard someone means that I must protect them. Keeping Jill in that room helpless and alone wasn't protection."

Kristoff was silent for a moment. "Do you have a knife on you right now, Declan?"

"Yes."

"Hold it to Jillian's throat."

Before I could make a move to scramble away from him, Declan grabbed me from behind and I gasped as I felt the cold, sharp press of silver at my throat. It was so close to my skin that any move would force him to slice it straight into me. I stopped breathing as I clutched at his arm.

"Kristoff"—Declan struggled to speak—"don't make me kill her."

"I know this is hard for you. But sometimes we have to do things that are difficult because there's no other choice."

Even though I was trying desperately not to move, I felt the sting of the blade and the warm trickle of blood sliding down my throat.

"Declan . . ." I gasped. "Please . . . fight this . . ."

"I can't," came the strangled reply. "Fuck. Kristoff—please . . ."

A long, tense moment went by before Kristoff spoke again. "You may drop the knife, Declan."

A moment later I heard the clang of metal as it hit the ground. Declan's fingers dug painfully into my shoulders, his breathing labored. I exhaled shakily, but didn't try to pull away from him. He fought it and that must have been very difficult for him.

Kristoff watched us carefully. "Go get my brother and Stephen and bring them in here, please."

Declan let go of me and strode across the room, opening the door between two six-foot-tall oil paintings of oak trees and lush, sunny meadows, and disappeared.

I held a hand to my throat.

"I spared your life," Kristoff said evenly. "I wouldn't do so for anyone else who'd crossed me as much as you have."

I struggled to breathe and scanned the room. Two guards stood at the far wall next to the tall archway leading toward the front hallway. "You obviously need me."

His lips curved to the side. "You think so?"

"The only reason I'm still breathing is because you like what I did to Alex. I proved myself to you."

"I expected you to fail. You didn't. But despite that and despite what you did to the guard earlier, you don't have the killer instinct, do you?" He didn't wait for my answer.

"However, you could still be a valuable weapon. The government researchers who held you originally saw that, too, didn't they?"

I was so popular at the moment both vampires and humans wanted to use me for my blood. I should start charging an hourly rate.

"The Nightshade was developed to kill vampires, but I wasn't the one it was supposed to be given to—it should have been injected into a trained agent. It's a fluke that it's in me."

He nodded. "Fate works in mysterious ways."

Declan returned with Matthias, pushing him in the room ahead of him. He seemed unharmed and furious. Another man entered the room as well, tall, dark-skinned, with a shaved head and the expected pale gray eyes.

Kristoff stood. "Welcome to my home, Stephen."

The man scanned his surroundings. "It's been a long time."

"Too long. But I'm glad for the chance to renew our friendship. Thank you for coming out on such short notice. I promise my gift for you will be well worth it."

My stomach twisted. I couldn't let him give Sara to this monster so he could drink her blood. Anything I had to do to prevent that, I'd do it. But, damn it. I didn't know how to stop this.

Stephen's gaze went to Matthias. "Your brother looks terrible. It looks like you've been taking out your vengeance on him rather extensively."

Kristoff laughed. "You know our rivalry has gone on for some time. But right now I'm the one with the power."

Matthias kneeled on the ground, his forehead coated in a sheen of perspiration. His bloody shirt was gone and his chest was pale and bare. He looked weak from earlier. He'd need a lot more time to recover from having his heart torn out and shoved back in. Despite his pallor, his expression was fierce. "Stephen, you son of a bitch—you're the reason Alex is dead."

Stephen cocked his head, his face showing nothing but bland interest. "Actually, I believe we can thank your brother's secret weapon for that. But I'm happy to reap the rewards of it. I'll make an excellent leader of the Amarantos. Bring it back to its prior glory that Alex attempted to smother with his misplaced morals all of these years."

Matthias looked at me and I saw the worry in his gaze. It didn't help ease my mind very much that everything would work out for the best this morning. His attention moved to his brother and his eyes narrowed.

"My poor brother," Kristoff said. "You do look a wreck. But I have the dhampyr here now and will allow you to drink from her whenever you like."

"I'm guessing there will be a price for that."

"Like what?"

"For me to stand back and let you offer my daughter up as a sacrifice to help you gain friends and influence people. But I won't sign my own child's death warrant."

Kristoff considered this. "I have to say that I'm impressed. You never put anyone but yourself first in the past."

Matthias's expression shadowed. "I've changed."

"You've become much too fond of humans over the years. It's made you soft."

"No, it's made me think about my actions before I set any master plan into play."

"Master plan. I don't think you're capable of having one of those anymore. You've been much too focused on pleasure and wasting your gift of immortality for the last thirty years."

"You call it a gift. I'm not so convinced anymore."

Kristoff smiled and glanced at me as I warily watched their exchange. "He plays the part of hero well, while making me out to be the villain."

"The soap operas always have a good twin and a bad twin," I said.

"Are you sure which is which, Jillian?"

I glared at him. "I think so."

"Then it would probably surprise you to learn that it was Matthias who discovered the immortality ritual. It was he who founded the Amarantos Society. And it was his master plan for vampires to become a stronger race and take hold of the world, making humans our blood servants." Kristoff spread his hands. "If he told you any differently, he was lying to you."

The news crashed over me and took my breath away for a minute. I felt as if I'd been struck. I looked at Matthias. "Is any of that true?"

His expression was unreadable. "All of it is."

Stephen stood close by with his arms crossed. He wore a suit that looked designer, modern, and very expensive that was tailor-fit for his tall, lean frame. "Matthias read about the immortality ritual in one of his ancient books of magic and wanted to learn more about it and any other method to make himself more powerful. That's why he founded the society. The entire purpose of the Amarantos is to discover ways to lengthen life and gain power. It was a spell using dark magic that originally created vampirism in the first place; the ritual is simply an extension of that."

"I drew the line when it came to the blood sacrifice of a child. But my brother drew his line in a different location." Matthias's voice was flat. "Kristoff, you've seen for yourself the ritual's effects. It's unnatural for anyone to live forever. All things must have a beginning and an end."

Kristoff moved to stand face-to-face with his brother. "I totally agree."

I eyed him, waiting for the punch line. He was admitting that it was wrong? Declan stood silently six feet to my left. He didn't meet my gaze when I glanced at him. However, his brow was furrowed.

"If you touch my child I will destroy you," Matthias said, breaking the silence in the room. "You can't give her to Stephen."

Kristoff frowned. "I never planned to give her to him. That's not why he's here."

My gaze shot to him. "I don't understand. You—you told Stephen to come here so he could use Sara for her blood."

"No. I never said anything of the sort."

"Then why is he here?"

He moved toward me and grasped my chin in his hand to raise my gaze to his. "He's here for you, Jillian."

My eyes widened. "Me?"

"After what you did to Alex, he was impressed. I planned to use you as an assassin, but I feel that giving you to Stephen is a sign of faith between us."

He was going to gift me to Stephen as a slave—one he could use to kill his enemies. The thought made me equally furious and scared to death that I wouldn't be able to find a way out of this mess.

The vampire's face showed no expression. "I didn't see her kill him with my own eyes. For all I know, she smuggled a stake into the nightclub. I need evidence that it was her blood before I'll be satisfied."

"Of course." Kristoff nodded toward Declan. "Fetch the others."

Declan soundlessly left the room and returned less than a minute later with Sara's nanny and Noah.

Oh, shit. Not Noah. I'd wondered where he'd disappeared to when he left the tunnels. Now I knew.

"Bring them closer," Kristoff instructed.

Noah looked worried, as he should. Both Noah's and the nanny's eyes turned to black when they got within six feet of me and hunger branched across their faces.

"The problem with Jillian," Kristoff explained to Stephen, "is that she's not a dedicated killer. Luckily her blood is more than enough to lure the vampires close enough that they find it impossible to resist the need to feed from her."

I shook my head, feeling frantic and trapped. "Please, don't do this."

"Would you rather it be Sara I was offering up to Stephen like you originally thought?"

"Of course not." I looked over my shoulder. "Declan—"

"Say nothing, Declan," Kristoff commanded.

His jaw was tense and I saw emotion in his gray eye, but Declan didn't speak or move. Anything Kristoff said, he had to obey. The thought sickened me right down to my soul.

Stephen studied the two hungry vampires from a dozen feet away. His distance to me was the only reason he seemed unaffected by the Nightshade himself. "The young man accompanied Jillian to Alex's nightclub last night."

"He did."

"Are they friends?"

"I believe so."

"He'll still bite her if he was able to resist her before?"

"I can help with that. Noah," Kristoff said. "Look at me."

"No, don't look at him—" My voice was strangled.

But it was too late. He looked, and Kristoff captured him in his hypnotic gaze.

"You find Jillian's blood irresistible don't you?" Kristoff asked.

"Yes," Noah said, his brow furrowed and his jawline tense. "But if I bite her, I'll die. That's a bit of a deterrent."

"Noah—"

"Yes?"

"Bite Jillian and drink her blood."

When Noah turned to me I saw a wash of blankness in his eyes from being influenced. Without hesitation, he lunged for me, and it was just like what happened the night he came back after being sired—a zombielike hunger replaced rational thought and action.

I screamed as he grabbed hold of me, his lips peeled back from his fangs, and lunged for my throat.

Declan grabbed hold of Noah's shirt and wrenched him back from me, throwing him so hard across the room that Noah stumbled and slammed his head against the wall. It was exactly like the other night. Only this time Noah was still conscious, scrambling to get back to his feet and come toward me again. Declan stalked over to him, grabbing him by the front of his shirt.

"This is for your own good," he said, before slamming Noah's head against the floor.

This time he was definitely unconscious. I didn't have much time to feel relieved about that when the nanny grabbed me. I shrieked as she sank her fangs deeply into my arm, paralyzing me immediately so I could only stare down at her with horror as she drank my blood.

After a few seconds, she looked up at me, her brows knitting together. "I was so hungry."

"Sorry to hear that."

And then she was gone. The ashes that remained of her fluttered gently to the ground at my feet.

I scanned the large room to see that everyone present looked surprised by this turn of events.

"Interesting," Stephen said after a moment. He sounded pleased with what he'd seen. "She's as deadly as you said she is."

Kristoff looked sternly over at Declan. "Why did you stop him from drinking from her?"

Declan rose from the floor from his crouched position over Noah. "Because he would have died."

"That was the point."

Declan's expression was tense. "I didn't want him to die."

Stephen studied Declan for a moment. "This is the dhampyr who killed many vampires in the past—the one everyone thought was indestructible?"

"Yes."

"It's against our laws to sire a dhampyr. You know very well why that is."

"*My* laws. And I broke them this one time. I was curious to see what would happen. He's adapted remarkably well to his siring. He's very impressive."

Stephen pursed his lips and scanned Declan from eye patch to shitkickers. "I agree. But he's unpredictable."

"As a brand-new fledgling, he's strong enough to resist Jillian's blood while many older vampires have been too weak to resist—as you just witnessed."

I looked across the room to Matthias. He'd watched everything that had happened carefully and he met my gaze now. I couldn't tell what he was thinking. Telepathy wasn't part of our bond. Or perhaps it required a great deal more concentration than I had to spare at the moment. His attention moved to Stephen, whom he watched very carefully as if analyzing every word he spoke.

Did he have a plan to get out of here? Or perhaps now that he knew his daughter wasn't in any immediate danger, he was simply going to bide his time until he got his strength back. While I didn't like that he'd kept the truth from me about his role in some of the things he'd attributed to his brother, I was hoping he had one of those master plans—or, hell, another of his disappearing acts—up his sleeve.

Unfortunately, he wasn't wearing any sleeves at the moment.

"Your son is very strong willed," Stephen said.

Kristoff nodded. "But he bends to my word. What I tell him to do, he does—but I must be specific. I thought he'd make an excellent bodyguard for me, but now I'm not so sure. He fights me, even now. It's because of Jillian. I believe Declan would choose her life over mine."

Stephen laughed. "You're surprised about that? He's still a man. When I take her with me they'll be separated. That should help matters."

"That's not good enough." Kristoff's cool gaze scanned the former dhampyr. "Declan, you'll do exactly as I say, won't you?"

"Yes," he replied tightly.

"Anything I ask?"

"Your word is my command."

My stomach sank. I didn't like where this was heading.

Kristoff held his son's gaze for a moment longer. "Drink Jillian's blood. Now."

There was no time to run. He moved even faster than he had when he'd held the knife to my throat.

"Declan, no!" I cried out as he grabbed me from behind, pulled my black hair away from my throat, and sank his sharp fangs into me.

⸺ 24

DECLAN WAS GOING TO DIE.

No—please. Not like this.

I tried to fight him, but it was too late. My arms fell slackly to my sides as his bite paralyzed me. Declan hadn't been a vampire long enough to learn how to take away the pain, I wasn't sure if any vampire could now that I'd been claimed by Matthias, so this hurt like hell. Instead, I was numbed by knowing what this meant. Pain was actually the last thing on my mind.

I felt cold, sickening fear as he drank from me. I couldn't do a damn thing to stop this from happening.

It was too late anyway.

When he released me, we stared at each other in shock. My dark blood was on his lips. He touched it and looked down at his fingertips as the realization of what he'd just done sank in. "Fuck. I'm so sorry, Jill."

I reached for him. "Declan—no—"

He convulsed in pain and fell hard to the ground on his knees.

I clamped my hand over my mouth to keep from screaming, but the sound still wrenched from my throat. I waited in terror to see him explode into fiery ash and scatter around me as the nanny had only a minute ago.

And there was nothing I could do, nothing I could say, that would change this. The man I loved was going to die and I'd never see him again, never touch him again, never kiss him again, and—

And he was still here.

In horrible pain.

But still here.

I collapsed to the ground next to him and touched his face. It was solid and real and this wasn't just a hallucination.

Kristoff crossed his arms as he watched us. "Exactly as I thought. Your blood won't kill him. It may in the future, but so close to his siring, he is still strong enough to resist."

I struggled to breathe. "What are you talking about?"

"Dhampyrs make very strong vampires. It's one of the reasons they aren't normally allowed to be sired. I wasn't sure just how strong he was. Now I know."

I was in shock, sickened by what I'd just experienced firsthand. It fought with the relief I felt that Declan was still alive. "So you made him drink my blood as some sort of experiment?"

"Yes, exactly."

Declan slowly recovered from the heartburn from hell. He pulled me against him into a tight hug.

My arms went around his shoulders. "Declan . . ."

"Shh, Jill." He whispered in my ear.

He slid something down the front of my dress. It was his knife. It cut me as it pressed against my skin, but I tried not to flinch. He wasn't trying to stab me with it, just transfer it to me. He was giving me a weapon to protect myself with.

He held my gaze, but didn't say anything. I didn't think he was currently capable of making full sentences. The intense pain he'd felt a minute ago was still in his gaze.

"So romantic." Kristoff shook his head. "Matthias, the woman you've claimed seems to belong to another. Doesn't that bother you?"

"You couldn't have known that would work," Matthias said flatly, ignoring the question. "Declan could still have died."

"But he didn't. I'll take that as a sign of good things to come." He turned. "So, Stephen, as you can see, Jillian is an admirable weapon. Just not when it comes to former dhampyrs."

"She seems to be."

"She'll be impossible to resist for your male and female enemies alike."

"Actually, all I saw was a weak-minded female and two fledglings whom you had to influence to bite her."

Frustration slid behind Kristoff's gaze. "Declan, bring her closer."

Declan's face tensed and he rose from the ground, wiping the back of his hand over his mouth to clear away the remainder of my tainted blood. He pulled me to my feet. It had only been two bites—three if I counted the guard from earlier—but it was enough blood loss for me to feel weaker than I had before. I hoped like hell I wouldn't pass out. I needed my head working right.

Declan pulled me closer to his father and Stephen. Stephen stiffened as I got within six feet of him and hunger branched across his face.

"Yes," he hissed. "I see what you mean. Her scent is dangerous."

"It is. She's dangerous even to me, aren't you, Jillian?" Kristoff grasped my face and brought me close to him, until only a couple inches separated us. I watched as he fought against his hunger, his lips curling into a tense smile. "It's a shame that you don't have the killer instinct to go along with your deadly blood."

I stared into his face that looked so much like Matthias's. "You're wrong about that."

He raised a pale eyebrow. "Am I?"

I stabbed him in the throat with Declan's knife, jamming the blade deep enough that I felt it scrape against bone.

I was sure this hadn't been Declan's intention in giving it to me. But the opportunity had presented itself, and I'd taken it. After all, I'd never been one to follow the rules.

Kristoff pushed me back from him so hard that I flew across the room, landing hard on my back and smacking my head against the floor. He grappled for the handle of the knife sticking out of his larynx and pulled it out, which produced a spray of blood. I could see the surprise in his furious and pained gaze.

The woman he'd thought lacked the killer instinct just stabbed him in the throat.

It was a start.

With the knife now clutched in his hand he rushed at me, all civility and calm, kingly exterior gone. He was going to kill me and be done with it. Forget using me as a weapon to hand over to his Amarantos buddy. Now he just wanted me dead.

I scrambled back, crablike, on the ground as he approached.

Declan stepped between us and I looked up at him with surprise. His hands were fisted at his sides.

Kristoff coughed and sputtered but didn't speak. *Couldn't* speak. It was the main reason I'd aimed for his throat—so he couldn't give Declan any more orders. We now had a window of opportunity before his healing kicked in and mended the damage I'd done.

Declan's shoulders tensed. "You wanted Jill to be a killer for you, but *I'm* the killer. Of vampires. And despite what you've done to me, nothing's changed."

He punched Kristoff in his already damaged throat. Kristoff recovered enough to slice the knife into Declan's shoulder, although I was sure he'd been aiming for his heart. Declan snarled and pulled the knife out, throwing it to the side.

"I can't kill you," he growled. "I don't give a fuck whose idea everything was to start with, you're the one with the power at the moment. And you need to be stopped. And there's only one way I can think of right now."

He grabbed his father by the front of his shirt and dragged him across the floor. Kristoff fought hard against him—their strengths were nearly equal to each other. Declan didn't have an easy time of it, but he reached the front door and kicked it open.

"No! Declan, don't!" I screamed.

He ignored me, instead launching both of them out into the morning sun.

I watched in horror as they disappeared from view before I scrambled up off the floor and staggered across the foyer just as I heard a scream.

It was Kristoff. His eyes were on fire.

I looked frantically for Declan. He stood in the sunlight, his gaze on me. He was squinting and grimacing against the brightness, shielding his face with his hand, but he was unhurt.

I let out a ragged sob of relief. Kristoff said himself that dhampyrs made strong vampires. I thought he'd meant physical strength, but he'd meant in what they could withstand. Sunlight was one of those things. My blood was another.

Kristoff might be immortal, but he could still be burned—it just wouldn't kill him.

Clamping his right hand over his burnt eyes, Kristoff stumbled back into the house, feeling his way. He fell to his knees just inside. His throat had begun to heal.

"Jade . . ." he managed to say. "Need . . . her blood."

The red-haired dhampyr was pressed up against the wall a little down the hallway. She was still holding Sara in her arms.

"Jade." Kristoff's ruined voice was painful to hear.

"Yes, your majesty?" she replied.

"Blood . . . *now.*"

She shook her head. "No more blood. I won't give

my blood to anyone else. I don't like how it makes me feel."

I gasped and pressed back against Declan, who'd also reentered the house, as Stephen walked swiftly toward us with the knife now in his hand.

"Stephen," Kristoff struggled to say. "Dhampyr . . . blood. I . . . need to heal . . . my eyes."

Stephen didn't reply. Matthias drew closer to us. I was very worried that Stephen would turn and thrust the blade into his chest.

He didn't.

Matthias looked down at his brother. His eyes might be blackened, but they were still there, unlike Alex's, which had been burned right out of his head. Kristoff had only been in the sunlight for a few moments.

"Matthias—" I began.

He met my gaze. "It's okay, Jillian."

"It's okay? What are you talking about?" I shook my head, my eyes going to the knife in Stephen's hand. And I was surprised when he handed this knife to Matthias hilt first. "What's going on?"

Stephen continued to study Kristoff, who knelt in pain in front of us. "You'll have to put his clothes on quickly."

Matthias nodded. "I will."

"I tried to kill as many of the guards as I could earlier. Anyone left—including the blood servants—won't know the difference when they next see you."

"Agreed."

"This one"—Stephen pushed at Kristoff with the toe of his shoe—"wasn't outside long enough to do any lasting damage. His eyes will eventually recover even without the dhampyr's blood."

Kristoff looked as confused as I felt. "What is this?"

There was disdain in Stephen's expression. "You thought you were strong after just being awakened, but you really should have taken a couple of weeks before jumping back into things with both feet. Unfortunately you jumped into an ocean with sharks out for your blood."

Kristoff pulled his hands away from his burnt eyes and I grimaced to see how bad they looked. "I . . . offered you . . . Jillian."

"I have no use for a woman with poisoned blood. If I need someone assassinated, I'll send a professional who knows how to use a silver stake. Much less messy or unpredictable."

"I don't understand."

"You don't?" Matthias said. "Then let me explain. From the moment I sensed an uprising from my subjects, I knew my days as king were numbered. They were fools to believe that you would be any better than I was. I set my plan into motion right back then. If I couldn't be king, if you were the only one they would accept as their leader, then so be it."

I felt the cold realization of what he was saying sink in. "You're going to take his place, aren't you?"

His gaze moved to me. "That's right."

"And you planned this the whole time."

"I did." His jaw was tight. "Things have not gone entirely according to plan. I meant to use your blood to weaken him. But in the end, all worked out as it should."

"A success." Stephen nodded.

"You were working together." My head throbbed at the sheer magnitude of Matthias's plan to reclaim his throne. "And Alex—what about Alex?"

Matthias's lips thinned. "I spoke to him on the phone a short time ago. It was his idea, knowing Kristoff hated him and that he'd likely think Stephen would be on his side as the new leader of a powerful organization of vampires. But what Kristoff didn't realize was that Stephen and I have been friends for some time now. A lot can change in thirty years."

I felt stunned by all of this. "Alex agreed to die. For you."

Pain slid behind his pale gray gaze. "Yes. And I'll never forget his sacrifice."

That was why he'd bitten me knowing what would happen. He was giving his life to help Matthias, someone he cared deeply for despite their challenges.

It had all been a part of Matthias's master plan. Everything—from not fighting harder against Meyers when he took the key, to claiming me, to Alex's death, and everything in between. And now he was going to take the place of his identical twin on the throne. He'd be the king again even though everyone would think he was his brother.

It was the ultimate disappearing act.

"Declan—" Kristoff's throat had begun to heal up so his words held more strength. "I command you to—"

Declan shoved a cloth into his temporarily blind father's mouth and held his arms tightly behind his back. "That's enough from you, I think."

Stephen glanced at Declan. "Help me take him into the other room so Matthias can change into his clothes."

Declan glanced at me. He looked as troubled as I was with this latest turn of events. But he finally gave a firm nod. "Fine."

He dragged his father back into the throne room with Matthias and Stephen following after him. That left me in the foyer all alone with a bleeding neck and severe shell shock.

Smiling widely, Jade approached me slowly with Sara cradled in her arms. "I love babies."

I stared at her for a long moment. "I'm happy for you."

WHEN MATTHIAS CAME TO FIND ME, I HAD TO TAKE A second look to make sure it wasn't his brother.

"Shit," I said under my breath. "Matthias, this is—"

"You'll have to call me Kristoff from now on. Only a few of my trusted circle will know the truth."

I rubbed my hand over my forehead. "This is too much for me to wrap my head around."

"All you need to understand is that everything turned

out the way it was supposed to. Kristoff was too much of a threat."

"A threat who was following your original plans."

His expression darkened. "I'm not the same as I was long ago. My priorities have shifted."

"And that makes you the better king."

"Yes." He frowned. "You look more upset about all of this than I would have expected. Had you grown fond of Kristoff?"

I laughed and it sounded vaguely hysterical. "No. No fondness here. I'll assume he has a date with a coffin in the basement?"

"Does that bother you?"

"Not as much as I might have thought."

I'd waited here by the front door silently for the last ten minutes, trying to make sense of everything I'd just witnessed and been through. I was still searching for answers. Maybe there weren't any. All I knew was that Kristoff's plans had been indefinitely put on hold. While Matthias wasn't perfect and he'd made some serious mistakes and poor judgment calls over the years, he was the only one I wanted to be leading the vampires currently in existence. If that was enough to keep the majority of them well behaved and out of sight, then it was good enough for me.

Matthias stayed out of the sliver of sunlight in the mostly shadowed foyer. "I won't tear out my brother's heart as he did to me. When he falls unconscious from lack of blood hopefully this time he'll stay that way."

I paced to the door, looking out at the ocean through the small shuttered window next to it. "If he could read your mind, why didn't he see any of this coming?"

He smiled, and I could see the tips of his sharp fangs. "He only saw what I wanted him to. I've been preparing myself a long time for this possibility. My mind is strong, stronger than I let on, and I could shield many things from him and not have him realize I was doing it."

I bit my bottom lip. "I guess I should feel privileged

that you chose me to be a pawn in such a huge game of chess."

He touched my chin to raise my gaze to his. "You're not a pawn. If this was really a chessboard, you'd be the queen."

I blinked. "I don't want to be the queen."

He was quiet for a moment. "Then you need to leave, Jillian. Take your nieces and don't return. Your life is away from here. But if you ever change your mind, you'll know where to find me."

"The bond holds between us, even though the drama is over."

He backed away from me to lean against the wall, his arms crossed over his chest. "I'm sure there will be plenty of drama in the future—especially if my ruse is ever discovered. But I think I have plenty of time."

I looked at him, from his dark blond hair to the stolen outfit he now wore. "You really think you can impersonate him?"

He looked down at himself. "We're identical."

"I can tell the difference."

He raised a pale brow. "I don't doubt it."

"Your majesty!" A male voice called from the other end of the foyer. It was Meyers. "I heard a disturbance earlier, but it looks as if everything's under control now. Is there anything I can do to help?"

"Yes. Come here." Matthias's voice was steady.

Meyers did as he was asked and glanced around. "Where is everyone?"

"Gone."

"Gone?" He looked confused. "Gone where?"

"Same place you're going." Matthias reached out, grabbed Meyers's head, and twisted it sharply. I heard the crack as his neck broke. He fell to the ground in a heap. Matthias looked at my shocked expression and shrugged. "I did warn him I'd kill him for betraying me. Why wait?"

I looked down at the dead man, surprised I didn't feel

any twinge of regret that I'd witnessed another murder. Either I was becoming seriously desensitized or he'd totally deserved that. Probably a bit of both. "Remind me not to get on your bad side."

"That would be very difficult." His gaze moved to his right and he watched as Declan approached us. "Time for you to go, Jillian."

My throat felt thick. The prospect of leaving Matthias was harder than I thought it would be, even knowing everything I now did about him. He was a deceptive, power-hungry, vengeful vampire. But there was so much more to him than that, and I felt it strongly in our bond. There was as much good in Matthias as there was bad. I knew Sara would be safe in her father's care, there was no question in my mind about that.

Declan stopped a couple feet away from me. "Jill?"

I looked at him, more relief flowing through me that he was alive after drinking my blood. I'd been so afraid that was the end. "We need to take Meg and Julie back to my sister."

"We can do that." He turned to face Matthias. "Is there a problem here?"

Matthias looked at the former dhampyr for a long, drawn-out moment. "No problem. Take the children. I promise no one will try to stop you."

"What about Jade?"

"She's under my care now. No one will abuse her again. And I think—despite her shortcomings—that she could make an excellent nanny for Sara."

Declan let out a hoarse laugh. "You might be right about that."

"As you leave here, try to keep one very important thing in mind."

"What's that?"

He smiled. "Jillian's a very dangerous woman."

"Trust me, I'm well aware."

Noah staggered into the foyer, holding his head be-

tween his hands. "What the hell happened?" He looked at
Matthias and his eyes widened. "Oh, shit. I mean—
Kristoff, your majesty, what can I do to assist you?"

The vampire king studied his most recent fledgling
with amusement. "I'm not Kristoff."

Noah glanced at me. "I knew that. I totally knew that."

25

I SAID GOOD-BYE TO EVERYONE—MATTHIAS, NOAH, even Jade. I didn't know when I'd see them again, but I was sure I would. There was no reason for me to stay here any longer. I had to forge some sort of normalcy in my life—starting with finally seeing my sister again.

Returning Meg and Julie to her was the perfect excuse.

"Are we going home now?" Meg asked as we left the house.

I nodded. "You are."

"I miss mommy," Julie said.

"Me, too." I directed them into the back of one of Kristoff's black sedans that Matthias was letting us permanently borrow.

Leaving the luxurious beach house, which on the surface looked like somewhere I would have once killed to live in—the irony was not lost on me—was a real relief. Away from the shadows and trouble, and out into the sunshine that felt so good on my skin. Declan had found a pair of dark sunglasses, which he currently wore, and he stood next to the car with the keys in his hand.

I glared at him as I approached.

He eyed me in return. "What?"

"Did you know the sun wouldn't blind you?"

He shrugged. "I had a hunch, but I didn't know for sure."

The anger that I'd felt earlier bubbled up again. "So you nearly went blind to stop Kristoff."

"A few moments wouldn't have done any permanent damage. I would have healed in a few months."

"Months." I shook my head. "Honestly, you make me so mad. There were better ways to deal with him."

"I guess I stopped thinking properly when I saw him lunge at you with that knife. I just reacted." His eyebrows raised. "Will you ever forgive me?"

"This time." I let out a long, shaky breath. "Just don't let it happen again."

"I'll try my best." He placed his hand on the roof of the car and looked up at the large house. "You sure you want to leave him?"

There was tightness in his voice.

My anger at his tendency toward risky behavior faded. "You're jealous."

He scrubbed a hand over his scalp. "You're his soul mate now because of your bond. He's a king, he's powerful, he's—"

"Rich and superhot," I finished for him. "That song and dance is getting old, vampire. Get in the car."

He studied me for a long moment. "Yes, ma'am."

The hour-long drive along the coast from Malibu back to Los Angeles gave me time to think, to clear my head, and to try to come to terms with everything that had happened. I could never completely fault Matthias for claiming me. It was the one thing that was going to keep the Nightshade in my blood from killing me. But the poison was still inside me and it wasn't going anywhere. My blood and the Nightshade formula were the same thing now. It was a disturbing thought, but something I had to accept, since there was no alternative.

The vampire next to me in the driver's seat showed signs that being this close to me for a prolonged amount of time bothered him. His hunger showed on his face—faintly at the moment—but it was there. He couldn't hide that from me.

"How often do you need to . . ." I swallowed hard. *"Feed?"*

His lips thinned. "Daily. But I can get it from blood banks, from hospitals. I don't need to—" He glanced at the kids in the backseat in case they were listening in, but they were currently snoozing. "It'll be fine. I can control it."

He sounded confident. If there was anyone I believed in, anyone I didn't think would lie to me about something like this, it was Declan. "Good."

"I thought being . . . what I am now . . . would feel different, that I'd feel different, but I feel the same—unless I'm"—he drew in a ragged breath—"really hungry. I'm hungry right now."

"You'll be fine." I touched his arm and he flinched. I pulled my hand back and placed it in my lap.

His reaction worried me. I hated to think that being near me was this difficult for him.

"Can you stop at a gas station?" I asked. "I need to clean myself up before I see Cathy."

"The fang marks are nearly healed."

I touched my throat remembering the fear I'd felt—mostly for Declan—when he'd bitten me. I'd never been so afraid in my entire life. I was sure he'd die.

But he was still here, in one piece . . .

Emotion welled in my chest, but I pushed back against it. There'd be time for that later.

Declan pulled into a gas station and I grabbed some breakfast for the girls. A coffee for me. I cleaned myself up as much as I could in the washroom. I'd have to buy some new clothes as soon as possible. The little black dress and high heels I still wore were currently my only possessions. I didn't think I'd wear a little black dress again. Like, ever.

I stared into the mirror for a long time. I looked pale, a bit thin, but strangely vibrant and alive. I knew it was because of my bond with Matthias. He was regaining the rest of his strength with every passing hour. He was immortal. He was powerful. And I got to siphon a little of that energy for myself, even from a distance. I looked a little closer at the mirror to realize with surprise that my eyes, previously as jet black as my hair, were cornflower blue again.

"Gift with purchase," I murmured as I drew my fingers through my hair to try to get the tangles out of it.

I left the washroom feeling better, stronger, and happier than I had in a very long time. A wash of optimism flowed over me. If I could survive the last couple of weeks, I think I could survive just about anything. There would be plenty of challenges ahead, I knew that. I wasn't completely normal and I never would be again. But maybe that was okay.

The girls ate their muffins and drank their bottles of orange juice in the backseat and I settled again into the passenger side.

"My eyes are blue," I announced with a smile.

"I noticed." Declan shifted into drive and we headed the rest of the way to my sister's house. I grew more nervous the closer we got. It had been my goal all along to see her again, to know at that moment everything would be all right. The time was finally here and I was so happy to bring her daughters back to her, unharmed, and completely oblivious to whatever danger they'd been close to. There was no evidence of a police presence, no search parties, no crowds or news cameras, so I assumed she still had no idea what had happened.

Ignorance was seriously bliss.

"Here it is, on the right with the Toyota in the driveway," I said as we pulled onto her treelined street. He parked at the curb and I got out to open the door for the girls.

I leaned into the car. "I'll just be—"

"You should stay here, Jill." Declan's grip was tight on the steering wheel, his gaze straight forward on the road.

A breath caught in my chest. "What?"

He nodded, still not looking directly at me. "I've been giving this a lot of thought, and it's the right thing to do. You're here, with your sister, just as you wanted. You're healthy, in no danger of dying. I'll go back to the compound and make sure all remaining paperwork and files on you are destroyed. You don't have to be afraid that anyone will be after you—I'll make sure no one knows you exist. Stay in nice, normal residential areas and you shouldn't have any problems with rogue vamps. You can have your life back any way you want it to be. A bright future."

I heard him, but his words weren't properly registering with me. "But, I thought we were—"

"What did you think?" His jaw was tense, his knuckles whitening on the steering wheel, and he finally looked at me. His sunglasses covered any expression in his single gray eye. "What were your plans now? To live on the road, motel to motel, constantly in danger? With a vampire who has difficulties controlling himself around your scent?"

"My blood doesn't kill you."

"No, but it's too tempting, Jill. And the pain I felt from tasting it—fuck, it nearly put me out of commission. I almost didn't get myself together enough after that to stop Kristoff. I can't concentrate around you."

"But—"

"What exactly did you think would happen next?"

My eyes stung. I hadn't expected this. "I—I hadn't really given it much thought."

"Exactly. Which is why I had to. Look, I'm planning on continuing on as I always have. Hunting down rogues. It's all I know and I'm used to doing it alone. You can tell just by looking at my scars it's a fucking dangerous business. And there's no place in it for someone like you."

I glanced at the girls waiting up on the curb. They hadn't run to the front door yet; they were waiting for me to accompany them.

"Come on, Aunt Jill," Meg said. "I want to see my mommy."

I turned back to Declan. "Listen, I—"

He shook his head. "No, Jill. This is your chance to be normal again. There's no future for us. Being around you it's—it's torture for me. That's no damn way to live. I can't deal with it. I don't want to deal with it. It's safer for us to be apart."

I tried to swallow, but it was difficult. "Safer for you or for me?"

"Both."

All I could do was nod. "You're right, of course. About everything."

"Yeah, I am."

I'd known it from the beginning—me and Declan, we were different. Too different. Our worlds didn't mesh, when it came right down to it. As soon as we got off the metaphorical roller-coaster ride we'd been on together, it was time to go our separate ways.

"Okay." I blinked hard, refusing to let myself cry over this. Not now. Maybe later, but not now. "Girls, say good-bye to Declan."

"Good-bye, Declan," they said in unison.

"Good luck." My voice sounded thick as I closed the passenger side door. I turned away and began walking up the driveway. The girls trailed after me. I didn't want to look back, but I glanced over my shoulder, feeling my heart sink as the black car drove off down the road as if he'd been in a bat-out-of-hell hurry to get away from me.

It was over.

Time for the rest of my life to begin.

I marched up to the door and inhaled deeply through my nose and let it out slowly through my mouth. I hesitated only a moment before I rang the doorbell.

It didn't take long before it opened and my sister stood there, her light blond hair, currently back in a haphazard ponytail, the exact same shade mine used to be.

She grinned. "Jill! I'm so happy to see you!"

I almost laughed at how completely at ease she seemed. "I'm happy to see you, too, Cathy."

"Mommy!" The girls ran past me into the house and hugged their mother.

"Did you have a good time last night?" Cathy asked.

"Yeah, it was fun," Meg said, smiling. "And we found Aunt Jill."

I felt on the verge of tears of relief at their complete and utter calm reaction to what had happened. Luckily they'd been kept out of the drama. Only I knew exactly what had happened and how much danger they'd been in. Seeing the girls reunited with their mother gave me a feeling of elation and relief, as if everything I'd been through had been completely worth it.

Cathy then grabbed me into a fierce hug so tight it almost hurt. "I was worried about you since you disappeared. Why didn't you call me?"

I hugged her back. "I'm sorry. I should have."

She pulled back from me and there were emotions sliding through her gaze—relief, happiness, and a little bit of annoyance with her uncommunicative sister, who didn't follow rules like a normal person. "What the hell happened to you, anyway? They told me you went out for a coffee break at work and that scary man grabbed you. He had a gun. Where the hell have you been all this time?"

I tried not to think about the scary man with the gun. He'd destroyed my normal life by dragging me into his. And I missed him already so much it felt as if I'd been stabbed through my heart. That pain fought with the pure joy I felt at seeing Cathy again.

"It's a long story," I said. "But I'm back and everything's going to be okay now."

Her expression turned quizzical. "What on earth did you do to your hair?"

I touched it absently. "It's different now. Do you like it?"

She leaned back and pursed her lips. "I think I can get used to it."

My hair was different. Permanently. Kind of like me. I knew I'd changed at a cellular level, just like my hair had. Like my blood had. It hadn't been all that long since I'd been ripped out of my normal life, kicking and screaming, but everything was different now.

She glanced over her shoulder to see the girls in the family room, turning on the television. "Did they have a good time with you and . . ." She frowned. "I forget his name. The handsome blond man with the gray eyes."

I wasn't surprised she didn't remember past Kristoff's strong mental influence. "They did."

She shook her head. "Where were you all this time? The man—the one who grabbed you—"

"He's gone." I squeezed my eyes shut for a moment, then opened them up and smiled at her. "It's okay."

She stroked my long black hair back from my face and tucked it behind my ear. "I have so many questions, I don't even know where to begin. But nothing really matters as much as the fact that you're back. Everything can go back to normal now, Jill. Everything. And I'm not letting you out of my sight ever again." She laughed. "This is better than I ever could have hoped for."

"It's exactly what I hoped for, too." I hugged her again, my chest felt tight. "I love you so much, Cathy."

"I love you, too."

"Please take care of yourself and the girls, okay?"

She pulled back from me, a frown creasing her brow. "What?"

I smiled, a truly genuine smile. "I need to go."

"Go? Go where?"

"I'll be in touch, I promise. Soon. Please don't worry about me."

I turned and left the house, walking down the driveway to the sidewalk. Seeing Cathy again, returning the girls safely, it was everything I thought it would be. It made me happy. It made me remember my life before—how normal and regulated everything was. There was a comfortable structure to having a job, having a set of friends, a sister and nieces I visited regularly. I could have that again, I'd just seen it.

But I wasn't the same person I'd been. I felt it deep inside me. I didn't belong there—not anymore. And that was okay. It was a part of my life, but not the sum total of it. I could have followed the rules. Could have stayed there. Hell, I was sure Cathy wouldn't have had a problem with me moving in and starting my life over here in Los Angeles.

But there were other things in store for me now.

"Jill!" Cathy called from her front door. "Where the hell are you going?"

I just waved at her. She probably thought I was crazy. Maybe I was. But I knew this was the right choice for me. I walked down the sidewalk in my short black dress, the high heels pinching my feet.

No matter what happened now, everything was going to be okay.

I believed it.

The car came to a stop at the curb beside me a few minutes later. I squeezed my eyes shut and prayed that it wasn't some jerk who wanted to give me a lift to the nearest motel room after mistaking me for a hooker.

"Are you getting in or what?" Declan asked through the open passenger side window.

I smiled, then grabbed the door handle, opened it up, and got in beside him. "I thought you were leaving."

"Me, too."

"But you came back."

"I did." His jaw was tight and his attention was on the road again.

"Isn't it torture to be close to me?"

"It is."

I bit my bottom lip and watched him carefully. "So why did you come back?"

He finally turned to look at me. "I guess I'm just a complete masochist who's fallen in love with you."

My heart swelled. "That was probably not a very smart decision."

"Tell me about it." His sunglasses were off, and I saw the raw emotion in his pale gray eye—emotion he'd never had to experience in the past thanks to his serum.

No more serum. No more dhampyr.

Just a vampire who could go out in the daylight. Who had survived my blood. Who'd dragged me into this life, and I was in no hurry to escape from him anymore. This was where I belonged, come what may. With Declan.

I looked out of the window back in the direction of my sister's house and my normal life. "So where are we headed next?"

"Honestly? I have no damn idea."

I smiled at him. "That sounds like a pretty good start to me."

He reached down to take my hand in his as we pulled away from the curb.

Turn the page for a special preview of the
next Living in Eden novel by Michelle Rowen

That Old Black Magic

Coming soon from Berkley Sensation!

"READY TO HEAR YOUR ULTIMATE FATE?"

Eden glanced warily at the shirtless demon sitting at the tiny dinette table in her tiny apartment with the daily newspaper's horoscope section in front of him. Seemed harmless enough, and yet a chill ran down her spine. Something about Darrak's statement felt like an omen. A bad one.

Maybe she was just being paranoid. Nothing new there.

She pushed back against the unpleasant vibe. "Sure."

Darrak absently raked his messy dark hair back from his forehead. "You're a Gemini, right?"

"Present and accounted for."

"Be prepared for a blast from the past as an old acquaintance, one whose destiny is irreversibly intertwined with yours, wants to reconnect. Also, buy more crunchy peanut butter as soon as possible."

She nodded. "Let me take a wild guess here . . . You added the last bit yourself."

"Doesn't make it any less true. We're out. And I love it."

"I'll put it on my grocery list."

"Life is good." He studied her for a moment longer before his grin began to fade at the edges. "What's wrong?"

"Wrong?" Eden crossed her arms. "Nothing's wrong. Nothing at all. Everything's wonderful. Fabulous, in fact."

"Overcompensating in your reply only leads me to believe that something's seriously wrong." When he stood the horoscope page fluttered to the carpeted floor at his feet. His brows drew together. "What is it?"

It was surprising how quickly Darrak could switch from amusement over a horoscope and a craving for crunchy peanut butter to deep concern for her well-being.

He wanted to know what was bothering her. That was a very dangerous question these days.

Ever since Eden woke this morning, she'd felt the unrequested tingle of magic moving down her arms and sparking off her fingertips. She didn't allow herself to tap into her recently acquired powers despite it being a constant itch for her. Magic—at least *her* magic—came with nasty consequences.

She could control it, she kept telling herself. She *could*.

Sometimes she even believed it.

"You need to get dressed," she said instead of answering his question. Her gaze moved over his very bare and very distracting chest. "We have to leave for the office in five minutes."

Black jersey material immediately flowed over Darrak's skin. Since he'd come into Eden's life a month ago, she'd wanted to take him shopping at a mall, but other than a leather coat he occasionally wore—short sleeves in Toronto in chilly mid-November might be a tip-off that he wasn't exactly human—he magically conjured his own clothing, which seemed to solely consist of black jeans and black T-shirts.

She slid her hands into the pockets of her navy blue pants and turned away from him.

Darrak caught her arm. "It's your magic, isn't it?"

The peanut-butter-loving demon could be very insightful. "My magic?"

"I can feel it, you know. Right now. It's coming off you in waves."

"I'm fine. Don't worry about it."

She grabbed her purse, which was hanging off the back of one of the dinette chairs, to fish into it for her new BlackBerry. Andy McCoy, her partner at the investigation agency they co-owned, insisted they become more technically savvy now that their caseload had increased, so he'd bought them both brand-new phones. Triple-A Investigations had been on the brink of bankruptcy only a month ago, but now they were busy with new cases.

The sudden surge in business was directly related to Darrak coming into Eden's life. While working as an occasional psychic consultant for the police, she'd been possessed by the cursed demon after the death of his previous host, a serial killer gunned down right in front of her.

Darrak was able to take solid human form during daylight hours, but when the sun set, he became incorporeal and had to possess her body. She'd recently had the chance to end the possession once and for all, but that would have destroyed him completely. Her privacy was a great motivator to find a solution to their problem, but not at such a high price.

After all . . . she'd come to care a great deal for the demon since they'd first met.

Unfortunately, all roads in their search for mutually beneficial separation had led to dead ends. Some deader than others.

She finally tore her gaze away from the screen of her phone to look at him and cringed when she noticed the searching look in his ice blue eyes. "I said nothing's wrong. Please, Darrak, don't worry."

"Your phone is on fire."

He was right. A spark from her magic had ignited her

BlackBerry. She shrieked and threw it before it burned her. It skittered across the breakfast bar and landed with a *sizzle* in the kitchen sink. "Well, damn."

Before she had a chance to move, Darrak was right in front of her. He pulled out the chain she wore around her neck so her amulet lay flat against her freshly ironed white shirt.

"It's even darker than it was yesterday."

She clamped her hand over the visible state of her soul. The more she used her magic, the more damage it did. A black witch, even an extremely reluctant one like her, started with a pure white soul, but it grew darker and darker every time she accessed her very accessible black magic. Eden's amulet was still pale gray, but it had darker veins branching through it, making it look like a piece of marble.

She shook her head. "I haven't done anything."

"Then what are these?" He pushed her hand away and slid his index finger over the veins.

She grimaced. "A glitch."

"A glitch," Darrak repeated skeptically. "Not sure it works like that."

"Then I don't know what to tell you."

"Eden"—all amusement was gone from his voice now—"I'm worried about you."

A demon from Hell was worried about her immortal soul. It sounded like a joke. But Darrak wasn't any normal demon. And she wasn't any normal black witch.

Once upon a time, Darrak had been just as bad as any demon who'd ever existed—as immortal as he was immoral, sadistic, powerful, selfish, manipulative, and deadly. He'd even conspired with a demonic pal to overthrow Lucifer himself in an attempt to take his power as Prince of Hell. However, they'd failed. Rather spectacularly, in fact.

Darrak had been summoned into the human world over three hundred years ago, and a curse was put on him that destroyed his original body and his ability to manifest a new one. He'd been forced to possess humans ever since. A side effect of this was that he'd absorbed humanity slowly but surely and it infused his being. The demon had developed a conscience. Morals. A sense of right and wrong.

But that wasn't the whole story.

To add to Eden's growing paranormal résumé, she'd recently been shocked to learn that in addition to being a black witch she was also a nephilim.

A human mother plus an angel father equaled one very confused twenty-nine-year-old woman—black witch plus half angel in the same body. It wasn't exactly a combination that was working out perfectly, more like oil and water.

And the bonus prize—she was possessed by a demon.

It had been an interesting year to say the least.

Her angel side infused her with celestial energy, something she'd never even sensed before, apart from a smidgeon of unreliable psychic insight. But it was what Darrak had absorbed over the last month due to their situation. And he'd absorbed a lot of it.

Bottom line, a human conscience was the least of Darrak's troubles. A demon who'd been neck deep in celestial energy as he had been in the last month . . .

Well, it was changing him on a core level. Only he didn't exactly know it yet.

Eden knew it would shake his already shaky confidence, not to mention his entire identity, to find out he was becoming a little more . . . *angelic*. Whether he liked it or not.

The news could wait a little longer.

"Eden," Darrak prompted when she didn't speak for a while. "Are you going to talk to me or what?"

"You mean I have a choice?"

"No. No choices. This is not a choose-your-own-adventure novel. Your amulet is darkening and you say you're doing nothing to cause this. Is that right?"

Eden didn't want to deal with this, but sometimes fate

didn't give you a chance to catch your breath before it threw another bucket of water in your face.

She looked up at him. "I can feel it this morning stronger than ever. I'm honestly not sure how much longer I can control it."

Darrak took her face between his hands. "But you want to control it."

She touched his hand but didn't pull away from him. "Of course I do."

"I wish to hell I could protect you from all of this." His jaw tensed. "Looks like it's time to get some outside help."

He walked over to the kitchen counter and grabbed the phone.

"Who are you calling?" she asked.

Darrak held a finger up to her. She flopped down on a chair at the table, already exhausted from talking about something she would much prefer to continue trying to ignore—magically melted BlackBerry or not.

She really hoped Andy had taken out a warranty on the device.

"Stanley?" Darrak said after a moment. "Do you know who this is?" A pause. "No, it's okay. Don't be scared. I'm not going to do that to you." Another pause. "Seriously, I'm not. Evisceration is extremely messy and the clean up is a— Come on. Please stop crying. Be a man."

That Darrak's "outside help" required contacting Stanley didn't fill Eden with a great deal of confidence. Stanley worked as a minion for just about any supernatural creature who paid or threatened him. Not exactly her favorite guy in the city.

"Is he back?" Darrak asked. "He is? Why didn't you let me know this already? Oh, come on. Stop crying."

Eden's hands tingled. It was so tempting to throw out a spell right here, right now. It still seemed like just a dream that all of this had happened to her. Demons were real. Angels were real. Witches were real and they came in a few different varieties.

White witches—the good and beneficial nature lovers.

Among other things, Eden had heard they could make flowers grow and dying trees come back to life. How nice for them.

Gray witches—able to blend both white magic and black magic with the ability to do this successfully without damaging their souls provided they maintained a perfect balance.

And then there were black witches—able to destroy or kill things with a mere thought if they were so inclined. Not exactly the life of the party.

"We need to see him as soon as possible." Darrak paced back and forth between her kitchenette and the dinette area. "That sounds fine. Why are you still crying? Suck it up, dude. Seriously."

He hung up.

"You upset Stanley," Eden said. "Actually . . . I'm fine with that."

Darrak shrugged. "He's still intimidated by my fearsome archdemon reputation. Nice to know somebody still is."

"Are you going to share what that was all about?"

"We're seeing Maksim. Today."

She stared at him blankly for a moment. "The wizard."

"The one and only. Sounds like he's finally back from his vacation."

Maksim the wizard had gone on vacation after surviving a torture session by Theo—Darrak's former demon friend— a couple weeks ago. Before he went AWOL, the wizard was supposed to help them find a way to break his curse, even though rumor had it only the witch who'd originally cursed him could do something about that. Since she was now dead it was a moot point.

"You really think he can help me?" She didn't want to hope for too much from a simple phone call. Disappointment was a heartless bitch.

"I don't think he can hurt. Wizards and witches go hand in hand, after all. Didn't you read *Harry Potter*?"

Eden stared at him. "Well, yeah."

"I didn't read the books," he continued. "But I did get

to see the movies. A previous host was a fan. He even wore dress robes and pretended he'd been sorted into a house. Hufflepuff, if you can believe it. Who liked Hufflepuff best? I mean, seriously."

"Not sure that's really helpful in this situation."

"A wizard, especially one at Maksim's level, will know how to control black magic, even yours. I'm sure of it."

It was worth a shot. "Okay, so when do we see him?"

"Now."

"Now?" She glanced at the clock, which read eight thirty. "But Andy's going to want us in the office."

"He can wait a couple of hours. He can wait a whole day if necessary. Figuring out how to control your magic is much more important."

She took a deep breath. "Maybe you're right."

"Of course I'm right." Darrak's smile had returned, although this time it didn't completely reach his eyes. He still looked worried.

Which was worrying.

"Fine." Eden nodded and clenched her magically tingling hands into fists at her sides. "Then I guess we're off to see the wizard."

"Don't make me start singing." He snatched the fallen newspaper from the floor and put it back on the table. "You know, he just might be the person from your past whose destiny is intertwined with yours, according to your horoscope."

"I think I'd remember meeting a wizard named Maksim."

Darrak crossed his arms. "Then who do you think it was referring to?"

She waved her hand flippantly. "It was just a horoscope. It's fiction. Totally meaningless."

"If you say so."

Out of all the drama in Eden's life lately, an entertaining but silly horoscope was the least of her problems.

CAROLINE RILEY WATCHED FROM THE SHADOWS AS her daughter left the apartment building and headed toward her rusty Toyota. She was about to run up and give Eden a big hug, but she held back when the demon came into view.

He was tall with unruly dark hair almost long enough to brush his broad shoulders. He casually pulled on a black leather jacket as he trailed closely after Eden. He was very handsome, of course. Most demons had a highly attractive human visage they wore when not in their demonic form. It made it that much easier to prey upon humans.

He was going to be a problem.

She wondered why Eden would spend time with this evil creature and allow him into her home. Maybe he was threatening her. Blackmailing her.

Or . . . sleeping with her.

Was her daughter having an affair with a demon?

Eden had always been a rules follower, a perfect student, a hard worker, although one who'd always lacked any specific career direction. A smart girl like that wasn't one who'd have her head easily turned by one of Lucifer's minions.

Then again, despite Eden's natural beauty—that she'd inherited from her mother, of course—she'd never had much confidence in herself when it came to men, poor thing. This must have been what the demon had preyed upon.

Caroline had arrived just in time. Sure, she had other pressing matters to attend to, but rescuing her only child from the clutches of a demon had now risen to the very top of her to-do list.

It would be so nice to talk to Eden again. It had been much too long since they'd last spent time together.

Then again, Caroline *had* been dead for the last three months.

Nightshade

Jillian Conrad never believed in vampires. But she's just become a living, breathing weapon against them. Attacked by a desperate scientist, she is injected with a formula that is supposed to act as a deadly poison to vampires. And when the scientist is gunned down in front of her, his secrets die with him—including how to purge her system of this poison.

Declan Reyes is only half-vampire, but he hates them with all his heart. He knows that the poison in Jillian's veins could finally destroy the undead kingdom. The serum also makes her blood irresistible to all vampires—including Declan, whose bloodthirsty traits are driven into a frenzy by her.

Driven by duty to protect her and by instinct to crave her, Declan takes Jillian into his shadowy world of blood and battle. But he soon realizes his increasing need for her may be a different kind of hunger . . .

penguin.com

Coming soon
from *New York Times* bestselling author
MaryJanice Davidson

Undead and Undermined

Vampire queen Betsy Taylor has awoken in a Chicago morgue, again, naked as a corpse. Her last memory is reconciling with her husband, Eric Sinclair, after a time-traveling field trip, including an indirect route to hell (literally), with her sister, Laura. Now she's Jane Doe #291, wrapped in plastic with a toe tag. Betsy can't help but wonder, what happened in hell?

Betsy heads back to her St. Paul mansion and discovers that she and Laura didn't time-travel alone. What followed them had a wicked agenda: to kill Betsy in a time when she was still young and vulnerable and end her future reign as queen.

But it's not just Betsy's future that has taken an unexpected detour. Everyone in her circle, alive or undead, is feeling the chill. Betsy can't let the unthinkable happen. It would be a cold day in hell if she did.

M804T1110

Don't miss the new series from
New York Times bestselling author

YASMINE GALENORN

NIGHT MYST
An Indigo Court Novel

Eons ago, vampires tried to turn the Dark Fae in order to harness their magic, only to create a demonic
enemy more powerful than they imagined. Now Myst,
the queen of the Indigo Court, has enough power to
begin a long-prophesied supernatural war.

Cicely Waters, a witch who can control the wind, may
be the only one who can stop her—and save her be-
loved Fae prince from the queen's enslavement.

M714T0510